AN APACHE
PRINCESS

A Tale of the Indian Frontier

GENERAL CHARLES KING

An Apache Princess

Charles King

© 1st World Library, 2007
PO Box 2211
Fairfield, IA 52556
www.1stworldlibrary.com
First Edition

LCCN: 2007927762

Softcover ISBN: 978-1-4218-4510-4
Hardcover ISBN: 978-1-4218-4426-8
eBook ISBN: 978-1-4218-4594-4

Purchase *"An Apache Princess"*
as a traditional bound book at:
www.1stWorldLibrary.com/purchase.asp?ISBN=978-1-4218-4510-4

1ˢᵗ World Library Literary Society

Giving Back to the World

"If you want to work on the core problem, it's early school literacy."

- James Barksdale, former CEO of Netscape

"No skill is more crucial to the future of a child, or to a democratic and prosperous society, than literacy."

- Los Angeles Times

"Literacy... means far more than learning how to read and write... The aim is to transmit... knowledge and promote social participation."

- UNESCO

"Literacy is not a luxury, it is a right and a responsibility. If our world is to meet the challenges of the twenty-first century we must harness the energy and creativity of all our citizens."

- President Bill Clinton

"Parents should be encouraged to read to their children, and teachers should be equipped with all available techniques for teaching literacy, so the varying needs and capacities of individual kids can be taken into account."

- Hugh Mackay

CONTENTS

CHAPTER I

THE MEETING BY THE WATERS

Under the willows at the edge of the pool a young girl sat daydreaming, though the day was nearly done. All in the valley was wrapped in shadow, though the cliffs and turrets across the stream were resplendent in a radiance of slanting sunshine. Not a cloud tempered the fierce glare of the arching heavens or softened the sharp outline of neighboring peak or distant mountain chain. Not a whisper of breeze stirred the drooping foliage along the sandy shores or ruffled the liquid mirror surface. Not a sound, save drowsy hum of beetle or soft murmur of rippling waters, among the pebbly shallows below, broke the vast silence of the scene. The snow cap, gleaming at the northern horizon, lay one hundred miles away and looked but an easy one-day march. The black upheavals of the Matitzal, barring the southward valley, stood sullen and frowning along the Verde, jealous of the westward range that threw their rugged gorges into early shade. Above and below the still and placid pool and but a few miles distant, the pine-fringed, rocky hillsides came shouldering close to the stream, but fell away, forming a deep, semicircular basin toward the west, at the hub of which stood bolt-upright a tall, snowy flagstaff, its shred of bunting hanging limp and lifeless from the peak, and in the dull, dirt-colored buildings of adobe, ranged in rigid lines about the dull brown, flat-topped *mesa*, a thousand yards up stream above the pool, drowsed a little band of martial exiles, stationed here to keep the peace 'twixt scattered settlers and swarthy, swarming Apaches. The fort was their soldier home; the solitary girl a soldier's daughter.

She could hardly have been eighteen. Her long, slim figure, in its clinging riding habit, betrayed, despite roundness and supple grace, a certain immaturity. Her hands and feet were long and slender. Her sun-tanned cheek and neck were soft and rounded. Her mouth was delicately chiseled and the lips were pink as the heart of a Bridesmaid rose, but, being firmly closed, told no tale of the teeth within, without a peep at which one knew not whether the beauty of the sweet young face was really made or marred. Eyes, eyebrows, lashes, and a wealth of tumbling tresses of rich golden brown were all superb, but who could tell what might be the picture when she opened those pretty, curving lips to speak or smile? Speak she did not, even to the greyhounds stretched sprawling in the warm sands at her feet. Smile she could not, for the young heart was sore troubled.

Back in the thick of the willows she had left her pony, blinking lazily and switching his long tail to rid his flanks of humming insects, but never mustering energy enough to stamp a hoof or strain a thread of his horsehair *riata*. Both the long, lean, sprawling hounds lolled their red, dripping tongues and panted in the sullen heat. Even the girl herself, nervous at first and switching with her dainty whip at the crumbling sands and pacing restlessly to and fro, had yielded gradually to the drooping influences of the hour and, seated on a rock, had buried her chin in the palm of her hand, and, with eyes no longer vagrant and searching, had drifted away into maiden dreamland. Full thirty minutes had she been there waiting for something, or somebody, and it, or he, had not appeared.

Yet somebody else was there and close at hand. The shadow of the westward heights had gradually risen to the crest of the rocky cliffs across the stream. A soft, prolonged call of distant trumpet summoned homeward, for the coming night, the scattered herds and herd guards of the post, and, rising with a sigh of disappointment, the girl turned toward her now impatient pony when her ear caught the sound of a smothered hand-clap, and, whirling about in swift hope and surprise, her face once more darkened at sight of an Indian girl, Apache unquestionably, crouching in the leafy covert of the opposite willows and pointing silently down stream. For a moment, without love or fear in the eyes of either, the white girl and the brown gazed at each other across the intervening water mirror and spoke no word. Then, slowly, the former approached the brink, looked in the direction indicated by the little dingy index and saw nothing to warrant the recall. Moreover, she was annoyed to think that all this time, perhaps, the Indian girl had been lurking in that sheltering grove and stealthily watching her. Once more she turned away, this time with a toss of her head that sent the russet-brown tresses tumbling about her slim back and shoulders, and at once the hand-clap was repeated, low, but imperative, and Tonto, the biggest of the two big hounds, uplifted one ear and growled a challenge.

"What do you want?" questioned the white girl, across the estranging waters.

For answer the brown girl placed her left forefinger on her lips, and again distinctly pointed to a little clump of willows a dozen rods below, but on the westward side.

"Do you mean—someone's coming?" queried the first.

"Sh-sh-sh!" answered the second softly, then pointed again, and pointed eagerly.

The soldier's daughter glanced about her, uncertainly, a moment, then slowly, cautiously made her way along the sandy brink in the direction indicated, gathering the folds of her long skirt in her gauntleted hand and stepping lightly in her slender moccasins. A moment or two, and she had reached the edge of a dense little copse and peered cautiously within. The Indian girl was right. Somebody lay there, apparently asleep, and the fair young intruder recoiled in obvious confusion, if not dismay. For a moment she stood with fluttering heart and parting lips that now permitted reassuring glimpse of pearly white teeth. For a moment she seemed on the verge of panicky retreat, but little by little regained courage and self-poise. What was there to fear in a sleeping soldier anyhow? She knew who it was at a glance. She could, if she would, whisper his name. Indeed, she had been whispering it many a time, day and night, these last two weeks until— until certain things about him had come to her ears that made her shrink in spite of herself from this handsome, petted young soldier, this Adonis of her father's troop, Neil Blakely, lieutenant of cavalry.

"The Bugologist," they called him in cardroom circles at the "store," where men were fiercely intolerant of other pursuits than poker, for which pastime Mr. Blakely had no use whatever—no more use than had its votaries for him. He was a dreamy sort of fellow, with big blue eyes and a fair skin that were in themselves sufficient to stir the rancor of born frontiersmen, and they of Arizona in the days of old were an exaggeration of the type in general circulation on the Plains. He was something of a dandy in dress, another thing they loathed; something of a purist in speech, which was affectation unpardonable; something of a dissenter as to drink, appreciative of "Cucumungo" and claret, but distrustful of whisky— another thing to call down scorn illimitable from the elect of the mining camps and packing "outfits." But all these disqualifications might have been overlooked had the lieutenant displayed even a faint preference for poker. "The Lord loveth a cheerful giver—or loser" was the creed of the cardroom circle at the store, but beyond a casual or smiling peep at the game from the safe distance of the doorway, Mr. Blakely had vouchsafed no interest in affairs of that character. To the profane disgust of Bill Hyde, chief packer, and the malevolent, if veiled, criticism of certain "sporty" fellow soldiers, Blakely preferred to spend his leisure hours riding up and down the valley, with a butterfly net over his shoulders and a japanned tin box slung at his back, searching for specimens that were scarce as the Scriptures among his commentators.

Even on this hot October afternoon he had started on his entomological work, but, finding little encouragement and resting a while in the shade, he had dozed away on a sandy couch, his head on his arms, his broad-brimmed hat over his face, his shapely legs outstretched in lazy, luxurious enjoyment, his tall and slender form, arrayed in cool white blouse and trousers, really a goodly thing to behold. This day, too, he must have come afoot, but his net and box lay there beside him, and his hunt had been without profit, for both were apparently empty. Possibly he had devoted but little time to netting insects. Possibly he had thought to encounter bigger game. If so his zest in the sport must have been but languid, since he had so soon yielded to the drowsy influences of the day. There was resentment in the heart of the girl as this occurred to her, even though it would have angered her the more had anyone suggested she had come in hope of seeing or speaking with him.

And yet, down in the bottom of her heart, she knew that just such a hope had held her there even to the hour of recall. She knew that, since opportunities for meeting him within the garrison were limited, she had deliberately chosen to ride alone, and farther than she had ever ridden alone before, in hope of meeting him without. She knew that in the pursuit of his winged prey he never sought the open *mesa* or the ravines and gorges of the foothills. Only along the stream were they—and he—to be found. Only along the stream, therefore, had she this day ridden and, failing to see aught of him, had dismounted to think in quiet by the pool, so she told herself, but incidentally to wait and watch for him; and now she had found him, neither watching nor waiting, but in placid unconcern and slumber.

One reason why they met so seldom in garrison was that her father did not like him in the least. The captain was a veteran soldier, self-taught and widely honored, risen from the ranks. The lieutenant was a man of gentle breeding and of college education, a soldier by choice, or caprice, yet quite able at any time to quit the service and live a life of ease, for he had, they said, abundant means of his own. He had been first lieutenant of that troop at least five years, not five months of which had he served on duty with it. First one general, then another, had needed him as aide-de-camp, and when, on his own application, he had been relieved from staff duty to enable him to accompany his regiment to this then distant and inhospitable land, he had little more than reached Camp Sandy when he was sent by the department commander to investigate some irregularity at the Apache reservation up

the valley, and then, all unsoliciting, he had been placed in charge pending the coming of a new agent to replace the impeached one going home under guard, and the captain said things about his subaltern's always seeking "fancy duty" that were natural, yet unjust—things that reached Mr. Blakely in exaggerated form, and that angered him against his senior to the extent of open rupture. Then Blakely took the mountain fever at the agency, thereby still further delaying his return to troop duty, and then began another complication, for the contract doctor, though skillful in his treatment, was less assiduous in nursing than were the wife of the newly arrived agent and her young companion Lola, daughter of the agency interpreter and his Apache-Yuma wife.

When well enough to attempt light duty again, the lieutenant had rejoined at Sandy, and, almost the first face to greet him on his arrival was one he had never seen before and never forgot thereafter—the sweet, laughing, winsome face of Angela Wren, his captain's only child.

The regiment had marched into Arizona overland, few of the wives and daughters with it. Angela, motherless since her seventh year, was at school in the distant East, together with the daughters of the colonel then commanding the regiment. They were older; were "finishing" that summer, and had amazed that distinguished officer by demanding to be allowed to join him with their mother. When they left the school Angela could stand it no longer. She both telegraphed and wrote, begging piteously to be permitted to accompany them on the long journey by way of San Francisco, and so it had finally been settled. The colonel's household were now at regimental headquarters up at Prescott, and Angela was quite happy at Camp Sandy. She had been there barely four weeks when Neil Blakely, pale, fragile-looking, and still far from strong, went to report for duty at his captain's quarters and was met at the threshold by his captain's daughter.

Expecting a girl friend, Kate Sanders, from "down the row," she had rushed to welcome her, and well-nigh precipitated herself upon a stranger in the natty undress uniform of the cavalry. Her instant blush was something beautiful to see. Blakely said the proper things to restore tranquillity; smilingly asked for her father, his captain; and, while waiting for that warrior to finish shaving and come down to receive him, was entertained by Miss Wren in the little army parlor. Looking into her wondrous eyes and happy, blushing face, he forgot that there was rancor between his troop commander and himself, until the captain's stiff, unbending greeting reminded him. Thoughtless people at the post, however, were laughing over the situation a week thereafter. Neil Blakely, a squire of dames in San Francisco and other cities when serving on staff duty, a society "swell" and clubman, had obviously become deeply interested in this blithe young army girl, without a cent to her name—with nothing but her beauty, native grace, and sweet, sunshiny nature to commend her. And everyone hitherto had said Neil Blakely would never marry in the army.

And there was one woman at Sandy who saw the symptoms with jealous and jaundiced eyes—Clarice, wife of the major then commanding the little "four-company" garrison. Other women took much to heart the fact that Major Plume had cordially invited Blakely, on his return from the agency, to be their guest until he could get settled in his own quarters. The Plumes had rooms to spare—and no children. The major was twelve years older than his wife, but women said it often looked the other way. Mrs. Plume had aged very rapidly after his sojourn on recruiting duty in St. Louis. Frontier commissariat and cooking played hob with her digestion, said the major. Frontier winds and water dealt havoc to her complexion, said the women. But both complexion and digestion seemed to "take a brace," as irreverent youth expressed it, when Neil Blakely came to Sandy and the major's roof. True, he stayed but six and thirty hours and then moved into his own domicile—quarters No. 7—after moving out a most reluctant junior. Major Plume and Mrs. Plume had expected him, they were so kind as to say, to choose a vacant half set, excellent for bachelor purposes, under the roof that sheltered Captain Wren, Captain Wren's maiden sister and housekeeper, and Angela, the captain's daughter. This set adjoined the major's big central house, its south windows looking into the major's north gallery. "It would be so neighborly and nice," said Mrs. Plume. Instead, however, Mr. Blakely stood upon his prerogative as a senior subaltern and "ranked out" Mr. and Mrs. Bridger and baby, and these otherwise gentle folk, evicted and aggrieved, knowing naught of Blakely from previous association, and seeing no reason why he should wish to be at the far end of the row instead of the middle, with his captain, where he properly belonged, deemed themselves the objects of wanton and capricious treatment at his hands, and resented it according to their opportunities. Bridger, being a soldier and subordinate, had to take it out in soliloquy and swear-words, but his impetuous little helpmate—being a woman, a wife and mother, set both wits and tongue to work, and heaven help the man when woman has both to turn upon him! In refusing the room and windows that looked full-face into those of Mrs. Plume, Blakely had nettled her. In selecting the quarters occupied by Mr. and Mrs. Bridger he had slightly inconvenienced and sorely vexed the latter. With no incumbrances whatever, with fine professional record, with personal traits and reputation to make him enviable, with comparative wealth and, as a rule, superlative health,

Blakely started on his career as a subaltern at Sandy with three serious handicaps,—the disfavor of his captain, who knew and loved him little,—the prejudice of Mrs. Bridger, who knew and loved him not at all,—and the jealous pique of Mrs. Plume, who had known and loved him, possibly, too well.

There was little duty doing at Sandy at the time whereof we write. Men rose at dawn and sent the horses forth to graze all day in the foothills under heavy guard. It was too hot for drills, with the mercury sizzling at the hundred mark. Indian prisoners did the "police" work about the post; and men and women dozed and wilted in the shade until the late afternoon recall. Then Sandy woke up and energetically stabled, drilled, paraded under arms at sunset, mounted guard immediately thereafter, dined in spotless white; then rode, drove, flirted, danced, gossiped, made mirth, melody, or monotonous plaint till nearly midnight; then slept until the dawn of another day.

Indians there were in the wilds of the Mogollon to the southeast, and, sometimes at rare intervals straying from the big reservation up the valley, they scared the scattered settlers of the Agua Fria and the Hassayampa; but Sandy rarely knew of them except as prisoners. Not a hostile shot had been fired in the surrounding mountains for at least six months, so nobody felt the least alarm, and many only languid interest, when the white-coated officers reported the result of sunset roll-call and inspection, and, saluting Major Plume, the captain of "C" Troop announced in tones he meant should be heard along the row: "Mr. Blakely, sir, is absent!"

CHAPTER II

SCOT VERSUS SAXON

Three women were seated at the moment on the front veranda of the major's quarters—Mrs. Plume, Miss Janet Wren, the captain's sister, and little Mrs. Bridger. The first named had been intently watching the officers as, after the dismissal of their companies at the barracks, they severally joined the post commander, who had been standing on the barren level of the parade, well out toward the flagstaff, his adjutant beside him. To her the abrupt announcement caused no surprise. She had seen that Mr. Blakely was not with his troop. The jeweled hands slightly twitched, but her voice had the requisite and conventional drawl as she turned to Miss Wren: "Chasing some new butterfly, I suppose, and got lost. A—what time did—Angela return?"

"Hours ago, I fancy. She was dressed when I returned from hospital. Sergeant Leary seems worse to-day."

"That was nearly six," dreamily persisted Mrs. Plume. "I happened to be at the side window." In the pursuit of knowledge Mrs. Plume adhered to the main issue and ignored the invalid sergeant, whose slow convalescence had stirred the sympathies of the captain's sister.

"Yes, it was nearly that when Angela dismounted," softly said Mrs. Bridger. "I heard Punch galloping away to his stable."

"Why, Mrs. Bridger, are you sure?" And the spinster of forty-five turned sharply on the matron of less than half her years. "She had on her white muslin when she came to the head of the stairs to answer me."

Mrs. Bridger could not be mistaken. It was Angela's habit when she returned from her rides to dismount at the rear gateway; give Punch his *conge* with a pat or two of the hand; watch him a moment as he tore gleefully away, round to the stables to the westward of the big quadrangle; then to go to her room and dress for the evening, coming down an hour later, looking fresh and sweet and dainty as a dewy Mermet. As a rule she rode without other escort than the hounds, for her father would not go until the sun was very low and would not let her go with Blakely or Duane, the only bachelor troop officers then at Sandy. He had nothing against Duane, but, having set his seal against the other, felt it necessary to include them both. As a rule, therefore, she started about four, alone, and was home an hour later. Five young maidens dwelt that year in officers' row, daughters of the regiments,—for it was a mixed command and not a big one,—two companies each of infantry and cavalry, after the manner of the early 70's. Angela knew all four girls, of course, and had formed an intimacy with one—one who only cared to ride in the cool of the bright evenings when the officers took the hounds jack-rabbit hunting up the valley. Twice a week, when Luna served, they held these moonlit meets, and galloping at that hour, though more dangerous to necks, was less so to complexions. As a rule, too, Angela and Punch contented themselves with a swift scurry round the reservation, with frequent fordings of the stream for the joy it gave them both. They were rarely out of sight of the sentries and never in any appreciable danger. No Apache with hostile intent ventured near enough to Sandy to risk reprisals. Miners, prospectors, and ranchmen were few in numbers, but, far and wide they knew the captain's bonny daughter, and, like the men of her father's troop, would have risked their lives to do her a service. Their aversions as to Sandy were centered in the other sex.

Aunt Janet, therefore, had some reason for doubting the report of Mrs. Bridger. It was so unlike Angela to be so very late returning, although, now that Mrs. Bridger had mentioned it, she, too, remembered hearing the rapid thud of Punch's galloping hoofs homeward bound, as was she, at 5.45. Yet, barely five minutes thereafter, Angela, who usually spent half an hour splashing in her tub, appeared full panoplied, apparently, at the head of the stairs upon her aunt's arrival, and was even now somewhere down the row, hobnobbing with Kate Sanders. That Lieutenant Blakely should have missed retreat roll-call was in itself no very serious matter. "Slept through at his quarters, perhaps," said Plume. "He'll turn up in time for dinner." In fine the major's indifference struck the captain as an evidence of official weakness, reprehensible in a commander charged with the discipline of a force on hostile soil. What Wren intended was that Plume should be impressed by his formal word and manner, and direct the adjutant to look up the derelict instanter. As no such action was taken, however, he felt it due to himself to speak again. A just man was Wren, and faithful to the core in his own discharge of duty. What he could not abide was negligence on part of officer or man, on part of superior or inferior, and he sought to "stiffen" Plume forthwith.

"If he isn't in his quarters, shall I send a party out in search, sir?"

"Who? Blakely? Dear, no, Wren! What for?" returned the post commander, obviously nettled. "I fancy he'll not thank you for even searching his quarters. You may stumble over his big museum in the dark and smash things. No, let him alone. If he isn't here for dinner, I'll 'tend to it myself."

And so, rebuffed, as it happened, by an officer much his inferior in point of experience and somewhat in years, Wren silently and stiffly saluted and turned away. Virtually he had been given to understand that his suggestion was impertinent. He reached his quarters, therefore, in no pleasant mood, and found his sister waiting for him with Duty in her clear and shining eyes.

A woman of many a noble trait was Janet Wren,—a woman who had done a world of good to those in sickness, sorrow, or other adversity, a woman of boundless faith in herself and her opinions, but not too much hope or charity for others. The blood of the Scotch Covenanters was in her veins, for her mother had been born and bred in the shadow of the kirk and lived and died in the shadow of the cross. A woman with a mission was Janet, and one who went at it unflinchingly. She had loved her brother always, yet disapproved his marriage to so young and unformed a woman as was his wife. Later, she had deprecated from the start the soldier spirit, fierce in his Highland blood, that tore him from the teachings of their gentle mother and her beloved meenister, took him from his fair young wife when most she needed him and sent him straightway into the ranks of the one Highland regiment in the Union Army at the outbreak of the Civil War. His gallant colonel fell at First Bull Run, and

Sergeant Wren fought over his body to the fervent admiration of the Southerners who captured both. The first War Secretary, mourning a beloved brother and grateful to his defender, commissioned the latter in the regulars at once and, on his return from Libby, Wren joined the army as a first lieutenant. With genuine Scottish thrift, his slender pay had been hoarded for him, and his now motherless little one, by that devoted sister, and when, a captain at the close of the war, he came to clasp his daughter to his heart, he found himself possessed of a few hundreds more than fell to the lot of most of his associates. It was then that Janet, motherless herself, had stepped into the management of her brother's army home, and sought to dominate in that as she had in everything else from early girlhood. Wren loved her fondly, but he, too, had a will. They had many a clash. It was this, indeed, that led to Angela's going so early to an Eastern school. We are all paragons of wisdom in the management of other people's children. It is in dealing with our own our limitations are so obvious. Fond as she had become of Angela's sweet young mother, it must be owned that whom Janet loved in this way she often chastened. Neighbors swore it was not grief, nor illness, half so much as sister-in-law, that wore the gentle spirit to the snapping-point. The great strong heart of the soldier was well-nigh broken at his loss, and Janet, who had never seen him shed a tear since early boyhood, stood for once, at least, in awe and trembling at sight of his awful grief. Time and nature played their part and brought him, gradually, resignation, but never genuine solace. He turned to little Angela with almost passionate love and tenderness. He would, mayhap, have spoiled her had not frontier service kept him so much afield that it was Janet who really reared her,—but not according to the strict letter of her law. Wren knew well what that was and forbade.

Misfortunes came to Janet Wren while yet a comely woman of thirty-five. She could have married, and married well, a comrade captain in her brother's regiment; but him, at least, she held to be her own, and, loving him with genuine fervor and devotion, she sought to turn him in all things to her serious views of life, its manifold duties and responsibilities. She had her ideal of what a man should be—a monarch among other men, but one knowing no God but her God, no creed but her creed, no master but Duty, no mistress but herself, and no weakness whatsoever. A braver, simpler, kinder soul than her captain there dwelt not in the service of his country, but he loved his pipe, his song, his dogs, his horses, his troop, and certain soldier ways that, during his convalescence from wounds, she had not had opportunity to observe. She had nursed him back to life and love and, unwittingly, to his former harmless habits. These all she would have had him forswear, not for her sake so much, she said, but because they were in themselves sinful and beneath him. She sought to train him down too fine for the rugged metal of the veteran soldier, and the fabric snapped in her hands. She had sent him forth sore-hearted over her ceaseless importunity. She had told him he must not only give up all his ways, but, if he would make her happy, he must put the words of Ruth into his mouth, and that ended it. He transferred into another corps when she broke with him; carried his sore heart to the Southern plains, and fell in savage battle within another month.

Not long thereafter her little fortune, invested according to the views of a spiritual rather than a temporal adviser,—and much against her brother's wishes,—went the way of riches that have wings, and now, dependent solely upon him, welcomed to his home and fireside, she nevertheless strove to dominate as of yore. He had had to tell her Angela could not and should not be subjected to

Charles King

such restraints as the sister would have prescribed, but so long as he was the sole victim he whimsically bore it without vehement protest. "Convert me all you can, Janet, dear," he said, "but don't try to reform the whole regiment. It's past praying for."

Now, when other women whispered to her that while Mrs. Plume had been a belle in St. Louis and Mr. Blakely a young society beau, the magnitude of their flirtation had well-nigh stopped her marriage, Miss Wren saw opportunity for her good offices and, so far from avoiding, she sought the society of the major's brooding wife. She even felt a twinge of disappointment when the young officer appeared, and after the initial thirty-six hours under the commander's roof, rarely went thither at all. She knew her brother disapproved of him, and thought it to be because of moral, not military, obliquity. She saw with instant apprehension his quick interest in Angela and the child's almost unconscious response. With the solemn conviction of the maiden who, until past the meridian, had never loved, she looked on Angela as far too young and immature to think of marrying, yet too shallow, vain and frivolous, too corrupted, in fact, by that pernicious society school—not to shrink from flirtations that might mean nothing to the man but would be damnation to the girl. Even the name of this big, blue-eyed, fair-skinned young votary of science had much about it that made her fairly bristle, for she had once been described as an "austere vestal" by Lieutenant Blake, of the regiment preceding them at Sandy, the—th Cavalry—and a mutual friend had told her all about it—another handicap for Blakely. She had grown, it must be admitted, somewhat gaunt and forbidding in these later years, a thing that had stirred certain callow wits to differentiate between the Misses Wren as Angela and Angular, which, hearing, some few women reproved but all repeated. Miss Wren, the sister, was in fine a woman widely honored but little sought. It was Angela that all Camp Sandy would have met with open arms.

"R-r-robert," began Miss Wren, as the captain unclasped his saber belt and turned it over to Mickel, his German "striker." She would have proceeded further, but he held up a warning hand. He had come homeward angering and ill at ease. Disliking Blakely from the first, a "ballroom soldier," as he called him, and alienated from him later, he had heard still further whisperings of the devotions of a chieftain's daughter at the agency, above all, of the strange infatuation of the major's wife, and these had warranted, in his opinion, warning words to his senior subaltern in refusing that gentleman's request to ride with Angela. "I object to any such attentions—to any meetings whatsoever," said he, but sooner than give the real reason, added lamely, "My daughter is too young." Now he thought he saw impending duty in his sister's somber eyes and poise. He knew it when she began by rolling her r's— it was so like their childhood's spiritual guide and mentor, MacTaggart, erstwhile of the "Auld Licht" persuasion, and a power.

"Wait a bit, Janet," said he. "Mickel, get my horse and tell Sergeant Strang to send me a mounted orderly." Then, as Mickel dropped the saber in the open doorway and departed, he turned upon her.

"Where's Angela?" said he, "and what was she doing out after recall? The stable sergeant says 'twas six when Punch came home."

"R-r-robert, it is of that I wish to speak to you, and before she comes to dinner. Hush! She's coming now."

Down the row of shaded wooden porticos, at the major's next door, at Dr. Graham's, the Scotch surgeon and Wren's especial friend and crony, at the Lynns' and Sanders's beyond, little groups of women and children in cool evening garb, and officers in white, were gathered in merry, laughing chat. Nowhere, save in the eyes of one woman at the commanding officer's, and here at Wren's, seemed there anything ominous in the absence of this officer so lately come to join them. The voice of Angela, glad and ringing, fell upon the father's ears in sudden joy. Who could associate shame or subterfuge with tones so charged with merriment? The face of Angela, coming suddenly round the corner from the side veranda, beamed instantly upon him, sweet, trusting and welcoming, then slowly shadowed at sight of the set expression about his mouth, and the rigid, uncompromising, determined sorrow in the features of her aunt.

Before she could utter a word, the father questioned:

"Angela, my child, have you seen Mr. Blakely this afternoon?"

One moment her big eyes clouded, but unflinchingly they met his gaze. Then, something in the stern scrutiny of her aunt's regard stirred all that was mutinous within her; yet there was an irrepressible twitching about the corners of the rosy mouth, a twinkle about the big brown eyes that should have given them pause, even as she demurely answered:

"Yes."

"When?" demanded the soldier, his muscular hand clutching ominously at the wooden rail; his jaw setting squarely. "When—and where?"

But now the merriment with which she had begun changed slowly at sight of the repressed fury in his rugged Gaelic face. She, too, was trembling as she answered:

"Just after recall—down at the pool."

For an instant he stood glaring, incredulous. "At the pool! You! My bairnie!" Then, with sudden outburst of passionate wrath, "Go to your room!" said he.

"But listen—father, dear," she began, imploringly. For answer he seized her slender arm in almost brutal grasp and fairly hurled her within the doorway. "Not a word!" he ground between his clinched teeth. "Go instantly!" Then, slamming the door upon her, he whirled about as though to seek his sister's face, and saw beyond her, rounding the corner of the northwest set of quarters, coming in from the *mesa* roadway at the back, the tall, white figure of the missing man.

Another moment and Lieutenant Blakely, in the front room of his quarters, looking pale and strange, was being pounced upon with eager questioning by Duane, his junior, when the wooden steps and veranda creaked under a quick, heavy, ominous tread, and, with livid face and clinching hands, the troop commander came striding in.

"Mr. Blakely," said he, his voice deep with wrath and tremulous with passion, "I told you three days ago my daughter and you must not meet, and—you know why! To-day you lured her to a rendezvous outside the post—"

"Captain Wren!"

"Don't lie! I say you lured her, for my lass would never have met you—"

"You shall *un*say it, sir," was Blakely's instant rejoinder. "Are you mad—or what? I never set eyes on your daughter to-day—until a moment ago."

And then the voice of young Duane was uplifted, shouting for help. With a crash, distinctly heard out on the parade, Wren had struck his junior down.

CHAPTER III

MOCCASIN TRACKS

When Mr. Blakely left the post that afternoon he went afoot. When he returned, just after the sounding of retreat, he came in saddle. Purposely he avoided the road that led in front of the long line of officers' quarters and chose instead the water-wagon track along the rear. People among the laundresses' quarters, south of the *mesa* on which stood the quadrangular inclosure of Camp Sandy, eyed him curiously as he ambled through on his borrowed pony; but he looked neither to right nor left and hurried on in obvious discomposure. He was looking pale and very tired, said the saddler sergeant's wife, an hour later, when all the garrison was agog with the story of Wren's mad assault. He never seemed to see the two or three soldiers, men of family, who rose and saluted as he passed, and not an officer in the regiment was more exact or scrupulous in his recognition of such soldier courtesy as Blakely had ever been. They wondered, therefore, at his strange abstraction. They wondered more, looking after him, when, just as his stumbling pony reached the crest, the rider reined him in and halted short in evident embarrassment. They could not see what he saw—two young girls in gossamer gowns of white, with arms entwining each other's waists, their backs toward him, slowly pacing northward up the *mesa* and to the right of the road. Some old croquet arches, balls, and mallets lay scattered about, long since abandoned to dry rot and disuse, and, so absorbed were the damsels in their confidential chat,—bubbling over, too, with merry laughter,—they gave no heed to these until one, the taller of the pair, catching her slippered foot in the stiff, unyielding wire, plunged forward and fell, nearly dragging her companion with her. Blakely, who had hung back, drove his barbless heels into the pony's flanks, sent him lurching forward, and in less than no time was out of saddle and aiding her to rise, laughing so hard she, for a moment, could not speak or thank him. Save to flowing skirt, there was not the faintest damage, yet his eyes, his voice, his almost tremulous touch were all suggestive of deep concern, before, once more mounting, he raised his broad-brimmed hat and bade them reluctant good-night. Kate Sanders ran scurrying home an instant later, but Angela's big and shining eyes followed him every inch of the way until he once more dismounted at the upper end of the row and, looking back, saw her and waved his hat, whereat she ran, blushing, smiling, and not a little wondering, flustered and happy, into the gallery of their own quarters and the immediate presence of her father. Blakely, meanwhile, had summoned his servant:

"Take this pony at once to Mr. Hart," said he, "and say I'll be back again as soon as I've seen the commanding officer."

When Downs, the messenger, returned to the house about half an hour later, it was to find his master prostrate and bleeding on the bed in his room, Dr. Graham and the hospital attendant working over him, the major and certain of his officers, with gloomy faces and muttering tongues, conferring on the piazza in front, and one of the lieutenant's precious cases of bugs and butterflies a wreck of shattered glass. More than half the officers of the post were present. A bevy of women and girls had gathered in the dusk some distance down the row. The wondering Milesian whispered inquiry of silent soldiers lingering about the house, but the gruff voice of Sergeant Clancy bade them go about their business. Not until nearly an hour later was it generally known that Captain Wren had been escorted to his quarters by the post adjutant and ordered to remain therein in close arrest.

If some older and more experienced officer than Duane had been there perhaps the matter would not have proved so tragic, but the latter was utterly unstrung by Wren's furious attack and the unlooked-for result. Without warning of any kind, the burly Scot had launched his big fist straight at Blakely's jaw, and sent the slender, still fever-weakened form crashing through a case of specimens, reducing it to splinters that cruelly cut and tore the bruised and senseless face. A corporal of the guard, marching his relief in rear of the quarters at the moment, every door and window being open, heard the crash, the wild cry for help, rushed in, with his men at his heels, and found the captain standing stunned and ghastly, with the sweat starting from his brow, staring down at the result of his fearful work. From the front Captain Sanders and his amazed lieutenant came hurrying. Together they lifted the stricken and bleeding man to his bed in the back room and started a soldier for the doctor on the run. The sight of this man, speeding down the row, bombarded all the way with questions he could not stop to answer, startled every soul along that westward-facing front, and sent men and women streaming up the line toward Blakely's quarters at the north end. The doctor fairly brushed them from his path and Major Plume had no easy task persuading the tearful, pallid groups of army wives and daughters to retire to the neighboring quarters. Janet Wren alone refused point-blank. She would not go without first seeing her brother. It was she who took the arm of the awed, bewildered, shame-and conscience-stricken man and led him, with bowed and humbled head, the adjutant aiding on the other side, back to the door he had so sternly closed upon his only child, and that now as summarily shut on him. Dr. Graham had pronounced the young officer's injuries serious, and the post commander was angry to the very core.

One woman there was who, with others, had aimlessly hastened up the line, and who seemed now verging on hysterics—the major's wife. It was Mrs. Graham who rebukefully sent her own braw young brood scurrying homeward through the gathering dusk, and then possessed herself of Mrs. Plume. "The shock has unnerved you," she charitably, soothingly whispered: "Come away with me," but the major's wife refused to go. Hart, the big post trader, had just reached the spot, driving up in his light buckboard. His usually jovial face was full of sympathy and trouble. He could not believe the news, he said. Mr. Blakely had been with him so short a time beforehand and was coming down again at once, so Downs, the striker, told him, when some soldier ran in to say the lieutenant had been half killed by Captain Wren. Plume heard him talking and came down the low steps to meet and confer with him, while the others, men and women, listened eagerly, expectant of developments. Then Hart became visibly embarrassed. Yes, Mr. Blakely had come up from below and begged the loan of a pony, saying he must get to the post at once to see Major Plume. Hadn't he seen the major? No! Then Hart's embarrassment increased. Yes, something had happened. Blakely had told him, and in fact they—he—all of them had something very important on hand. He didn't know what to do now, with Mr.

Blakely unable to speak, and, to the manifest disappointment of the swift-gathering group, Hart finally begged the major to step aside with him a moment and he would tell him what he knew. All eyes followed them, then followed the major as he came hurrying back with heightened color and went straight to Dr. Graham at the sufferer's side. "Can I speak with him? Is he well enough to answer a question or two?" he asked, and the doctor shook his head. "Then, by the Lord, I'll have to wire to Prescott!" said Plume, and left the room at once. "What is it?" feebly queried the patient, now half-conscious. But the doctor answered only "Hush! No talking now, Mr. Blakely," and bade the others leave the room and let him get to sleep.

But tattoo had not sounded that still and starlit evening when a strange story was in circulation about the post, brought up from the trader's store by pack-train hands who said they were there when Mr. Blakely came in and asked for Hart—"wanted him right away, bad," was the way they put it. Then it transpired that Mr. Blakely had found no sport at bug-hunting and had fallen into a doze while waiting for winged insects, and when he woke it was to make a startling discovery—his beautiful Geneva watch had disappeared from one pocket and a flat note case, carried in an inner breast pocket of his white duck blouse, and containing about one hundred dollars, was also gone. Some vagrant soldier, possibly, or some "hard-luck outfit" of prospectors, probably, had come upon him sleeping, and had made way with his few valuables. Two soldiers had been down stream, fishing for what they called Tonto trout, but they were looked up instantly and proved to be men above suspicion. Two prospectors had been at Hart's, nooning, and had ridden off down stream toward three o'clock. *There* was a clew worth following, and certain hangers-on about the trader's, "layin' fer a job," had casually hinted at the prospect of a game down at Snicker's—a ranch five miles below. Here, too, was something worth investigating. If Blakely had been robbed, as now seemed more than likely, Camp Sandy felt that the perpetrator must still be close at hand and of the packer or prospector class.

But before the ranks were broken, after the roll-call, then invariably held at half-past nine, Hart came driving back in a buckboard, with a lantern and a passenger, the latter one of the keenest trailers among the sergeants of Captain Sanders' troop, and Sanders was with the major as the man sprang from the wagon and stood at salute.

"Found anything, sergeant?" asked Plume.

"Not a boot track, sir, but the lieutenant's own."

"No tracks at all—in that soft sand!" exclaimed the major, disappointed and unbelieving. His wife had come slowly forward from within doors, and, bending slightly toward them, stood listening.

"No boot tracks, sir. There's others though—Tonto moccasins!"

Plume stood bewildered. "By Jove! I never thought of that!" said he, turning presently on his second troop commander. "But who ever heard of Apaches taking a man's watch and leaving—him?"

"If the major will look," said the sergeant, quietly producing a scouting notebook such as was then issued by the engineer department, "I measured 'em and made rough copies here. There was *two*, sir. Both came, both went, by the path through the willows up stream. We didn't have time to follow. One is longer and slimmer than the other. If I may make so bold, sir, I'd have a guard down there to-night to keep people away; otherwise the tracks may be spoiled before morning."

"Take three men and go yourself," said the major promptly. "See anything of any of the lieutenant's property? Mr. Hart told you, didn't he?" Plume was studying the sergeant's pencil sketches, by the light of the trader's lantern, as he spoke, a curious, puzzled look on his soldierly face.

"Saw where the box had lain in the sand, sir, but no trace of the net," and Sergeant Shannon was thinking less of these matters than of his sketches. There was something he thought the major ought to see, and presently he saw.

"Why, sergeant, these may be Tonto moccasin tracks, but not grown men's. They are mere boys, aren't they?"

"Mere girls, sir."

There was a sound of rustling skirts upon the bare piazza. Plume glanced impatiently over his shoulder. Mrs. Plume had vanished into the unlighted hallway.

"That would account for their taking the net," said he thoughtfully, "but what on earth would the guileless Tonto maiden do with a watch or with greenbacks? They wouldn't dare show with them at the agency! How far did you follow the tracks?"

"Only a rod or two. Once in the willows they can't well quit them till they reach the shallows above the pool, sir. We can guard there to-night and begin trailing at dawn."

"So be it then!" and presently the conference closed.

Seated on the adjoining gallery, alone and in darkness, stricken and sorrowing, a woman had been silently observant of the meeting, and had heard occasional snatches of the talk. Presently she rose; softly entered the house and listened at a closed door on the northward side—Captain Wren's own room. An hour previous, tortured between his own thoughts and her well-meant, but unwelcome efforts to cheer him, he had begged to be left alone, and had closed his door against all comers.

Now, she as softly ascended the narrow stairway and paused for a moment at another door, also closed. Listening a while, she knocked, timidly, hesitatingly, but no answer came. After a while, noiselessly, she turned the knob and entered.

A dim light was burning on a little table by the white bedside. A long, slim figure, white-robed and in all the abandon of girlish grief, was lying, face downward, on the bed. Tangled masses of hair concealed much of the neck and shoulders, but, bending over, Miss Wren could partially see the flushed and tear-wet cheek pillowed on one slender white arm. Exhausted by long weeping, Angela at last had dropped to sleep, but the little hand that peeped from under the thick, tumbling tresses still clung to an odd and unfamiliar object—something the older woman had seen only at a distance before—something she gazed at in startled fascination this strange and solemn night—a slender, long-handled butterfly net of filmy gauze.

CHAPTER IV

A STRICKEN SENTRY

Sentry duty at Camp Sandy along in '75 had not been allowed to bear too heavily on its little garrison. There was nothing worth stealing about the place, said Plume, and no pawn-shop handy. Of course there were government horses and mules, food and forage, arms and ammunition, but these were the days of soldier supremacy in that arid and distant land, and soldiers had a summary way of settling with marauders that was discouraging to enterprise. Larceny was therefore little known until the law, with its delays and circumventions, took root in the virgin soil, and people at such posts as Sandy seldom shut and rarely locked their doors, even by night. Windows were closed and blanketed by day against the blazing sun and torrid heat, but, soon after nightfall, every door and window was usually opened wide and often kept so all the night long, in order that the cooler air, settling down from *mesa* and mountain, might drift through every room and hallway, licking up the starting dew upon the smooth, rounded surface of the huge *ollas*, the porous water jars that hung suspended on every porch, and wafting comfort to the heated brows of the lightly covered sleepers within. Pyjamas were then unknown in army circles, else even the single sheet that covered the drowsing soldier might have been dispensed with.

Among the quarters occupied by married men, both in officers' row and Sudsville under the plateau, doors were of little account in a community where the only intruder to be feared was heat, and so it had resulted that while the corrals, stables, and storehouses had their guards, only a single sentry paced the long length of the eastward side of the post, a single pair of eyes and a single rifle barrel being deemed amply sufficient to protect against possible prowlers the rear yards and entrances of the row. The westward front of the officers' homes stood in plain view, on bright nights at least, of the sentry at the guard-house, and needed no other protector. On dark nights it was supposed to look out for itself.

A lonely time of it, as a rule, had No. 5, the "backyard sentry," but this October night he lacked not for sensation. Lights burned until very late in many of the quarters, while at Captain Wren's and Lieutenant Blakely's people were up and moving about until long after midnight. Of course No. 5 had heard all about the dreadful affair of the early evening. What he and his fellows puzzled over was the probable cause of Captain Wren's furious assault upon his subaltern. Many a theory was afloat, Duane, with unlooked-for discretion, having held his tongue as to the brief conversation that preceded the blow. It was after eleven when the doctor paid his last visit for the night, and the attendant came out on the rear porch for a pitcher of cool water from the *olla*. It was long after twelve when the light in the upstairs room at Captain Wren's was turned low, and for two hours thereafter, with bowed head, the captain himself paced nervously up and down, wearing in the soft and sandy soil a mournful pathway parallel with his back porch. It was after three, noted Private Mullins, of that first relief, when from the rear door of the major's quarters there emerged two forms in feminine garb, and, there being no hindering fences, away they hastened in the dim starlight, past Wren's, Cutler's, Westervelt's, and Truman's quarters until they were swallowed up in the general gloom about Lieutenant Blakely's. Private Mullins could not say for certain whether they had entered the rear door or gone around under the deep shadows of the veranda. When next he saw them, fifteen minutes later, coming as swiftly and silently back, Mullins was wondering whether he ought not to challenge and have them account for themselves. His orders were to allow inmates of the officers' quarters to pass in or out at night without challenge, provided he "recognized them to be such." Now, Mullins felt morally certain that these two were Mrs. Plume and Mrs. Plume's vivacious maid, a French-Canadian damsel, much admired and sought in soldier circles at the post, but Mullins had not seen their faces and could rightfully insist it was his duty and prerogative to do so. The question was, how would the "commanding officer's lady" like and take it? Mullins therefore shook his head. "I hadn't the nerve," as he expressed it, long afterwards. But no such frailty oppressed the occupant of the adjoining house. Just as the two had reached the rear of Wren's quarters, and were barely fifty steps from safety, the captain himself, issuing again from the doorway, suddenly appeared upon the scene, and in low, but imperative tone accosted them. "*Who* are you?" said he, bending eagerly, sternly over them. One quick look he gave, and, almost instantly recoiling, exclaimed "Mrs. Plume! I beg—" Then, as though with sudden recollection, "No, madam, I do *not* beg your pardon," and, turning on his heel, abruptly left them. Without a word, but with the arm of the maid supporting, the taller woman sped swiftly across the narrow intervening space and was lost again within the shadows of her husband's home.

Private Mullins, silent and probably unseen witness of this episode, slowly tossed his rifle from the port to the shoulder; shook his puzzled head; stared a moment at the dim figure of Captain Wren again in the starlit morning, nervously tramping up and down his narrow limit; then mechanically sauntered down the roadway, pondering much over what he had seen and heard during the brief period of his early morning watch. Reaching the south, the lower, end of his post, he turned again. He had but ten minutes left of his two-hour tramp. The second relief was due to start at 3.30, and should reach him at 3.35. He was wondering would the officer of the day "come nosin' round" within that time, asking him his orders, and was everything all right on his post? And had he observed anything unusual? There was Captain Wren, like a caged tiger, tramping up and down behind his quarters. At least he had been, for now he had disappeared. There were, or rather had been, the two ladies in long cloaks flitting in the shadows from the major's quarters to those of the invalid lieutenant. Mullins certainly did not wish to speak about them to any official visitor, whatever he might whisper later to Norah Shaughnessy, the saddler sergeant's daughter—Norah, who was nurse girl at the Trumans', and knew all the ins and outs of social life at Sandy—Norah, at whose window, under the north gable, he gazed with love in his eyes as he made his every round. He was a good soldier, was Mullins, but glad this night to get off post. Through the gap between the second and third quarters he saw the lights at the guard-house and could faintly see the black silhouette of armed men in front of them. The relief was forming sharp on time, and presently Corporal Donovan would be bringing Trooper Schultz, of "C" Troop, straight across the parade in search of him. The major so allowed his sentry on No. 5 to be relieved at night. Mullins thanked the saints with pious fervor that no more ladies would be like to flit across his vision, that night at least, when, dimly through the dusk, against the spangled northern sky, he sighted another figure crouching across the upper end of his post and making straight for the lighted entrance at the rear of the lieutenant's quarters. Someone else, then, had interest at Blakely's—someone coming stealthily from without. A minute later certain wakeful ears were startled by a moaning cry for aid.

Just what happened, and how it happened, within the minute, led to conflicting stories on the morrow. First man examined by Major Plume was Lieutenant Truman of the Infantry, who happened to be officer of the day. He had been over at Blakely's about midnight, he said; had found the patient sleeping under the influence of soothing medicine, and, after a whispered word with Todd, the hospital attendant, had tiptoed out again, encountering Downs, the lieutenant's striker, in the darkness on the rear porch. Downs said he was that excited he couldn't sleep at all, and Mr. Truman had come to the conclusion that Downs's excitement was due, in large part, to local influences totally disconnected with the affairs of the early evening. Downs was an Irishman who loved the "craytur," and had been known to resort to unconventional methods of getting it. At twelve o'clock, said Mr. Truman, the striker had obviously been priming. Now Plume's standing orders were that no liquor should be sold to Downs at the store and none to other soldiers except in "pony" glasses and for use on the spot. None could be carried away unconsumed. The only legitimate spirits, therefore, to which Downs could have access were those in Blakely's locked closet—spirits hitherto used only in the preservation of specimens, and though probably not much worse than the whisky sold at the store, disdainfully referred to by votaries as "Blakely's bug juice." Mr. Truman, therefore, demanded of Downs the possession of the lieutenant's keys, and, with aggrieved dignity of mien, Downs had referred him to the doctor, whose suspicions had been earlier aroused. Intending to visit his sentries after the change of guard at 1.30, Truman had thrown himself into a reclining chair in his little parlor, while Mrs. Truman and the little Trumans slumbered peacefully aloft. After reading an hour or so the lieutenant fell into a doze from which he awoke with a start. Mrs. Truman was bending over him. Mrs. Truman had been aroused by hearing voices in cautious, yet excited, colloquy in the shadows of Blakely's back porch. She felt sure that Downs was one and thought from the sound that he must be intoxicated, so Truman shuffled out to see, and somebody, bending double in the dusk, scurried away at his approach. He heard rather than saw. But there was Downs, at least, slinking back into the house, and him Truman halted and accosted. "Who was that with you?" he asked, and Downs thickly swore he hadn't seen a soul. But all the while Downs was clumsily stuffing something into a side pocket, and Truman, seizing his hand, dragged it forth into the light. It was one of the hospital six-ounce bottles, bearing a label indicative of glycerine lotion, but the color of the contained fluid belied the label. A sniff was sufficient. "Who gave you this whisky?" was the next demand, and Downs declared 'twas a hospital "messager" that brought it over, thinking the lieutenant might need it. Truman, filled with wrath, had dragged Downs into the dimly lighted room to the rear of that in which lay Lieutenant Blakely, and was there upbraiding and investigating when startled by the stifled cry that, rising suddenly on the night from the open *mesa* just without, had so alarmed so many in the garrison. Of what had led to it he had then no more idea than the dead.

Corporal Donovan, next examined, said he was marching Schultz over to relieve Mullins on No. 5, just after half-past three, and heading for the short cut between the quarters of Captains Wren and Cutler, which was about where No. 5 generally met the relief, when, just as they were halfway between the flagstaff and the row, Schultz began to limp and said there must be a pebble in his boot. So they halted. Schultz kicked off his boot and shook it upside down, and, while he was tugging at it again, they both heard a sort of gurgling, gasping cry out on the *mesa*. Of course Donovan started and ran that way, leaving Schultz to follow, and, just back of Captain Westervelt's, the third house from the northward end, he almost collided with Lieutenant Truman, officer of the day, who ordered him to run for Dr. Graham and fetch him up to Lieutenant Blakely's quick. So of what had taken place he, too, was ignorant until later.

It was the hospital attendant, Todd, whose story came next and brought Plume to his feet with consternation in his eyes. Todd said he had been sitting at the lieutenant's bedside when, somewhere about three o'clock, he had to go out and tell Downs to make less noise. Downs was completely upset by the catastrophe to his officer and, somehow, had got a few comforting drinks stowed away, and these had started him to singing some confounded Irish keen that grated on Todd's nerves. He was afraid it would disturb the patient and he was about to go out and remonstrate when the singing stopped and presently he heard Downs's voice in excited conversation. Then a woman's voice in low, urgent, persuasive whisper became faintly audible, and this surprised Todd beyond expression. He had thought to go and take a look and see who it could be, when there was a sudden swish of skirts and scurry of feet, and then Mr. Truman's voice was heard. Then there was some kind of sharp talk from the lieutenant to Downs, and then, in a sort of a lull, there came that uncanny cry out on the *mesa*, and, stopping only long enough to see that the lieutenant was not roused or disturbed, Todd hastened forth. One or two dim figures, dark and shadowy, were just visible on the eastward *mesa*, barely ten paces away, and thither the attendant ran. Downs, lurching heavily, was just ahead of him. Together they came upon a little group. Somebody went running southward—Lieutenant Truman, as Todd learned later—hurrying for the doctor. A soldier equipped as a sentry lay moaning on the sand, clasping a bloody hand to his side, and over him, stern, silent, but agitated, bent Captain Wren.

CHAPTER V

THE CAPTAIN'S DEFIANCE

Within ten minutes of Todd's arrival at the spot the soft sands of the *mesa* were tramped into bewildering confusion by dozens of trooper boots. The muffled sound of excited voices, so soon after the startling affair of the earlier evening, and hurrying footfalls following, had roused almost every household along the row and brought to the spot half the officers on duty at the post. A patrol of the guard had come in double time, and soldiers had been sent at speed to the hospital for a stretcher. Dr. Graham had lost no moment of time in reaching the stricken sentry. Todd had been sent back to Blakely's bedside and Downs to fetch a lantern. They found the latter, five minutes later, stumbling about the Trumans' kitchen, weeping for that which was lost, and the sergeant of the guard collared and cuffed him over to the guard-house— one witness, at least, out of the way. At four o'clock the doctor was working over his exhausted and unconscious patient at the hospital. Mullins had been stabbed twice, and dangerously, and half a dozen men with lanterns were hunting about the bloody sands where the faithful fellow had dropped, looking for a weapon or a clew, and probably trampling out all possibility of finding either. Major Plume, through Mr. Doty, his adjutant, had felt it necessary to remind Captain Wren that an officer in close arrest had no right to be away from his quarters. Late in the evening, it seems, Dr. Graham had represented to the post commander that the captain was in so nervous and overwrought a condition, and so distressed, that as a physician he recommended his patient be allowed the limits of the space adjoining his quarters in which to walk off his superabundant excitement. Graham had long been the friend of Captain Wren and was his friend as well as physician now, even though deploring his astounding outbreak, but Graham had other things to demand his attention as night wore on, and there was no one to speak for Wren when the young adjutant, a subaltern of infantry, with unnecessary significance of tone and manner, suggested the captain's immediate return to his proper quarters. Wren bowed his head and went in stunned and stubborn silence. It had never occurred to him for a moment, when he heard that half-stifled, agonized cry for help, that there could be the faintest criticism of his rushing to the sentry's aid. Still less had it occurred to him that other significance, and damning significance, might attach to his presence on the spot, but, being first to reach the fallen man, he was found kneeling over him within thirty seconds of the alarm. Not another living creature was in sight when the first witnesses came running to the spot. Both Truman and Todd could swear to that.

In the morning, therefore, the orderly came with the customary compliments to say to Captain Wren that the post commander desired to see him at the office.

It was then nearly nine o'clock. Wren had had a sleepless night and was in consultation with Dr. Graham when the summons came. "Ask that Captain Sanders be sent for at once," said the surgeon, as he pressed his comrade patient's hand. "The major has his adjutant and clerk and possibly some other officers. You should have at least one friend."

"I understand," briefly answered Wren, as he stepped to the hallway to get his sun hat. "I wish it might be you." The orderly was already speeding back to the office at the south end of the brown rectangle of adobe and painted pine, but Janet Wren, ministering, according to her lights, to Angela in the little room aloft, had heard the message and was coming down. Taller and more angular than ever she looked as, with flowing gown, she slowly descended the narrow stairway.

"I have just succeeded in getting her to sleep," she murmured. "She has been dreadfully agitated ever since awakened by the voices and the running this morning, and she must have cried herself to sleep last night. R-r-r-obert, would it not be well for you to see her when she wakes? She does not know—I could not tell her—that you are under arrest."

Graham looked more "dour" than did his friend of the line. Privately he was wondering how poor Angela could get to sleep at all with Aunt Janet there to soothe her. The worst time to teach a moral lesson, with any hope of good effect, is when the recipient is suffering from sense of utter injustice and wrong, yet must perforce listen. But it is a favorite occasion with the "ower guid." Janet thought it would be a long step in the right direction to bring her headstrong niece to the belief that all the trouble was the direct result of her having sought, against her father's wishes, a meeting with Mr. Blakely. True, Janet had now some doubt that such had been the case, but, in what she felt was only stubborn pride, her niece refused all explanation. "Father would not hear me at the time," she sobbed. "I am condemned without a chance to defend myself or—him." Yet Janet loved the bonny child devotedly and would go through fire and water to serve her best interests, only those best interests must be as Janet saw them. That anything very serious might result as a consequence of her brother's violent assault on Blakely, she had never yet imagined. That further complications had arisen which might blacken his record she never could credit for a moment. Mullins lay still unconscious, and not until he recovered strength was he to talk with or see anyone. Graham had given faint hope of recovery, and declared that everything depended on his patient's having no serious fever or setback. In a few days he might be able to tell his story. Then the mystery as to his assailant would be cleared in a breath. Janet had taken deep offense that the commanding officer should have sent her brother into close arrest without first hearing of the extreme provocation. "It is an utterly unheard-of proceeding," said she, "this confining of an officer and gentleman without investigation of the affair," and she glared at Graham, uncomprehending, when, with impatient shrug of his big shoulders, he asked her what had they done, between them, to Angela. It was his wife put him up to saying that, she reasoned, for Janet's Calvinistic dogmas as to daughters in their teens were ever at variance with the views of her gentle neighbor. If Angela had been harshly dealt with, undeserving, it was Angela's duty to say so and to say why, said Janet. Meantime, her first care was her wronged and misjudged brother. Gladly would she have gone to the office with him and stood proudly by his side in presence of his oppressor, could such a thing be permitted. She marveled that Robert should now show so little of tenderness for her who had served him loyally, if masterfully, so very long. He merely laid his hand on hers and said he had been summoned to the commanding officer's, then went forth into the light and left her.

Major Plume was seated at his desk, thoughtful and perplexed. Up at regimental headquarters at Prescott Wren was held in high esteem, and the major's brief telegraphic message had called forth anxious inquiry and something akin to veiled disapprobation. Headquarters could not see how it was possible for Wren to assault Lieutenant Blakely without some grave reason. Had Plume investigated? No, but that was coming now, he said to himself, as Wren entered and stood in silence before him.

The little office had barely room for the desks of the commander and his adjutant and the table on which were spread the files of general orders from various superior headquarters—regimental, department, division, the army, and the War Secretary. No curtains adorned the little windows, front and rear. No rug or carpet vexed the warping floor. Three chairs, kitchen pattern, stood against the pine partition that shut off the sight, but by no means the hearing, of the three clerks scratching at their flat-topped desks in the adjoining den. Maps of the United States, of the Military Division of the Pacific, and of the Territory, as far as known and surveyed, hung about the wooden walls. Blue-prints and photographs of scout maps, made by their predecessors of the—th Cavalry in the days of the Crook campaigns, were scattered with the order files about the table. But of pictures, ornamentation, or relief of any kind the gloomy box was destitute as the dun-colored flat of the parade. Official severity spoke in every feature of the forbidding office as well as in those of the major commanding.

There was striking contrast, too, between the man at the desk and the man on the rack before him. Plume had led a life devoid of anxiety or care. Soldiering he took serenely. He liked it, so long as no grave hardship threatened. He had done reasonably good service at corps headquarters during the Civil War; had been commissioned captain in the regulars in '61, and held no vexatious command at any time perhaps, until this that took him to far-away Arizona. Plume was a gentlemanly fellow and no bad garrison soldier. He really shone on parade and review at such fine stations as Leavenworth and Riley, but had never had to bother with mountain scouting or long-distance Indian chasing on the plains. He had a comfortable income outside his pay, and when he was wedded, at the end of her fourth season in society, to a prominent, if just a trifle *passee* belle, people thought him a more than lucky man, until the regiment was sent to Arizona and he to Sandy. Gossip said he went to General Sherman with appeal for some detaining duty, whereupon that bluff and most outspoken warrior exclaimed: "What, what, what! Not want to go with the regiment? Why, here's Blakely begging to be relieved from Terry's staff because he's mad to go." And this, said certain St. Louis commentators, settled it, for Mrs. Plume declared for Arizona.

Well garbed, groomed, and fed was Plume, a handsome, soldierly figure. Very cool and placid was his look in the spotless white that even then by local custom had become official dress for Sandy; but beneath the snowy surface his heart beat with grave disquiet as he studied the strong, rugged, somber face of the soldier on the floor.

Wren was tall and gaunt and growing gray. His face was deeply lined; his close-cropped beard was silver-stranded; his arms and legs were long and sinewy and powerful; his chest and shoulders burly; his regimental dress had not the cut and finish of the commander's. Too much of bony wrist and hand was in evidence, too little of grace and curve. But, though he stood rigidly at attention, with all semblance of respect and subordination, the gleam in his deep-set eyes, the twitch of the long fingers, told of keen and pent-up feeling, and he looked the senior soldier squarely in the face. A sergeant, standing by the adjutant's desk, tiptoed out into the clerk's room and closed the door behind him, then set himself to listen. Young Doty, the adjutant, fiddled nervously with his pen and tried to go on signing papers, but failed. It was for Plume to break the awkward silence, and he did not quite know how. Captain Westervelt, quietly entering at the moment, bowed to the major and took a chair. He had evidently been sent for.

"Captain Wren," presently said Plume, his fingers trembling a bit as they played with the paper folder, "I have felt constrained to send for you to inquire still further into last night's affair—or affairs. I need not tell you that you may decline to answer if you consider your interests are—involved. I had hoped this painful matter might be so explained as to—as to obviate the necessity of extreme measures, but your second appearance close to Mr. Blakely's quarters, under all the circumstances, was so—so extraordinary that I am compelled to call for explanation, if you have one you care to offer."

For a moment Wren stood staring at his commander in amaze. He had expected to be offered opportunity to state the circumstances leading to his now deeply deplored attack on Mr. Blakely, and to decline the offer on the ground that he should have been given that opportunity before being submitted to the humiliation of arrest. He had intended to refuse all overtures, to invite trial by court-martial or investigation by the inspector general, but by no manner of means to plead for reconsideration now; and here was the post commander, with whom he had never served until they came to Sandy, a man who hadn't begun to see the service, the battles, and campaigns that had fallen to his lot, virtually accusing him of further misdemeanor, when he had only rushed to save or succor. He forgot all about Sanders or other witnesses. He burst forth impetuously:

"Extraordinary, sir! It would have been most extraordinary if I hadn't gone with all speed when I heard that cry for help."

Plume looked up in sudden joy. "You mean to tell me you didn't—you weren't there till after—the cry?"

Wren's stern Scottish face was a sight to see. "Of what can you possibly be thinking, Major Plume?" he demanded, slowly now, for wrath was burning within him, and yet he strove for self-control. He had had a lesson and a sore one.

"I will answer that—a little later, Captain Wren," said Plume, rising from his seat, rejoicing in the new light now breaking upon him. Westervelt, too, had gasped a sigh of relief. No man had ever known Wren to swerve a hair's breadth from the truth. "At this moment time is precious if the real criminal is to be caught at all. You were first to reach the sentry. Had you seen no one else?"

In the dead silence that ensued within the room the sputter of hoofs without broke harshly on the ear. Then came spurred boot heels on the hollow, heat-dried boarding, but not a sound from the lips of Captain Wren. The rugged face, twitching with pent-up indignation the moment before, was now slowly turning gray. Plume stood facing him in growing wonder and new suspicion.

"You heard me, did you not? I asked you did you see anyone else during—along the sentry post when you went out?"

A fringed gauntlet reached in at the doorway and tapped. Sergeant Shannon, straight as a pine, stood expectant of summons to enter and his face spoke eloquently of important tidings, but the major waved him away, and, marveling, he slowly backed to the edge of the porch.

"Surely you can answer that, Captain Wren," said Plume, his clear-cut, handsome face filled with mingled anxiety and annoy. "Surely you *should* answer, or—"

The ellipsis was suggestive, but impotent. After a painful moment came the response:

"Or—take the consequences, major?" Then slowly— "Very well, sir—I must take them."

CHAPTER VI

A FIND IN THE SANDS

The late afternoon of an eventful day had come to camp Sandy—just such another day, from a meteorological viewpoint, as that on which this story opened nearly twenty-four hours earlier by the shadows on the eastward cliffs. At Tuesday's sunset the garrison was yawning with the *ennui* born of monotonous and uneventful existence. As Wednesday's sunset drew nigh and the mountain shadows overspread the valley, even to the opposite crests of the distant Mogollon, the garrison was athrill with suppressed excitement, for half a dozen things had happened since the flag went up at reveille.

In the first place Captain Wren's arrest had been confirmed and Plume had wired department headquarters, in reply to somewhat urgent query, that there were several counts in his indictment of the captain, any one of which was sufficient to demand a trial by court-martial, but he wished, did Plume, for personal and official reasons that the general commanding should send his own inspector down to judge for himself.

The post sergeant major and the three clerks had heard with sufficient distinctness every word that passed between the major and the accused captain, and, there being at Sandy some three hundred inquisitive souls, thirsting for truth and light, it could hardly be expected of this quartette that it should preserve utter silence even though silence had been enjoined by the adjutant. It was told all over the post long before noon that Wren had been virtually accused of being the sentry's assailant as well as Lieutenant Blakely's. It was whispered that, in some insane fury against the junior officer, Wren had again, toward 3.30, breaking his arrest, gone up the row with the idea of once more entering Blakely's house and possibly again attacking him. It was believed that the sentry had seen and interposed, and that, enraged at being balked by an enlisted man, Wren had drawn a knife and stabbed him. True, no knife had been found anywhere about the spot, and Wren had never been known to carry one. But now a dozen men, armed with rakes, were systematically going over the ground under the vigilant eye of Sergeant Shannon—Shannon, who had heard the brief, emphatic interview between the major and the troop commander and who had been almost immediately sent forth to supervise this search, despite the fact that he had but just returned from the conduct of another, the result of which he imparted to the ears of only two men, Plume, the post commander, and Doty, his amazed and bewildered adjutant. But Shannon had with him a trio of troopers, one of whom, at least, had not been proof against inquisitive probing, for the second sensation of the day was the story that one of the two pairs of moccasin tracks, among the yielding sands of the willow copse, led from where Mr. Blakely had been dozing to where the pony Punch had been drowsing in the shade, for there they were lost, as the maker had evidently mounted and ridden away. All Sandy knew that Punch had no other rider than pretty Angela Wren.

A third story, too, was whispered in half a dozen homes, and was going wild about the garrison, to the effect that Captain Wren, when accused of being Mullins's assailant, had virtually declared that he had seen other persons prowling on the sentry's post and that they, not he, were the guilty ones; but when bidden to name or describe them, Wren had either failed or refused; some said one, some said the other, and the prevalent belief in Sudsville circles, as well as in the barracks, was that Captain Wren was going crazy over his troubles. And now there were women, ay, and men, too, though they spake with bated breath, who had uncanny things to say of Angela—the captain's only child.

And this it was that led to sensation No. 4—a wordy battle of the first magnitude between the next-door neighbor of the saddler sergeant and no less a champion of maiden probity than Norah Shaughnessy—the saddler sergeant's buxom daughter. All the hours since early morning Norah had been in a state of nerves so uncontrollable that Mrs. Truman—who knew of Norah's fondness for Mullins and marveled not that Mullins always preferred the loneliness and isolation of the post on No. 5—decided toward noon to send the girl home to her mother for a day or so, and Norah thankfully went, and threw herself upon her mother's ample breast and sobbed aloud. It was an hour before she could control herself, and her agitation was such that others came to minister to her. Of course there was just one expla- nation—Norah was in love with Mullins and well-nigh crazed with grief over his untimely taking off, for later reports from the hospital were most depressing. This, at least, was sufficient explanation until late in the afternoon. Then, restored to partial composure, the girl was sitting up and being fanned in the shade of her father's roof-tree, when roused by the voice of the next-door neighbor before mentioned—Mrs. Quinn, long time laundress of Captain Sanders's troop and jealous as to Wren's, was telling what *she* had heard of Shannon's discoveries, opining that both Captain Wren and the captain's daughter deserved investigation. "No wan need tell *me* there was others prowling about Mullins's post at three in the marnin.' As for Angela—" But here Miss Shaughnessy bounded from the wooden settee, and, with amazing vim and vigor, sailed spontaneously into Mrs. Quinn.

"No wan need tell *you*—ye say! No wan need tell *you*, ye black-tongued scandlum! Well, then, *I* tell ye Captain Wren did see others prowlin' on poor Pat Mullins's post an' others than him saw them too. Go you to the meejer, soon as ye like and say *I* saw them, and if Captain Wren won't tell their names there's them that will."

The shrill tones of the infuriated girl were plainly audible all over the flats whereon were huddled the little cabins of log and adobe assigned as quarters to the few married men among the soldiery. These were the halcyon days of the old army when each battery, troop, or company was entitled to four laundresses and each laundress to one ration. Old and young, there were at least fifty pairs of ears within easy range of the battle that raged forthwith, the noise of which reached even to the shaded precincts of the trader's store three hundred yards away. It was impossible that such a flat-footed statement as Norah's should not be borne to the back doors of "The Row" and, repeated then from lip to lip, should soon be told to certain of the officers. Sanders heard it as he came in from stable duty, and Dr. Graham felt confident that it had been repeated under the major's roof when at 6 P. M. the post commander desired his professional services in behalf of Mrs. Plume, who had become unaccountably, if not seriously, ill.

Graham had but just returned from a grave conference with Wren, and his face had little look of the family physician as he reluctantly obeyed the summons. As another of the auld licht school of Scotch Presbyterians, he also had conceived deep-rooted prejudice to that frivolous French aide-de-camp of the major's wife. The girl did dance and flirt and ogle to perfection, and half a dozen strapping sergeants were now at sword's points all on account of this objectionable Eliza. Graham, of course, had heard with his ears and fathomed with his understanding the first reports of Wren's now famous reply to his commanding officer; and though Wren would admit no more to him than he had to the major, Graham felt confident that the major's wife was one of the mysterious persons seen by Wren, and declared by Norah, in the dim starlight of the early morning, lurking along the post of No. 5. Graham had no doubt that Elise was the other. The man most concerned in the case, the major himself, was perhaps the only one at sunset who never seemed to suspect that Mrs. Plume could have been in any way connected with the affair. He met the doctor with a world of genuine anxiety in his eyes.

"My wife," said he, "is of a highly sensitive organization, and she has been completely upset by this succession of scandalous affairs. She and Blakely were great friends at St. Louis three years ago; indeed, many people were kind enough to couple their names before our marriage. I wish you could—quiet her," and the sounds from aloft, where madame was nervously pacing her room, gave point to the suggestion. Graham climbed the narrow stairs and tapped at the north door on the landing. It was opened by Elise, whose big, black eyes were dilated with excitement, while Mrs. Plume, her blonde hair tumbling down her back, her *peignoir* decidedly rumpled and her general appearance disheveled, was standing in mid-floor, wringing her jeweled hands. "She looks like sixty," was the doctor's inward remark, "and is probably not twenty-six."

Her first question jarred upon his rugged senses.

"Dr. Graham, when will Mr. Blakely be able to see—or read?"

"Not for a day or two. The stitches must heal before the bandages can come off his eyes. Even then, Mrs. Plume, he should not be disturbed," was the uncompromising answer.

"Is that wretch, Downs, sober yet?" she demanded, standing and confronting him, her whole form quivering with strong, half-suppressed emotion.

"The wretch is sobering," answered Graham gravely. "And now, madame, I'll trouble you to take a chair. Do you," with a glance of grim disfavor, "need this girl for the moment? If not, she might as well retire."

"I need my maid, Dr. Graham, and I told Major Plume distinctly I did not need you," was the impulsive reply, as the lady strove against the calm, masterful grasp he laid on her wrist.

"That's as may be, Mrs. Plume. We're often blind to our best interests. Be seated a moment, then I'll let you tramp the soles of your feet off, if you so desire." And so he practically pulled her into a chair; Elise, glaring the while, stood spitefully looking on. The antipathy was mutual.

"You've slept too little of late, Mrs. Plume," continued the doctor, lucklessly hitting the mark with a home shot instantly resented, for the lady was on her feet again.

"Sleep! People do nothing but sleep in this woebegone hole!" she cried. "I've had sleep enough to last a lifetime. What I want is to wake—wake out of this horrible nightmare! Dr. Graham, you are a friend of Captain Wren's. What under heaven possessed him, with his brutal strength, to assault so sick a man as Mr. Blakely? What possible pretext could he assert?" And again she was straining at her imprisoned hand and seeking to free herself, Graham calmly studying her the while, as he noted the feverish pulse. Not half an hour earlier he had been standing beside the sick bed of a fair young girl, one sorely weighted now with grave anxieties, yet who lay patient and uncomplaining, rarely speaking a word. They had not told the half of the web of accusation that now enmeshed her father's feet, but what had been revealed to her was more than enough to banish every thought of self or suffering and to fill her fond heart with instant and loving care for him. No one, not even Janet, was present during the interview between father and child that followed. Graham found him later locked in his own room, reluctant to admit even him, and lingering long before he opened the door; but even then the tear-stains stood on his furrowed face, and the doctor knew he had been sobbing his great heart out over the picture of his child—the child he had so harshly judged and sentenced, all unheard. Graham had gone to him, after seeing Angela, with censure on his tongue, but he never spoke the words. He saw there was no longer need.

"Let the lassie lie still the day," said he, "with Kate, perhaps, to read to her. Your sister might not choose a cheering book. Then perhaps we'll have her riding Punch again to-morrow." But Graham did not smile when meeting Janet by the parlor door.

He was thinking of the contrast in these two, his patients, as with professional calm he studied the troubled features of the major's wife when the voice of Sergeant Shannon was heard in the lower hall, inquiring for the major, and in an instant Plume had joined him. In that instant, too, Elise had sped, cat-like, to the door, and Mrs. Plume had followed. Possibly for this reason the major led the sergeant forth upon the piazza and the conversation took place in tones inaudible to those within the house; but, in less than a minute, the doctor's name was called and Graham went down.

"Look at this," said Plume. "They raked it out of the sand close to where Mullins was lying." And the major held forth an object that gleamed in the last rays of the slanting sunshine. It was Blakely's beautiful watch.

CHAPTER VII

"WOMAN-WALK-IN-THE-NIGHT"

The dawn of another cloudless day was breaking and the dim lights at the guard-house and the hospital burned red and bleary across the sandy level of the parade. The company cooks were already at their ranges, and a musician of the guard had been sent to rouse his fellows in the barracks, for the old-style reveille still held good at many a post in Arizona, before the drum and fife were almost entirely abandoned in favor of the harsher bugle, by the infantry of our scattered little army. Plume loved tradition. At West Point, where he had often visited in younger days, and at all the "old-time" garrisons, the bang of the morning gun and the simultaneous crash of the drums were the military means devised to stir the soldier from his sleep. Then, his brief ablutions were conducted to the accompaniment of the martial strains of the field musicians, alternating the sweet airs of Moore and Burns, the lyrics of Ireland and Auld Reekie, with quicksteps from popular Yankee melodies of the day, winding up with a grand flourish at the foot of the flagstaff, to whose summit the flag had started at the first alarum; then a rush into rattling "double quick" that summoned the laggards to scurry into the silently forming ranks, and finally, with one emphatic rataplan, the morning concert abruptly closed and the gruff voices of the first sergeants, in swift-running monotone, were heard calling the roll of their shadowy companies, and, thoroughly roused, the garrison "broke ranks" for the long routine of the day.

We have changed all that, and not for the better. A solitary trumpeter steps forth from the guard-house or adjutant's office and, at the appointed time, drones a long, dispiriting strain known to the drill books as "Assembly of the Trumpeters," and to the army at large as "First Call." Unassisted by other effort, it would rouse nobody, but from far and near the myriad dogs of the post—"mongrel, hound, and cur of low degree"—lift up their canine voices in some indefinable sympathy and stir the winds of the morning with their mournful yowls. Then, when all the garrison gets up cursing and all necessity for rousing is ended, the official reveille begins, sounded by the combined trumpeters, and so, uncheered by concord of sweet sounds, the soldier begins his day.

The two infantry companies at Sandy, at the time whereof we tell, were of an honored old regiment that had fought with Worth at Monterey—one whose scamps of drum boys and fifers had got their teachings from predecessors whose nimble fingers had trilled the tunes of old under the walls of the Bishop's Palace and in the resounding Halls of the Montezumas. Plume and Cutler loved their joyous, rhythmical strains, and would gladly have kept the cavalry clarions for purely cavalry calls; but reveille and guard-mounting were the only ones where this was practicable, and an odd thing had become noticeable. Apache Indians sometimes stopped their ears, and always looked impolite, when the brazen trumpets sounded close at hand; whereas they would squat on the sun-kissed sands and listen in stolid, unmurmuring bliss to every note of the fife and drum. Members of the guard were always sure of sympathetic spectators during the one regular ceremony—guard-mounting—held just after sunset, for the Apache prisoners at the guard-house begged to be allowed to remain without the prison room until a little after the "retreat" visit of the officer of the day, and, roosting along the guard-house porch, to gaze silently forth at the little band of soldiery in the center of the parade, and there to listen as silently to the music of the fife and drum. The moment it was all over they would rise without waiting for directions, and shuffle stolidly back to their hot wooden walls. They had had the one intellectual treat of the day. The savage breast was soothed for the time being, and Plume had come to the conclusion that, aside from the fact that his Indian prisoners were better fed than when on their native heath, the Indian prison pen at Sandy was not the place of penance the department commander had intended. Accessions became so frequent; discharges so very few.

Then there was another symptom: Sentries on the north and east front, Nos. 4 and 5, had been a bit startled at first at seeing, soon after dawn, shadowy forms rising slowly from the black depths of the valley, hovering uncertainly along the edge of the *mesa* until they could make out the lone figure of the morning watcher, then slowly, cautiously, and with gestures of amity and suppliance, drawing gradually nearer. Sturdy Germans and mercurial Celts were, at the start, disposed to "shoo" away these specters as being hostile, or at least incongruous. But officers and men were soon made to see it was to hear the morning music these children of the desert flocked so early. The agency lay but twenty miles distant. The reservation lines came no nearer; but the fame of the invader's big maple tom-tom (we wore still the deep, resonant drum of Bunker Hill and Waterloo, of Jemappes, Saratoga, and Chapultepec, not the modern rattle pan borrowed from Prussia), and the trill of his magical pipe had spread abroad throughout Apache land to the end that no higher reward for good behavior could be given by the agent to his swarthy charges than the begged-for *papel* permitting them, in lumps of twenty, to trudge through the evening shades to the outskirts of the soldier castle on the *mesa*, there to wait the long night through until the soft tinting of the eastward heavens and the twitter of the birdlings in the willows along the stream, gave them courage to begin their timid approach.

And this breathless October morning was no exception. The sentry on the northward line, No. 4, had recognized and passed the post surgeon soon after four o'clock, hastening to hospital in response to a summons from an anxious nurse. Mullins seemed far too feverish. No. 4 as well as No. 5 had noted how long the previous evening Shannon and his men kept raking and searching about the *mesa* where Mullins was stabbed in the early morning, and they were in no mood to allow strangers to near them unchallenged. The first shadowy forms to show at the edge had dropped back abashed at the harsh reception accorded them. Four's infantry rifle and Five's cavalry carbine had been leveled at the very first to appear, and stern voices had said things the Apache could neither translate nor misunderstand. The would-be audience of the morning concert ducked and waited. With more light the sentry might be more kind. The evening previous six new prisoners had been sent down under strong guard by the agent, swelling the list at Sandy to thirty-seven and causing Plume to set his teeth—and an extra sentry. Now, as the dawn grew broader and the light clear and strong, Four and Five were surprised, if not startled, to see that not twenty, but probably forty Apaches, with a sprinkling of squaws, were hovering all along the *mesa*, mutely watching for the signaled permission to come in. Five, at least, considered the symptom one of sufficient gravity to warrant report to higher authority, and full ten minutes before the time for reveille to begin, his voice went echoing over the arid parade in a long-draw, yet imperative "Corporal of the Gua-a-rd, No. 5!"

Whereat there were symptoms of panic among the dingy white-shirted, dingy white-turbaned watchers along the edge, and a man in snowy white fatigue coat, pacing restlessly up and down in rear, this time, of the major's quarters, whirled suddenly about and strode out on the *mesa*, gazing northward in the direction of the sound. It was Plume himself, and Plume had had a sleepless night.

At tattoo, by his own act and direction, the major had still further strained the situation. The discovery of Blakely's watch, buried loosely in the sands barely ten feet from where the sentry fell, had seemed to him a matter of such significance that, as Graham maintained an expression of professional gravity and hazarded no explanation, the major sent for the three captains still on duty, Cutler, Sanders, and Westervelt, and sought their views. One after another each picked up and closely examined the watch, within and without, as though expectant of finding somewhere concealed about its mechanism full explanation of its mysterious goings and comings. Then in turn, with like gravity, each declared he had no theory to offer, unless, said Sanders, Mr. Blakely was utterly mistaken in supposing he had been robbed at the pool. Mr. Blakely had the watch somewhere about him when he dismounted, and then joggled it into the sands, where it soon was trampled under foot. Sanders admitted that Blakely was a man not often mistaken, and that the loss reported to the post trader of the flat notebook was probably correct. But no one could be got to see, much less to say, that Wren was in the slightest degree connected with the temporary disappearance of the watch. Yet by this time Plume had some such theory of his own.

Sometime during the previous night, along toward morning, he had sleepily asked his wife, who was softly moving about the room, to give him a little water. The "monkey" stood usually on the window sill, its cool and dewy surface close to his hand; but he remembered later that she did not then approach the window—did not immediately bring him the glass. He had retired very late, yet was hardly surprised to find her wide awake and more than usually nervous. She explained by saying Elise had been quite ill, was still suffering, and might need her services again. She could not think, she said, of sending for Dr. Graham after all he had had to vex him. It must have been quite a long while after, so soundly had Plume slept, when she bent over him and said something was amiss and Mr. Doty was at the front door waiting for him to come down. He felt oddly numb and heavy and stupid as he hastily dressed, but Doty's tidings, that Mullins had been stabbed on post, pulled him together, as it were, and, merely running back to his room for his canvas shoes, he was speedily at the scene. Mrs. Plume, when briefly told what had happened, had covered her face with her hands and buried face and all in the pillow, shuddering. At breakfast-time Plume himself had taken her tea and toast, both mistress and maid being still on the invalid list, and, bending affectionately over her, he had suggested her taking this very light refreshment and then a nap. Graham, he said, should come and prescribe for Elise. But madame was feverishly anxious. "What will be the outcome? What will happen to—Captain Wren?" she asked.

Plume would not say just what, but he would certainly have to stand court-martial, said he. Mrs. Plume shuddered more. What good would that do? How much better it would be to suppress everything than set such awful scandal afloat. The matter was now in the hands of the department commander, said Plume, and would have to take its course. Then, in some way, from her saying how ill the captain was looking, Plume gathered the impression that she had seen him since his arrest, and asked the question point-blank. Yes, she admitted,—from the window,—while she was helping Elise. Where was he? What was he doing? Plume had asked, all interest now, for that must have been very late, in fact, well toward morning. "Oh, nothing especial, just looking at his watch," she thought, "he probably couldn't sleep." Yes, she was sure he was looking at his watch.

Then, as luck would have it, late in the day, when the mail came down from Prescott, there was a little package for Captain Wren, expressed, and Doty signed the receipt and sent it by the orderly. "What was it?" asked Plume. "His watch, sir," was the brief answer. "He sent it up last month for repairs." And Mrs. Plume at nine that night, knowing nothing of this, yet surprised at her husband's pertinacity, stuck to her story. She was sure Wren was consulting or winding or doing something with a watch, and, sorely perplexed and marveling much at the reticence of his company commanders, who seemed to know something they would not speak of, Wren sent for Doty. He had decided on another interview with Wren.

Meanwhile "the Bugologist" had been lying patiently in his cot, saying little or nothing, in obedience to the doctor's orders, but thinking who knows what. Duane and Doty occasionally tiptoed in to glance inquiry at the fanning attendant, and then tiptoed out. Mullins had been growing worse and was a very sick man. Downs, the wretch, was painfully, ruefully, remorsefully sobered over at the post of the guard, and of Graham's feminine patients the one most in need, perhaps, of his ministration was giving the least trouble. While Aunt Janet paced restlessly about the lower floor, stopping occasionally to listen at the portal of her brother, Angela Wren lay silent and only sometimes sighing, with faithful Kate Sanders reading in low tone by the bedside.

The captains had gone back to their quarters, conferring in subdued voices. Plume, with his unhappy young adjutant, was seated on the veranda, striving to frame his message to Wren, when the crack of a whip, the crunching of hoofs and wheels, sounded at the north end of the row, and down at swift trot came a spanking, four-mule team and Concord wagon. It meant but one thing, the arrival of the general's staff inspector straight from Prescott.

It was the very thing Plume had urged by telegraph, yet the very fact that Colonel Byrne was here went to prove that the chief was far from satisfied that the major's diagnosis was the right one. With soldierly alacrity, however, Plume sprang forward to welcome the coming dignitary, giving his hand to assist him from the dark interior into the light. Then he drew back in some chagrin. The voice of Colonel Byrne was heard, jovial and reassuring, but the face and form first to appear were those of Mr. Wayne Daly, the new Indian agent at the Apache reservation. Coming by the winding way of Cherry Creek, the colonel must have found means to wire ahead, then to pick up this civil functionary some distance up the valley, and to have some conference with him before ever reaching the major's bailiwick. This was not good, said Plume. All the same, he led them into his cozy army parlor, bade his Chinese servant get abundant supper forthwith, and, while the two were shown to the spare room to remove the dust of miles of travel, once more returned to the front piazza and his adjutant.

"Captain Wren, sir," said the young officer at once, "begs to be allowed to see Colonel Byrne this evening. He states that his reasons are urgent."

"Captain Wren shall have every opportunity to see Colonel Byrne in due season," was the answer. "It is not to be expected that Colonel Byrne will see him until after he has seen the post commander. Then it will probably be too late," and that austere reply, intended to reach the ears of the applicant, steeled the Scotchman's heart against his commander and made him merciless.

The "conference of the powers" was indeed protracted until long after 10.30, yet, to Plume's surprise, the colonel at its close said he believed he would go, if Plume had no objection, and see Wren in person and at once. "You see, Plume, the general thinks highly of the old Scot. He has known him ever since First Bull Run and, in fact, I am instructed to hear what Wren may have to say. I hope you will not misinterpret the motive."

"Oh, not at all—not at all!" answered the major, obviously ill pleased, however, and already nettled that, against all precedent, certain of the Apache prisoners had been ordered turned out as late as 10 P. M. for interview with the agent. It would leave him alone, too, for as much as half an hour, and the very air seemed surcharged with intrigue against the might, majesty, power, and dominion of the post commander. Byrne, a soldier of the old school, might do his best to convince the major that in no wise was the confidence of the general commanding abated, but every symptom spoke of something to the contrary. "I should like, too, to see Dr. Graham to-night," said the official inquisitor ere he quitted the piazza to go to Wren's next door. "He will be here to meet you on your return," said Plume, with just a bit of stateliness, of ruffled dignity in manner, and turned once more within the hallway to summon his smiling Chinaman.

Something rustling at the head of the stairs caused him to look up quickly. Something dim and white was hovering, drooping, over the balustrade, and, springing aloft, he found his wife in a half-fainting condition, Elise, the invalid, sputtering vehemently in French and making vigorous effort to pull her away. Plume had left her at 8.30, apparently sleeping at last under the influence of Graham's medicine. Yet here she was again. He lifted her in his arms and laid her upon the broad, white bed. "Clarice, my child," he said, "you *must* be quiet. You must not leave your bed. I am sending for Graham and he will come to us at once."

"I *will* not see him! He *shall* not see me!" she burst in wildly. "The man maddens me with his—his insolence."

"Clarice!"

"Oh, I mean it! He and his brother Scot, between them— they would infuriate a—saint," and she was writhing in nervous contortions.

"But, Clarice, how?"

"But, monsieur, no!" interposed Elise, bending over, glass in hand. "Madame will but sip of this—Madame will be tranquil." And the major felt himself thrust aside. "Madame must not talk to-night. It is too much."

But madame would talk. Madame would know where Colonel Byrne was gone, whether he was to be permitted to see Captain Wren and Dr. Graham, and that wretch Downs. Surely the commanding officer must have *some* rights. Surely it was no time for investigation—*this* hour of the night. Five minutes earlier Plume was of the same way of thinking. Now he believed his wife delirious.

"See to her a moment, Elise," said he, breaking loose from the clasp of the long, bejeweled fingers, and, scurrying down the stairs, he came face to face with Dr. Graham.

"I was coming for you," said he, at sight of the rugged, somber face. "Mrs. Plume—"

"I heard—at least I comprehend," answered Graham, with uplifted hand. "The lady is in a highly nervous state, and my presence does not tend to soothe her. The remedies I left will take effect in time. Leave her to that waiting woman; she best understands her."

"But she's almost raving, man. I never knew a woman to behave like that."

"Ye're not long married, major," answered Graham. "Come into the air a bit," and, taking his commander's arm, the surgeon swept him up the starlit row, then over toward the guard-house, and kept him half an hour watching the strange interview between Mr. Daly, the agent, and half a dozen gaunt, glittering-eyed Apaches, from whom he was striving to get some admission or information, with Arahawa, "Washington Charley," as interpreter. One after another the six had shaken their frowsy heads. They admitted nothing—knew nothing.

"What do you make of it all?" queried Plume.

"Something's wrang at the reservation," answered Graham. "There mostly is. Daly thinks there's running to and fro between the Tontos in the Sierra Ancha country and his wards above here. He thinks there's more out than there should be—and more a-going. What'd you find, Daly?" he added, as the agent joined them, mechanically wiping his brow. Moisture there was none. It evaporated fast as the pores exuded.

"They know well enough, damn them!" said the new official. "But they think I can be stood off. I'll nail 'em yet—to-morrow," he added. "But could you send a scout at once to the Tonto basin?" and Daly turned eagerly to the post commander.

Plume reflected. Whom could he send? Men there were in plenty, dry-rotting at the post for lack of something to limber their joints; but officers to lead? There was the rub! Thirty troopers, twenty Apache Mohave guides, a pack train and one or, at most, two officers made up the usual complement of such expeditions. Men, mounts, scouts, mules and packers, all, were there at his behest; but, with Wren in arrest, Sanders and Lynn back but a week from a long prod through the Black Mesa country far as Fort Apache, Blakely invalided and Duane a boy second lieutenant, his choice of cavalry officers was limited. It never occurred to him to look beyond.

"What's the immediate need of a scout?" said he.

"To break up the traffic that's going on—and the rancherias they must have somewhere down there. If we don't, I'll not answer for another month." Daly might be new to the neighborhood, but not to the business.

"I'll confer with Colonel Byrne," answered Plume guardedly. And Byrne was waiting for them, a tall, dark shadow in the black depths of the piazza. Graham would have edged away and gone to his own den, but Plume held to him. There was something he needed to say, yet could not until the agent had retired. Daly saw,—perhaps he had already imbibed something of the situation,—and was not slow to seek his room. Plume took the little kerosene lamp; hospitably led the way; made the customary tender of a "night-cap," and polite regrets he had no ice to offer therewith; left his unwonted guest with courteous good-night and cast an eye aloft as he came through the hall. All there was dark and still, though he doubted much that Graham's sedatives had yet prevailed. He had left the two men opposite the doorway. He found them at the south end of the piazza, their heads together. They straightened up to perfunctory talk about the Medical Director, his drastic methods and inflammable ways; but the mirth was forced, the humor far too dry. Then silence fell. Then Plume invaded it:

"How'd you find Wren—mentally?" he presently asked. He felt that an opening of some kind was necessary.

"Sound," was the colonel's answer, slow and sententious. "Of course he is much—concerned."

"About—his case? Ah, will you smoke, colonel?"

"About Blakely. I believe not, Plume; it's late."

Plume struck a light on the sole of his natty boot. "One would suppose he would feel very natural anxiety as to the predicament in which he has placed himself," he ventured.

"Wren worries much over Blakely's injuries, which accident made far more serious than he would have inflicted, major, even had he had the grounds for violence that he thought he had. Blakely was not the only sufferer, and is not the only cause, of his deep contrition. Wren tells me that he was even harsher to Angela. But that is all a family matter." The colonel was speaking slowly, thoughtfully.

"But—these later affairs—that Wren couldn't explain—or wouldn't." Plume's voice and color both were rising.

"Couldn't is the just word, major, and couldn't especially —to you," was the significant reply.

Plume rose from his chair and stood a moment, trembling not a little and his fingers twitching. "You mean—" he huskily began.

"I mean this, my friend," said Byrne gently, as he, too, arose, "and I have asked Graham, another friend, to be here—that Wren would not defend himself to you by even mentioning—others, and might not have revealed the truth even to me had he been the only one cognizant of it. But, Plume, *others* saw what he saw, and what is now known to many people on the post. Others than Wren were abroad that night. One other was being carefully, tenderly brought home—*led* home—to your roof. You did not know—Mrs. Plume was a somnambulist?"

In the dead silence that ensued the colonel put forth a pitying hand as though to stay and support the younger soldier, the post commander. Plume stood, swaying a bit, and staring. Presently he strove to speak, but choked in the effort.

"It's the only proper explanation," said Graham, and between them they led the major within doors.

And this is how it happened that he, instead of Wren, was

pacing miserably up and down in the gathering dawn, when the sentry startled all waking Sandy with his cry for the corporal. This is how, far ahead of the corporal, the post commander reached the alarmed soldier, with demand to know the cause; and, even by the time he came, the cause had vanished from sight.

"Apaches, sir, by the dozen,—all along the edge of the *mesa*," stammered No. 5. He could have convinced the corporal without fear or thought of ridicule, but his voice lacked confidence when he stood challenged by his commanding officer. Plume heard with instant suspicion. He was in no shape for judicial action.

"Apaches!" This in high disdain. "Trash, man! Because one sentry has a scuffle with some night prowler is the next to lose his nerve? You're scared by shadows, Hunt. That's what's the matter with you!"

It "brought to" a veteran trooper with a round turn. Hunt had served his fourth enlistment, had "worn out four blankets" in the regiment, and was not to be accused of scare.

"Let the major see for himself, then," he answered sturdily. "Come in here, you!" he called aloud. "Come, the whole gang of ye. The concert's beginning!" Then, slowly along the eastward edge there began to creep into view black polls bound with dirty white, black crops untrammeled by any binding. Then, swift from the west, came running footfalls, the corporal with a willing comrade or two, wondering was Five in further danger. There, silent and regretful, stood the post commander, counting in surprise the score of scarecrow forms now plainly visible, sitting, standing, or squatting along the *mesa* edge. Northernmost in view, nearly opposite

Blakely's quarters, were two, detached from the general assembly, yet clinging close together—two slender figures, gowned, and it was at these the agent Daly was staring, as he, too, came running to the spot.

"Major Plume," cried he, panting, "I want those girls arrested, at once!"

Charles King

CHAPTER VIII

"APACHE KNIVES DIG DEEP!"

At five o'clock of this cloudless October morning Colonel Montgomery Byrne, "of the old Army, sir," was reviling the fates that had set him the task of unraveling such a skein as he found at Sandy. At six he was blessing the stars that sent him. Awakened, much before his usual hour, by half-heard murmur of scurry and excitement, so quickly suppressed he believed it all a dream, he was thinking, half drowsily, all painfully, of the duty devolving on him for the day, and wishing himself well out of it, when the dream became real, the impression vivid. His watch told him reveille should now be sounding. His ears told him the sounds he heard were not those of reveille, yet something had roused the occupants of Officers' Row, and then, all on a sudden, instead of the sweet strains of "The Dawn of the Day" or "Bonnie Lass o' Gawrie" there burst upon the morning air, harsh and blustering, the alarum of the Civil War days, the hoarse uproar of the drum thundering the long roll, while above all rang the loud clamor of the cavalry trumpet sounding "To Horse."

"Fitz James was brave, but to his heart
The life blood leaped with sudden start."

Byrne sprang from his bed. He was a soldier, battle-tried, but this meant something utterly new to him in war, for, mingling with the gathering din, he heard the shriek of terror-stricken women. Daly's bed was empty. The agent was gone. Elise aloft was jabbering *patois* at her dazed and startled mistress. Suey, the Chinaman, came clattering in, all flapping legs and arms and pigtail, his face livid, his eyes staring. "Patcheese! Patcheese!" he squealed, and dove under the nearest bed. Then Byrne, shinning into boots and breeches and shunning his coat, grabbed his revolver and rushed for the door.

Across the parade, out of their barracks the "doughboys" came streaming, no man of them dressed for inspection, but rather, like sailors, stripped for a fight; and, never waiting to form ranks, but following the lead of veteran sergeants and the signals or orders of officers somewhere along the line, went sprinting straight for the eastward *mesa*. From the cavalry barracks, the northward sets, the troopers, too, were flowing, but these were turned stableward, back of the post, and Byrne, with his night-shirt flying wide open, wider than his eyes, bolted round through the space between the quarters of Plume and Wren, catching sight of the arrested captain standing grim and gaunt on his back piazza, and ran with the foremost sergeants to the edge of the plateau, where, in his cool white garb, stood Plume, shouting orders to those beneath.

There, down in the Sandy bottom, was explanation of it all. Two soldiers were bending over a prostrate form in civilian dress. Two swarthy Apaches, one on his face, the other, ten rods away, writhing on his side, lay weltering in blood. Out along the sandy barren and among the clumps of mezquite and greasewood, perhaps as many as ten soldiers, members of the guard, were scattering in rude skirmish order; now halting and dropping on one knee to fire, now rushing forward; while into the willows, that swept in wide concave around the flat, a number of forms in dirty white, or nothing at all but streaming breechclout, were just disappearing.

Northward, too, beyond the post of No. 4, other little squads and parties could be faintly seen scurrying away for the shelter of the willows, and as Byrne reached the major's side, with the to-be-expected query "Whatin-hell'sthematter?" the last of the fleeing Apaches popped out of sight, and Plume turned toward him in mingled wrath and disgust:

"That—ass of an agent!" was all he could say, as he pointed to the prostrate figure in pepper and salt.

Byrne half slid, half stumbled down the bank and bent over the wounded man. Dead he was not, for, with both hands clasped to his breast, Daly was cradling from side to side and saying things of Apaches totally unbecoming an Indian agent and a man of God. "But who did it? and how?—and why?" demanded Byrne of the ministering soldiers.

"Tried to 'rest two Patchie girls, sir," answered the first, straightening up and saluting, "and her feller wouldn't stand it, I reckon. Knifed the agent and Craney, too. Yonder's the feller."

Yonder lay, face downward, as described, a sinewy young brave of the Apache Mohave band, his newer, cleaner shirt and his gayly ornamented sash and headgear telling of superior rank and station among his kind. With barely a glance at Craney, squatted beside a bush, and with teeth and hands knotting a kerchief about a bleeding arm,

Byrne bent over the Apache and turned the face to the light.

"Good God!" he cried, at the instant, "it's Quonathay—Raven Shield! Why, *you* know him, corporal!"—this to Casey, of Wren's troop, running to his side. "Son of old Chief Quonahelka! I wouldn't have had this happen for all the girls on the reservation. Who were they? Why did he try to arrest them? Here! I'll have to ask him—stabbed or not!" And, anxious and angering, the colonel hastened over toward the agent, now being slowly aided to his feet. Plume, too, had come sidelong down the sandy bank with Cutler, of the infantry, asking where he should put in his men. "Oh, just deploy across the flats to stand off any possible attack," said Plume. "Don't cross the Sandy, and, damn it all! get a bugler out and sound recall!" For now the sound of distant shots came echoing back from the eastward cliffs. The pursuit had spread beyond the stream. "I don't want any more of those poor devils hurt. There's mischief enough already," he concluded.

"I should say so," echoed the colonel. "What was the matter, Mr. Daly? Whom did you seek to arrest?—and why?"

"Almost any of 'em," groaned Daly. "There were a dozen there I'd refused passes to come again this week. They were here in defiance of my orders, and I thought to take that girl Natzie,—she that led Lola off,—back to her father at the agency. It would have been a good lesson. Of course she fought and scratched. Next thing I knew a dozen of 'em were atop of us—some water, for God's sake!—and lift me out of this!"

Then with grave and watch-worn face, Graham came hurrying to the spot, all the way over from Mullins's bedside at the hospital and breathing hard. Dour indeed was the look he gave the groaning agent, now gulping at a gourd held to his pale lips by one of the men. The policy of Daly's predecessor had been to feather his own nest and let the Indian shift for himself, and this had led to his final overthrow. Daly, however, had come direct from the care of a tribe of the Pueblo persuasion, peace-loving and tillers of the soil, meek as the Pimas and Maricopas, natives who fawned when he frowned and cringed at the crack of his whip. These he had successfully, and not dishonestly, ruled, but that very experience had unfitted him for duty over the mountain Apache, who cringed no more than did the lordly Sioux or Cheyenne, and truckled to no man less than a tribal chief. Blakely, the soldier, cool, fearless, and resolute, but scrupulously just, they believed in and feared; but this new blusterer only made them laugh, until he scandalized them by wholesale arrest and punishment. Then their childlike merriment changed swiftly to furious and scowling hate,—to open defiance, and finally, when he dared lay hands on a chosen daughter of the race, to mutiny and the knife. Graham, serving his third year in the valley, had seen the crisis coming and sought to warn the man. But what should an army doctor know of an Apache Indian? said Daly, and, fatuous in his own conceit, the crisis found him unprepared.

"Go you for a stretcher," said the surgeon, after a quick look into the livid face. "Lay him down gently there," and kneeling, busied himself with opening a way to the wound. Out over the flats swung the long skirmish line, picturesque in the variety of its undress, Cutler striding vociferous in its wake, while a bugler ran himself out of breath, far to the eastward front, to puff feeble and abortive breath into unresponsive copper. And still the same flutter of distant, scattering shots came drifting back from the brakes and canons in the rocky wilds beyond the stream. The guard still pursued and the Indians still led, but they who knew anything well knew it could not be long before the latter turned on the scattering chase, and Byrne strode about, fuming with anxiety. "Thank God!" he cried, as a prodigious clatter of hoofs, on hollow and resounding wood, told of cavalry coming across the *acequia*, and Sanders galloped round the sandy point in search of the foe—or orders. "Thank God! Here, Sanders —pardon me, major, there isn't an instant to lose—Rush your men right on to the front there! Spread well out, but don't fire a shot unless attacked in force! Get those— chasing idiots and bring them in! By God, sir, we'll have an Indian war on our hands as it is!" And Sanders nodded and dug spurs to his troop horse, and sang out: "Left front into line—gallop!" and the rest was lost in a cloud of dust and the blare of cavalry trumpet.

Then the colonel turned to Plume, standing now silent and sore troubled. "It was the quickest way," he said apologetically. "Ordinarily I should have given the order through you, of course. But those beggars are armed to a man. They left their guns in the crevices of yonder rocks, probably, when they came for the morning music. We must have no fight over this unless they force it. I wish to heaven we hadn't killed—these two," and ruefully he looked at the stark forms—the dead lover of Natzie, the gasping tribesman just beyond, dying, knife in hand. "The general has been trying to curb Daly for the last ten days," continued he, "and warned him he'd bring on trouble. The interpreter split with him on Monday last, and there's been mischief brewing ever since. If only we could have kept Blakely there—all this row would have been averted!"

If only, indeed! was Plume thinking, as eagerly, anxiously he scanned the eastward shore, rising jagged, rocky, and forbidding from the willows of the stream bed. If only, indeed! Not only all this row of which Byrne had seen so much, but all this other row, this row within a row, this intricacy of mishaps and misery that involved the social universe of Camp Sandy, of which as yet the colonel, presumably, knew so very little; of which, as post commander, Plume had yet to tell him! An orderly came running with a field glass and a scrap of paper. Plume glanced at the latter, a pencil scrawl of his wife's inseparable companion, and, for aught he knew, confidante. "Madame," he could make out, and "*affreusement*" something, but it was enough. The orderly supplemented: "Leece, sir, says the lady is very bad—"

"Go to her, Plume," with startling promptitude cried the colonel. "I'll look to everything here. It's all coming out right," for with a tantara—tantara-ra-ra Sanders's troop, spreading far and wide, were scrambling up the shaly slopes a thousand yards away. "Go to your wife and tell her the danger's over," and, with hardly another glance at the moaning agent, now being limply hoisted on a hospital stretcher, thankfully the major went. "The lady's very bad, is she?" growled Byrne, in fierce aside to Graham. "That French hag sometimes speaks truth, in spite of herself. How d'you find him?" This with a toss of the head toward the vanishing stretcher.

"Bad likewise. These Apache knives dig deep. There's Mullins now—"

"Think *that* was Apache?" glared Byrne, with sudden light in his eyes, for Wren had told his troubles—all.

"Apache *knife*—yes."

"What the devil do you mean, Graham?" and the veteran

soldier, who knew and liked the surgeon, whirled again on him with eyes that looked not like at all.

The doctor turned, his somber gaze following the now distant figure of the post commander, struggling painfully up the yielding sand of the steep slope to the plateau. The stretcher bearers and attendants were striding away to hospital with the now unconscious burden. The few men, lingering close at hand, were grouped about the dead Apaches. The gathering watchers along the bank were beyond earshot. Staff officer and surgeon were practically alone and the latter answered:

"I mean, sir, that if that Apache knife had been driven in by an Apache warrior, Mullins would have been dead long hours ago—which he isn't."

Byrne turned a shade grayer.

"Could *she* have done that?" he asked, with one sideward jerk of his head toward the major's quarters.

"I'm not saying," quoth the Scot. "I'm asking was there anyone else?"

CHAPTER IX

A CARPET KNIGHT, INDEED

The flag at Camp Sandy drooped from the peak. Except by order it never hung halfway. The flag at the agency fluttered no higher than the cross-trees, telling that Death had loved some shining mark and had not sued in vain. Under this symbol of mourning, far up the valley, the interpreter was telling to a circle of dark, sullen, and unresponsive faces a fact that every Apache knew before. Under the full-masted flag at the post, a civilian servant of the nation lay garbed for burial. Poor Daly had passed away with hardly a chance to tell his tale, with only a loving, weeping woman or two to mourn him. Over the camp the shadow of death tempered the dazzling sunshine, for all Sandy felt the strain and spoke only with sorrow. He meant well, did Daly, that was accorded him now. He only lacked "savvy" said they who had dwelt long in the land of Apache.

Over at the hospital two poor women wept, and twice their number strove to soothe. Janet Wren and Mrs. Graham were there, as ever, when sorrow and trouble came. Mrs. Sanders and Mrs. Cutler, too, were hovering about the mourners, doing what they could, and the hospital matron, busy day and night of late, had never left her patient until he needed her no more, and then had turned to minister to those he left behind—the widow and the fatherless. Over on the shaded verandas other women met and murmured in the soft, sympathetic drawl appropriate to funereal occasion, and men nodded silently to each other. Death was something these latter saw so frequently it brought but little of terror. Other things were happening of far greater moment that they could not fathom at all.

Captain Wren, after four days of close arrest, had been released by the order of Major Plume himself, who, pending action on his application for leave of absence, had gone on sick report and secluded himself within his quarters. It was rumored that Mrs. Plume was seriously ill, so ill, indeed, she had to be denied to every one of the sympathizing women who called, even to Janet, sister of their soldier next-door neighbor, but recently a military prisoner, yet now, by law and custom, commander of the post.

Several things had conspired to bring about this condition of affairs. Byrne, to begin with, had been closely questioning Shannon, and had reached certain conclusions with regard to the stabbing of Mullins that were laid before Plume, already stunned by the knowledge that, sleeping as his friendly advisers declared, or waking, as his inner consciousness would have it, Clarice, his young and still beautiful wife, had left her pillow and gone by night toward the northern limit of the line of quarters. If Wren were tried, or even accused, that fact would be the first urged in his defense. Plume's stern accusation of Elise had evoked from her nothing but a voluble storm of protest. Madame was ill, sleepless, nervous—had gone forth to walk away her nervousness. She, Elise, had gone in search and brought her home. Downs, the wretch, when as stoutly questioned, declared he had been blind drunk; saw nobody, knew nothing, and must have taken the lieutenant's whisky. Plume shrank from asking Norah questions. He could not bring himself to talking of his wife to the girl of the laundresses' quarters, but he knew now that he must drop that much of the case against Wren.

Then came the final blow. Byrne had gone to the agency, making every effort through runners, with promises of immunity, to coax back the renegades to the reservation, and so avert another Apache war. Plume, in sore perplexity, was praying for the complete restoration of Mullins—the only thing that could avert investigation— when, as he entered his office the morning of this eventful day, Doty's young face was eloquent with news.

One of the first things done by Lieutenant Blakely when permitted by Dr. Graham to sit and speak, was to dictate a letter to the post adjutant, the original of which, together with the archives of Camp Sandy, was long since buried among the hidden treasures of the War Department. The following is a copy of the paper placed by Mr. Doty in the major's hands even before he could reach his desk:

CAMP SANDY, A. T.,

October —, 187—

LIEUTENANT J. J. DOTY,

8th U. S. Infantry,

Post Adjutant.

Sir: I have the honor to submit for the consideration of

the post commander, the following:

Shortly after retreat on the—th inst. I was suddenly accosted in my quarters by Captain Robert Wren,—th Cavalry, and accused of an act of treachery to him;—an accusation which called forth instant and indignant denial. He had, as I now have cause to know, most excellent reason for believing his charge to be true, and the single blow he dealt me was the result of intense and natural wrath. That the consequences were so serious he could not have foreseen.

As the man most injured in the affair, I earnestly ask that no charges be preferred. Were we in civil life I should refuse to prosecute, and, if the case be brought before a court-martial it will probably fail—for lack of evidence.

Very Respectfully,

Your Obedient Servant,

NEIL D. BLAKELY,

1st Lieut.,—th Cavalry.

Now, Doty had been known to hold his tongue when a harmful story might be spread, but he could no more suppress his rejoicing over this than he could the impulse to put it in slang. "Say, aint this just a corker?" said this ingenuous youth, as he spread it on his desk for Graham's grimly gleaming eyes. Plume had read it in dull, apathetic, unseeing fashion. It was the morning after the Apache *emeute*. Plume had stared hard at his adjutant a moment, then, whipping up the sun hat that he had dropped on his desk, and merely saying, "I'll return—shortly," had sped to his darkened quarters and not for an hour had he reappeared. Then the first thing he asked for was that letter of Mr. Blakely's, which, this time, he read with lips compressed and twitching a bit at the corners. Then he called for a telegraph blank and sent a wire to intercept Byrne at the agency. "I shall turn over command to Wren at noon. I'm too ill for further duty," was all he said. Byrne read the rest between the lines.

But Graham went straightway to the quarters of Captain Wren, a rough pencil copy of that most unusual paper in his hand. "R-robert Wren," said he, as he entered, unknocking and unannounced, "will ye listen to this? Nay, Angela, lass, don't go." When strongly moved, as we have seen, our doctor dropped to the borderland of dialect.

In the dim light from the shaded windows he had not at first seen the girl. She was seated on a footstool, her hands on her father's knee, her fond face gazing up into his, and that strong, bony hand of his resting on her head and toying with the ribbon, the "snood," as he loved to call it, with which she bound her abundant tresses. At sound of the doctor's voice, Janet, ever apprehensive of ill, had come forth from the dining room, silver brush and towel in hand, and stood at the doorway, gazing austerely. She could not yet forgive her brother's friend his condemnation of her methods as concerned her brother's child. Angela, rising to her full height, stood with one hand on the back of her father's chair, the other began softly stroking the grizzled crop from his furrowed forehead.

No one spoke a word as Graham began and slowly, to the uttermost line, read his draft of Blakely's missive. No one spoke for a moment after he had finished. Angela, with parted lips and dilated eyes, had stood at first drinking in each syllable, then, with heaving bosom, she slowly turned, her left hand falling by her side. Wren sat in silence, his deep-set eyes glowering on the grim reader, a dazed look on his rugged face. Then he reached up and drew the slim, tremulous hand from his forehead and snuggled it against his stubbly cheek, and still he could not speak. Janet slowly backed away into the darkness of the dining room. The situation had softening tendencies and Janet's nature revolted at sentiment. It was Graham's voice that again broke the silence.

"For a vain carpet knight, 'whose best boast was to wear a braid of his fair lady's hair,' it strikes me our butterfly chaser has some points of a gentleman," said he, slowly folding his paper. "I might say more," he continued presently, retiring toward the hall. Then, pausing at the doorway, "but I won't," he concluded, and abruptly vanished.

An hour later, when Janet in person went to answer a knock at the door, she glanced in at the parlor as she passed, and that peep revealed Angela again seated on her footstool, with her bonny head pillowed on her father's knee, his hand again toying with the glossy tresses, and both father and child looked up, expectant. Yes, there stood the young adjutant, officially equipped with belt and sword and spotless gloves. "Can I see the captain?" he asked, lifting his natty *kepi*, and the captain arose and strode to the door.

"Major Plume presents his compliments—and this letter, sir," stammered the youth, blushing, too, at sight of Angela, beaming on him from the parlor door. "And— you're in command, sir. The major has gone on sick report."

That evening a solemn *cortege* filed away down the winding road to the northward flats and took the route to the little cemetery, almost all the garrison following to the grave all that was mortal of the hapless agent. Byrne, returned from the agency, was there to represent the general commanding the department. Wren stalked solemnly beside him as commander of the post. Even the women followed, tripping daintily through the sand. Graham watched them from the porch of the post hospital. He could not long leave Mullins, tossing in fever and delirium. He had but recently left Lieutenant Blakely, sitting up and placidly busying himself in patching butterfly wings, and Blakely had even come to the front door to look at the distant gathering of decorous mourners. But the bandaged head was withdrawn as two tall, feminine forms came gravely up the row, one so prim and almost antique, the other so lithe and lissome. He retreated to the front room, and with the one available eye at the veiled window, followed her, the latter, until the white flowing skirt was swept from the field of his vision. He had stood but a few hours previous on the spot where he had received that furious blow five nights before, and this time, with cordial grasp, had taken the huge hand that dealt it between his white and slender palms. "Forgive us our trespasses as we forgive those," Wren had murmured, as he read the deeply regretful words of his late accuser and commander, for had not he in his turn, and without delay, also to eat humble pie? There was something almost pathetic in the attitude of the big soldier as he came to the darkened room and stood before his junior and subordinate, but the latter had stilled the broken, clumsy, faltering words with which this strong, masterful man was striving to make amend for bitter wrong. "I won't listen to more, Captain Wren," he said. "You had reasons I never dreamed of—then. Our eyes have been opened" (one of his was still closed). "You have said more than enough. Let us start afresh now—with better understanding."

"It—it is generous in you, Blakely. I misjudged everything—everybody, and now,—well, you know there are still Hotspurs in the service. I'm thinking some man may be ass enough to say you got a blow without resenting—"

Blakely smiled, a contorted and disunited smile, perhaps, and one much trammeled by adhesive plaster. Yet there was placid unconcern in the visible lines of his pale face. "I think I shall know how to answer," said he. And so for the day, and without mention of the name uppermost in the thoughts of each, the two had parted—for the first time as friends.

But the night was yet to come.

CHAPTER X

"WOMAN-WALK-IN-THE-NIGHT" AGAIN

So swift had been the succession of events since the first day of the week, few of the social set at Sandy could quite realize, much less fathom, all that had happened, and as they gathered on the verandas, in the cool of the evening after Daly's funeral, the trend of talk was all one way. A man who might have thrown light on certain matters at issue had been spirited away, and there were women quite ready to vow it was done simply to get him beyond range of their questioning. Sergeant Shannon had been sent to the agency on some mission prescribed by Colonel Byrne. It was almost the last order issued by Major Plume before turning over the command.

Byrne himself still lingered at the post, "watching the situation," as it was understood, and in constant telegraphic correspondence with the general at Prescott and the commander of the little guard over the agency buildings at the reservation—Lieutenant Bridger, of the Infantry. With a sergeant and twenty men that young officer had been dispatched to that point immediately after the alarming and unlooked-for catastrophe of the reveille outbreak. Catastrophe was what Byrne called it, and he meant what he said, not so much because it had cost the life of Daly, the agent, whose mistaken zeal had precipitated the whole misunderstanding, but rather because of the death of two such prominent young warriors as "Shield" and his friend, who had fallen after dealing the fatal blow to him who had laid violent hands, so they regarded it, on two young girls, one a chieftain's daughter and both objects of reverent and savagely sentimental interest. "If war doesn't come at once," said Byrne, "it will be because the Apache has a new sense or a deep-laid scheme. Look out for him."

No news as yet had come from the runners sent forth in search of the scattered fugitives, who would soon be flocking together again in the fastnesses of the Mogollon to the east or the Red Rock country northward—the latter probably, as being nearer their friends at the reservation and farther from the few renegade Tontos lurking in the mountains toward Fort Apache. Byrne's promise to the wanderers, sent by these runners, was to the effect that they would be safe from any prosecution if they would return at once to the agency and report themselves to the interpreter and the lieutenant commanding the guard. He would not, he said, be answerable for what might happen if they persisted in remaining at large. But when it was found that, so far from any coming in, there were many going out, and that Natzie's father and brother had already gone, Byrne's stout heart sank. The message came by wire from the agency not long after the return of the funeral party, and while the evening was yet young. He sent at once for Wren, and, seated on the major's front piazza, with an orderly hovering just out of earshot, and with many an eye anxiously watching them along the row, the two veterans were holding earnest conference. Major Plume was at the bedside of his wife, so said Graham when he came down about eight. Mrs. Plume, he continued, was at least no worse, but very nervous. Then he took himself back to the hospital.

Another topic of talk along the line was Blakely's watch and its strange recovery, and many were the efforts to learn what Blakely himself had to say about it. The officers, nearly all of them, of course, had been at intervals to see Blakely and inquire if there were not something that they could do, this being the conventional and proper thing, and they who talked with him, with hardly an exception, led up to the matter of the watch and wished to know how he accounted for its being there on the post of No. 5. It was observed that, upon this topic and the stabbing of Private Mullins, Mr. Blakely was oddly reticent. He had nothing whatever to suggest as explanation of either matter. The watch was taken from the inner pocket of his thin white coat as he lay asleep at the pool, of this he felt confident, but by whom he would not pretend to say. Everybody knew by this time that Angela Wren had seen him sleeping, and had, in a spirit of playful mischief, fetched away his butterfly net, but who would accuse Angela of taking his watch and money? Of course such things had been, said one or two wise heads, but—not with girls like Angela.

But who could say what, all this while, Angela herself was thinking? Once upon a time it had been the way of our young folk well over the North and West to claim forfeit in the game of "Catching the weasel asleep." There had been communities, indeed, and before co-education became a fad at certain of our great universities, wherein the maid caught napping could hold it no sin against watchful swain, or even against her, that he then and there imprinted on her lips a kiss. On the other hand, the swain found sleeping might not always expect a kiss, but must pay the penalty, a pair of dainty gloves. Many a forfeit, both lip and glove, had there been claimed and allowed in army days whereof we write, and Angela, stealing upon Blakely as he dozed beneath the willows, and liking him well and deploring her father's pronounced aversion to him—perhaps even resenting it an undutiful bit—had found it impossible to resist the temptation to softly disengage that butterfly net from the loosely clasping fingers, and swiftly, stealthily, delightedly to scamper away with it against his waking. It was of this very exploit, never dreaming of the fateful consequences, she and Kate Sanders were so blissfully bubbling over, fairly shaking with maiden merriment when the despoiled victim, homeward bound, caught sight of them upon the *mesa*. Ten minutes more, and in full force she had been made to feel the blow of her father's fierce displeasure. Twenty minutes more, and, under the blow of her father's furious wrath, Blakely had been felled like a log.

When with elongated face and exaggerated gloom of manner Aunt Janet came to make her realize the awful consequences of her crime, Angela's first impulse had been to cry out against her father's unreasoning rage. When she learned that he was in close arrest,—to be tried, doubtless, for his mad assault,—in utter revulsion of feeling, in love and tenderness, in grief and contrition inexpressible, she had thrown herself at his feet and, clasping his knees, had sobbed her heart out in imploring his forgiveness for what she called her wicked, heedless, heartless conduct. No one saw that blessed meeting, that scene of mutual forgiveness, of sweet reconciliation; too sweet and serene, indeed, for Janet's stern and Calvinistic mold.

Are we ever quite content, I wonder, that others' bairnies should be so speedily, so entirely, forgiven? All because of this had all Janet's manifestations of sympathy for Robert to be tempered with a fine reserve. As for Angela, it would never do to let the child so soon forget that this should be an awful lesson. Aunt Janet's manner, therefore, when, butterfly net in hand, she required of her niece full explanation of the presence in the room of this ravished trophy, was something fraught with far too much of future punishment, of wrath eternal. Even in her chastened mood Angela's spirit stood *en garde*. "I have told father everything, auntie," she declared. "I leave it all to him," and bore in silence the comments, without the utterance of which the elder vestal felt she could not conscientiously quit the field. "Bold," "immodest," "unmaidenly," "wanton," were a choice few of Aunt Janet's expletives, and these were unresented. But when she concluded with "I shall send this—thing to him at once, with my personal apologies for the act of an irresponsible child," up sprang Angela with rebellion flashing from her eyes. She had suffered punishment as a woman. She would not now be treated as a child. To Janet's undisguised amaze and disapprobation, Wren decided that Angela herself should send both apology and net. It was the first missive of the kind she had ever written, but, even so, she would not submit it for either advice or criticism—even though its composition cost her many hours and tears and sheets of paper. No one but the recipient had so much as a peep at it, but when Blakely read it a grave smile lighted his pallid and still bandaged face. He stowed the little note in his desk, and presently took it out and read it again, and still again, and then it went slowly into the inner pocket of his white sack coat and was held there, while he, the wearer, slowly paced up and down the veranda late in the starlit night. This was the evening of Daly's funeral, the evening of the day on which he and his captain had shaken hands and were to start afresh with better understanding.

Young Duane was officer of the day and, after the tattoo

inspection of his little guard, had gone for a few minutes to the hospital where Mullins lay muttering and tossing in his feverish sleep; then, meeting Wren and Graham on the way, had tramped over to call on Blakely, thinking, perhaps, to chat a while and learn something. Soon after "taps" was sounded, however, the youngster joined the little group gossiping in guarded tones on the porch at Captain Sanders', far down the row, and, in response to question, said that "Bugs"—that being Blakely's briefest *nom de guerre*—must be convalescing rapidly, he "had no use for his friends," and, as the lad seemed somewhat ruffled and resentful, what more natural than that he should be called upon for explanation? Sanders and his wife were present, and Mrs. Bridger, very much alive with inquiry and not a little malicious interest. Kate, too, was of the party, and Doty, the adjutant, and Mesdames Cutler and Westervelt—it was so gloomy and silent, said these latter, at their end of the row. Much of the talk had been about Mrs. Plume's illness and her "sleep-walking act," as it had been referred to, and many had thought, but few had spoken, of her possible presence on the post of No. 5 about the time that No. 5 was stabbed. They knew *she* couldn't have done it, of course, but then how strange that she should have been there at all! The story had gained balloon-like expanse by this time, and speculation was more than rife. But here was Duane with a new grievance which, when put into Duane's English, reduced itself to this: "Why, it was like as if Bugs wanted to get rid of me and expected somebody else," and this they well remembered later. Nobody else was observed going to Blakely's front door, at least, but at eleven o'clock he himself could still be dimly heard and seen pacing steadily up and down his piazza, apparently alone and deep in thought. His lights, too, were turned down, a new man from the troop having asked for and assumed the duties formerly devolving on the wretch Downs, now doing time within the garrison prison. Before eleven, however, this new martial domestic had gone upstairs to bed and Blakely was all alone, which was as he wished it, for he had things to plan and other things to think of that lifted him above the possibility of loneliness.

Down the line of officers' quarters only in two or three houses could lights be seen. Darkness reigned at Plume's, where Byrne was still rooming. Darkness reigned at Wren's and Graham's, despite the fact that the lords of these manors were still abroad, both at the bedside of Trooper Mullins. A dozen people were gathered by this time at Sanders'. All the other verandas, except Blakely's with its solitary watcher, seemed deserted. To these idlers of the soft and starlit night, sitting bareheaded about the gallery and chatting in the friendly way of the frontier, there came presently a young soldier from the direction of the adjutant's office at the south end. "The night operator," he explained. "Two dispatches have just come for Colonel Byrne, and I thought maybe—"

"No, Cassidy," said Doty. "The colonel is at his quarters. Dispatch, is it? Perhaps I'd better go with you," and, rising, the young officer led the way, entering on tiptoe the hall of the middle house where, far back on a table, a lamp was burning low. Tapping at an inner door, he was bidden to enter. Byrne was in bed, a single sheet over his burly form, but he lay wide awake. He took the first dispatch and tore it open eagerly. It was from Bridger at the agency:

Runners just in say Natzie and Lola had turned back from trail to Montezuma Well, refusing to go further from their dead. Can probably be found if party go at dawn or sooner. Alchisay with them. More Indians surely going out from here.

Byrne's brow contracted and his lips compressed, but he gave no other sign. "Is Captain Wren still up?" he briefly asked, as he reached for the other dispatch.

"Over at the hospital, sir," said Doty, and watched this famous campaigner's face as he ripped open the second brown envelope. This time he was half out of bed before he could have half finished even that brief message. It was from the general:

> News of trouble must have reached Indians at San Carlos. Much excitement there and at Apache. Shall start for Camp McDowell to-morrow as soon as I have seen Plume. He should come early.

The colonel was in his slippers and inexpressibles in less than no time, but Plume aloft had heard the muffled sounds from the lower floor, and was down in a moment. Without a word Byrne handed him the second message and waited until he had read, then asked: "Can you start at dawn?"

"I can start now," was the instant reply. "Our best team can make it in ten hours. Order out the Concord, Mr. Doty." And Doty vanished.

"But Mrs. Plume—" began the colonel tentatively.

"Mrs. Plume simply needs quiet and to be let alone," was the joyless answer. "I think perhaps—I am rather in the way."

"Well, I know the general will appreciate your promptness. I—did not know you had asked to see him," and Byrne looked up from under his shaggy brows.

"I hadn't exactly, but my letter intimated as much. There is so very much I—I cannot write about—that of course he's bound to hear,—I don't mean you, Colonel Byrne,— and he ought to know the—facts. Now I'll get ready at once and—see you before starting."

"Better take an escort, Plume."

"One man on driver's seat. That's all, sir. I'll come in presently, in case you have anything to send," said Plume, and hurried again upstairs.

It was barely midnight when Plume's big black wagon, the Concord, all spring and hickory, as said the post quartermaster, went whirling away behind its strapping team of four huge Missouri mules. It was 12.30 by the guard-house clock and the call of the sentries when Wren came home to find Angela, her long, luxuriant hair tumbling down over her soft, white wrapper, waiting for him at the front door. From her window she had seen him coming; had noted the earlier departure of the wagon; had heard the voice of Major Plume bidding good-by, and wondered what it meant—this midnight start of the senior officer of the post. She had been sitting there silent, studying the glittering stars, and wondering would there be an answer to her note? Would he be able to write just yet? Was there reason, really, why he *should* write, after all that had passed? Somehow she felt that write he certainly would, and soon, and the thought kept her from sleeping. It was because she was anxious about Mullins, so she told herself and told her father, that she had gone fluttering down to meet him at the door. But no sooner had he answered, "Still delirious and yet holding his own," than she asked where and why Major Plume had gone.

"The general wired for him," answered Wren. "And what is my tall girlie doing, spiering from windows this time of night? Go to bed, child." She may be losing beauty sleep, but not her beauty, thought he fondly, as she as fondly kissed him and turned to obey. Then came a heavy footfall on the gallery without, and a dark form, erect and soldierly, stood between them and the dim lights of the guard-house. It was a corporal of the guard.

"No. 4, sir, reports he heard shots—two—way up the valley."

"Good God!" Wren began, then throttled the expletive half spoken. Could they have dared waylay the major— and so close to the post? A moment more and he was hurrying over to his troop quarters; five minutes, and a sergeant and ten men were running with him to the stables; ten, and a dozen horses, swiftly saddled, were being led into the open starlight; fifteen, and they were away at a lunging bronco lope, a twisting column of twos along the sandy road, leaving the garrison to wake and wonder. Three, four, five miles they sped, past Boulder Point, past Rattlesnake Hill, and still no sign of anything amiss, no symptom of night-raiding Apache, for indeed the Apache dreads the dark. Thrice the sergeant had sprung from his horse, lighted a match, and studied the trail. On and on had gone the mules and wagon without apparent break or interruption, until, far beyond the bluff that hid the road from sight of all at Sandy, they had begun the long, tortuous climb of the divide to Cherry Creek. No. 4 might have heard shots, but, if intended for the wagon, they had been harmless. It was long after one when Wren gave the word to put back to the post, and as they remounted and took the homeward trail, they rode for the first five minutes almost directly east, and, as they ascended a little slant of hillside, the sergeant in advance reined suddenly in. "Look there!" said he.

Far over among the rocky heights beyond the valley, hidden from the south from Sandy by precipitous cliffs that served almost as a reflector toward the reservation, a bright blaze had shot suddenly heavenward—a signal fire of the Apache. Some of them, then, were in the heart of that most intractable region, not ten miles northeast of the post, and signaling to their fellows; but the major must have slipped safely through.

Sending his horse to stable with the detachment, Wren had found No. 4 well over toward the east end of his post, almost to the angle with that of No. 5. "Watch well for signal fires or prowlers to-night," he ordered. "Have you seen any?"

"No signal fires, sir," answered the sentry. "Welch, who was on before me, thought he heard shots—"

"I know," answered Wren impatiently. "There was nothing in it. But we did see a signal fire over to the northeast, so they are around us, and some may be creeping close in to see what we're doing, though I doubt it. You've seen nothing?"

"Well, no, sir; we can't see much of anything, it's so dark. But there's a good many of the post people up and moving about, excited, I suppose. There were lights there at the lieutenant's, Mr. Blakely's, a while ago, and—voices." No. 4 pointed to the dark gable end barely forty yards away.

"That's simple enough," said Wren. "People would naturally come up to this end to see what had become of us, why we had gone, etc. They heard of it, I dare say, and some were probably startled."

"Yes, sir, it sounded like—somebody cryin'."

Wren was turning away. "What?" he suddenly asked.

No. 4 repeated his statement. Wren pondered a moment, started to speak, to question further, but checked himself and trudged thoughtfully away through the yielding sand. The nearest path led past the first quarters, Blakely's, on the eastward side, and as the captain neared the house he stopped short. Somewhere in the shadows of the back porch low, murmuring voices were faintly audible. One, in excited tone, was not that of a man, and as Wren stood, uncertain and surprised, the rear door was quickly opened and against the faint light from within two dark forms were projected. One, the taller, he recognized beyond doubt as that of Neil Blakely; the other he did not recognize at all. But he had heard the tone of the voice. He knew the form to be, beyond doubt, that of a young and slender woman. Then together the shadows disappeared within and the door was closed behind them.

CHAPTER XI

A STOP—BY WIRE

Three days later the infantry guard of the garrison were in sole charge. Wren and Sanders, with nearly fifty troopers apiece, had taken the field in compliance with telegraphic orders from Prescott. The general had established field headquarters temporarily at Camp McDowell, down the Verde Valley, and under his somewhat distant supervision four or five little columns of horse, in single file, were boring into the fastnesses of the Mogollon and the Tonto Basin. The runners had been unsuccessful. The renegades would not return. Half a dozen little nomad bands, forever out from the reservation, had eagerly welcomed these malcontents and the news they bore that two of their young braves had been murdered while striving to defend Natzie and Lola. It furnished all that was needed as excuse for instant descent upon the settlers in the deep valleys north of the Rio Salado, and, all unsuspecting, all unprepared, several of these had met their doom. Relentless war was already begun, and the general lost no time in starting his horsemen after the hostiles. Meantime the infantry companies, at the scattered posts and camps, were left to "hold the fort," to protect the women, children, and property, and Neil Blakely, a sore-hearted man because forbidden by the surgeon to attempt to go, was chafing, fuming, and retarding his recovery at his lonely quarters. The men whom he most liked were gone, and the few among the women who might have been his friends seemed now to stand afar off. Something, he knew not what, had turned garrison sentiment against him.

For a day or two, so absorbed was he in his chagrin over Graham's verdict and the general's telegraphic orders in the case, Mr. Blakely never knew or noticed that anything else was amiss. Then, too, there had been no opportunity of meeting garrison folk except the few officers who dropped in to inquire civilly how he was progressing. The bandages were off, but the plaster still disfigured one side of his face and neck. He could not go forth and seek society. There was really only one girl at the post whose society he cared to seek. He had his books and his bugs, and that, said Mrs. Bridger, was "all he demanded and more than he deserved." To think that the very room so recently sacred to the son and heir should be transformed into what that irate little woman called a "beetle shop"! It was one of Mr. Blakely's unpardonable sins in the eyes of the sex that he found so much to interest him in a pursuit that neither interested nor included them. A man with brains and a bank account had no right to live alone, said Mrs. Sanders, she having a daughter of marriageable age, if only moderately prepossessing. All this had the women to complain of in him before the cataclysm that, for the time at least, had played havoc with his good looks. All this he knew and bore with philosophic and whimsical stoicism. But all this and more could not account for the phenomenon of averted eyes and constrained, if not freezing, manner when, in the dusk of the late autumn evening, issuing suddenly from his quarters, he came face to face with a party of four young women under escort of the post adjutant—Mrs. Bridger and Mrs. Truman foremost of the four and first to receive his courteous, yet half embarrassed, greeting. They had to stop for half a second, as they later said, because really he confronted them, all unsuspected. But the other two, Kate Sanders and Mina Westervelt, with bowed heads and without a word, scurried by him and passed on down the line. Doty explained hurriedly that they had been over to the post hospital to inquire for Mullins and were due at the Sanders' now for music, whereupon Blakely begged pardon for even the brief detention, and, raising his cap, went on out to the sentry post of No. 4 to study the dark and distant upheavals in the Red Rock country, where, almost every night of late, the signal fires of the Apaches were reported. Not until he was again alone did he realize that he had been almost frigidly greeted by those who spoke at all. It set him to thinking.

Mrs. Plume was still confined to her room. The major had returned from Prescott and, despite the fact that the regiment was afield and a clash with the hostiles imminent, was packing up preparatory to a move. Books, papers, and pictures were being stored in chests, big and little, that he had had made for such emergencies. It was evident that he was expecting orders for change of station or extended leave, and they who went so far as to question the grave-faced soldier, who seemed to have grown ten years older in the last ten days, had to be content with the brief, guarded reply that Mrs. Plume had never been well since she set foot in Arizona, and even though he returned, she would not. He was taking her, he said, to San Francisco. Of this unhappy woman's nocturnal expedition the others seldom spoke now and only with bated breath. "Sleep-walking, of course!" said everybody, no matter what everybody might think. But, now that Major Plume knew that in her sleep his wife had wandered up the row to the very door—the back door—of Mr. Blakely's quarters, was it not strange that he had taken no pains to prevent a recurrence of so compromising an excursion, for strange stories were afloat. Sentry No. 4 had heard and told of a feminine voice, "somebody cryin' like" in the darkness of midnight about Blakely's, and Norah Shaughnessy—returned to her duties at the Trumans', yet worrying over the critical condition of her trooper lover, and losing thereby much needed sleep—had gained some new and startling information. One night she had heard, another night she had dimly seen, a visitor received at Blakely's back door, and that visitor a woman, with a shawl about her head. Norah told her mistress, who very properly bade her never refer to it again to a soul, and very promptly referred to it herself to several souls, one of them Janet Wren. Janet, still virtuously averse to Blakely, laid the story before her brother the very day he started on the warpath, and Janet was startled to see that she was telling him no news whatever. "Then, indeed," said she, "it is high time the major took his wife away," and Wren sternly bade her hold her peace, she knew not what she was saying! But, said Camp Sandy, who could it have been but Mrs. Plume or, possibly, Elise? Once or twice in its checkered past Camp Sandy had had its romance, its mystery, indeed its scandals, but this was something that put in the shade all previous episodes; this shook Sandy to its very foundation, and this, despite her brother's prohibition, Janet Wren felt it her duty to detail in full to Angela.

To do her justice, it should be said that Miss Wren had striven valiantly against the impulse,—had indeed mastered it for several hours,—but the sight of the vivid blush, the eager joy in the sweet young face when Blakely's new "striker" handed in a note addressed to Miss Angela Wren, proved far too potent a factor in the undoing of that magnanimous resolve. The girl fled with her prize, instanter, to her room, and thither, as she did not reappear, the aunt betook herself within the hour. The note itself was neither long nor effusive—merely a bright, cordial, friendly missive, protesting against the idea that any apology had been due. There was but one line which could be considered even mildly significant. "The little net," wrote Blakely, "has now a value that it never had before." Yet Angela was snuggling that otherwise unimportant billet to her cheek when the creaking stairway told her portentously of a solemn coming. Ten minutes more and the note was lying neglected on the bureau, and Angela stood at her window, gazing out over dreary miles of almost desert landscape, of rock and shale and sand and cactus, with eyes from which the light had fled, and a new, strange trouble biting at her girlish heart. Confound No. 4—and Norah Shaughnessy!

It had been arranged that when the Plumes were ready to start, Mrs. Daly and her daughter, the newly widowed and the fatherless, should be sent up to Prescott and thence across the desert to Ehrenberg, on the Colorado. While no hostile Apaches had been seen west of the Verde Valley, there were traces that told that they were watching the road as far at least as the Agua Fria, and a sergeant and six men had been chosen to go as escort to the little convoy. It had been supposed that Plume would prefer to start in the morning and go as far as Stemmer's ranch, in the Agua Fria Valley, and there rest his invalid wife until another day, thus breaking the fifty-mile stage through the mountains. To the surprise of everybody, the Dalys were warned to be in readiness to start at five in the morning, and to go through to Prescott that day. At five in the morning, therefore, the quartermaster's ambulance was at the post trader's house, where the recently bereaved ones had been harbored since poor Daly's death, and there, with their generous host, was the widow's former patient, Blakely, full of sympathy and solicitude, come to say good-bye. Plume's own Concord appeared almost at the instant in front of his quarters, and presently Mrs. Plume, veiled and obviously far from strong, came forth leaning on her husband's arm, and closely followed by Elise. Then, despite the early hour, and to the dismay of Plume, who had planned to start without farewell demonstration of any kind, lights were blinking in almost every house along the row, and a flock of women, some tender and sympathetic, some morbidly curious, had gathered to wish the major's wife a pleasant journey and a speedy recovery. They loved her not at all, and liked her none too well, but she was ill and sorrowing, so that was enough. Elise they could not bear, yet even Elise came in for a kindly word or two. Mrs. Graham was there, big-hearted and brimming over with helpful suggestion, burdened also with a basket of dainties. Captain and Mrs. Cutler, Captain and Mrs. Westervelt, the Trumans both, Doty, the young adjutant, Janet Wren, of course, and the ladies of the cavalry, the major's regiment, without exception, were on hand to bid the major and his wife good-bye. Angela Wren was not feeling well, explained her aunt, and Mr. Neil Blakely was conspicuous by his absence.

It had been observed that, during those few days of hurried packing and preparation, Major Plume had not once gone to Blakely's quarters. True, he had visited only Dr. Graham, and had begged him to explain that anxiety on account of Mrs. Plume prevented his making the round of farewell calls; but that he was thoughtful of others to the last was shown in this: Plume had asked Captain Cutler, commander of the post, to order the release of that wretch Downs. "He has been punished quite sufficiently, I think," said Plume, "and as I was instrumental in his arrest I ask his liberation." At tattoo, therefore, the previous evening "the wretch" had been returned to duty, and at five in the morning was found hovering about the major's quarters. When invited by the sergeant of the guard to explain, he replied, quite civilly for him, that it was to say good-by to Elise. "Me and her," said he, "has been good friends."

Presumably he had had his opportunity at the kitchen door before the start, but still he lingered, feigning professional interest in the condition of the sleek mules that were to haul the Concord over fifty miles of rugged road, up hill and down dale before the setting of the sun. Then, while the officers and ladies clustered thick on one side of the black vehicle, Downs sidled to the other, and the big black eyes of the Frenchwoman peered down at him a moment as she leaned toward him, and, with a whispered word, slyly dropped a little folded packet into his waiting palm. Then, as though impatient, Plume shouted "All right. Go on!" The Concord whirled away, and something like a sigh of relief went up from assembled Sandy, as the first kiss of the rising sun lighted on the bald pate of Squaw Peak, huge sentinel of the valley, looming from the darkness and shadows and the mists of the shallow stream that slept in many a silent pool along its massive, rocky base. With but a few hurried, embarrassed words, Clarice Plume had said adieu to Sandy, thinking never to see it again. They stood and watched her past the one unlighted house, the northernmost along the row. They knew not that Mr. Blakely was at the moment bidding adieu to others in far humbler station. They only noted that, even at the last, he was not there to wave a good-by to the woman who had once so influenced his life. Slowly then the little group dissolved and drifted away. She had gone unchallenged of any authority, though the fate of Mullins still hung in the balance. Obviously, then, it was not she whom Byrne's report had implicated, if indeed that report had named anybody. There had been no occasion for a coroner and jury. There would have been neither coroner nor jury to serve, had they been called for. Camp Sandy stood in a little world of its own, the only civil functionary within forty miles being a ranchman, dwelling seven miles down stream, who held some Territorial warrant as a justice of the peace.

But Norah Shaughnessy, from the gable window of the Trumans' quarters, shook a hard-clinching Irish fist and showered malediction after the swiftly speeding ambulance. "Wan 'o ye," she sobbed, "dealt Pat Mullins a coward and cruel blow, and I'll know which, as soon as ever that poor bye can spake the truth." She would have said it to that hated Frenchwoman herself, had not mother and mistress both forbade her leaving the room until the Plumes were gone.

Three trunks had been stacked up and secured on the hanging rack at the rear of the Concord. Others, with certain chests and boxes, had been loaded into one big wagon and sent ahead. The ambulance, with the Dalys and the little escort of seven horsemen, awaited the rest of the convoy on the northward flats, and the cloud of their combined dust hung long on the scarred flanks as the first rays of the rising sun came gilding the rocks at Boulder Point, and what was left of the garrison at Sandy turned out for reveille.

That evening, for the first time since his injury, Mr. Blakely took his horse and rode away southward in the soft moonlight, and had not returned when tattoo sounded. The post trader, coming up with the latest San Francisco papers, said he had stopped a moment to ask at the store whether Schandein, the ranchman justice of the peace before referred to, had recently visited the post.

That evening, too, for the first time since his dangerous

wound, Trooper Mullins awoke from his long delirium, weak as a little child; asked for Norah, and what in the world was the matter with him—in bed and bandages, and Dr. Graham, looking into the poor lad's dim, half-opening eyes, sent a messenger to Captain Cutler's quarters to ask would the captain come at once to hospital. This was at nine o'clock.

Less than two hours later a mounted orderly set forth with dispatches from the temporary post commander to Colonel Byrne at Prescott. A wire from that point about sundown had announced the safe arrival of the party from Camp Sandy. The answer, sent at ten o'clock, broke up the game of whist at the quarters of the inspector general. Byrne, the recipient, gravely read it, backed from the table, and vainly strove not to see the anxious inquiry in the eyes of Major Plume, his guest. But Plume cornered him.

"From Sandy?" he asked. "May I read it?"

Byrne hesitated just one moment, then placed the paper in his junior's hand. Plume read, turned very white, and the paper fell from his trembling fingers. The message merely said:

Mullins recovering and quite rational, though very weak. He says two women were his assailants. Courier with dispatches at once.

(Signed) CUTLER, Commanding.

CHAPTER XII

FIRE!

"It was not so much his wounds as his weakness," Dr. Graham was saying, later still that autumn night, "that led to my declaring Blakely unfit to take the field. He would have gone in spite of me, but for the general's order. He has gone now in spite of me, and no one knows where."

It was then nearly twelve o'clock, and "the Bugologist" was still abroad. Dinner, as usual since his mishap, had been sent over to him from the officers' mess soon after sunset. His horse, or rather the troop horse designated for his use, had been fed and groomed in the late afternoon, and then saddled at seven o'clock and brought over to the rear of the quarters by a stable orderly.

There had been some demur at longer sending Blakely's meals from mess, now reduced to an actual membership of two. Sandy was a "much married" post in the latter half of the 70's, the bachelors of the commissioned list being only three, all told,—Blakely, and Duane of the Horse, and Doty of the Foot. With these was Heartburn, the contract doctor, and now Duane and the doctor were out in the mountains and Blakely on sick report, yet able to be about. Doty thought him able to come to mess. Blakely, thinking he looked much worse than he felt, thanks to his plastered jowl, stood on his rights in the matter and would not go. There had been some demur on part of the stable sergeant of Wren's troop as to sending over the horse. Few officers brought eastern-bred horses to Arizona in those days. The bronco was best suited to the work. An officer on duty could take out the troop horse assigned to his use any hour before taps and no questions asked; but the sergeant told Mr. Blakely's messenger that the lieutenant wasn't for duty, and it might make trouble. It did. Captain Cutler sent for old Murray, the veteran sergeant, and asked him did he not know his orders. He had allowed a horse to be sent to a sick man—an officer not on duty—and one the doctor had warned against exercise for quite a time, at least. And now the officer was gone, so was the horse, and Cutler, being sorely torn up by the revelations of the evening and dread of ill befalling Blakely, was so injudicious as to hint to a soldier who had worn chevrons much longer than he, Cutler, had worn shoulder-straps, that the next thing to go would probably be his sergeant's bars, whereat Murray went red to the roots of his hair—which "continued the march" of the color,—and said, with a snap of his jaws, that he got those chevrons, as he did his orders, from his troop commander. A court might order them stricken off, but a captain couldn't, other than his own. For which piece of impudence the veteran went straightway to Sudsville in close arrest. Corporal Bolt was ordered to take over his keys and the charge of the stables until the return of Captain Wren, also this order—that no government horse should be sent to Lieutenant Blakely hereafter until the lieutenant was declared by the post surgeon fit for duty.

There were left at the post, of each of the two cavalry troops, about a dozen men to care for the stables, the barracks, and property. Seven of these had gone with the convoy to Prescott, and, when Cutler ordered half a dozen horsemen out at midnight to follow Blakely's trail and try to find him, they had to draw on both troop stables, and one of the designated men was the wretch Downs,—and Downs was not in his bunk,—not anywhere about the quarters or corrals. It was nearly one by the time the party started down the sandy road to the south, Hart and his buckboard and a sturdy brace of mules joining them as they passed the store. "We may need to bring him back in this," said he, to Corporal Quirk.

"An' what did ye fetch to bring him *to* wid?" asked the corporal. Hart touched lightly the breast of his coat, then clucked to his team. "Faith, there's more than wan way of tappin' it then," said Quirk, but the cavalcade moved on.

The crescent moon had long since sunk behind the westward range, and trailing was something far too slow and tedious. They spurred, therefore, for the nearest ranch, five miles down stream, making their first inquiry there. The inmates were slow to arise, but quick to answer. Blakely had neither been seen nor heard of. Downs they didn't wish to know at all. Indians hadn't been near the lower valley since the "break" at the post the previous week. One of the inmates declared he had ridden alone from Camp McDowell within three days, and there wasn't a 'Patchie west of the Matitzal. Hart did all the questioning. He was a business man and a brother. Soldiers, the ranchmen didn't like—soldiers set too much value on government property.

The trail ran but a few hundred yards east of the stream, and close to the adobe walls of the ranch. Strom, the proprietor, got out his lantern and searched below the point where the little troop had turned off. No recent hoof-track, southbound, was visible. "He couldn't have come this far," said he. "Better put back!" Put back they did, and by the aid of Hart's lantern found the fresh trail of a government-shod horse, turning to the east nearly two miles toward home. Quirk said a bad word or two; borrowed the lantern and thoughtfully included the flask; bade his men follow in file and plunged through the underbrush in dogged pursuit. Hart and his team now could not follow. They waited over half an hour without sign or sound from the trailers, then drove swiftly back to the post. There was a light in the telegraph office, and thither Hart went in a hurry. Lieutenant Doty, combining the duties of adjutant and officer of the day, was up and making the rounds. The sentries had just called off three o'clock.

"Had your trouble for nothing, Hart," hailed the youngster cheerily. "Where're the men?"

"Followed his trail—turned to the east three miles below here," answered the trader.

"Three miles *below*! Why, man, he wasn't below. He met them up Beaver Creek, an' brought 'em in."

"Brought who in?" asked Hart, dropping his whip. "I don't understand."

"Why, the scouts, or runners! Wren sent 'em in. He's had a sharp fight up the mountains beyond Snow Lake. Three men wounded. You couldn't have gone a mile before Blakely led 'em across No. 4's post. Ahorah and another chap—'Patchie-Mohaves. We clicked the news up to Prescott over an hour ago."

The tin reflector at the office window threw the light of the glass-framed candle straight upon Hart's rubicund face, and that face was a study. He faltered a bit before he asked:

"Did Blakely seem all right?—not used up, I mean?"

"Seemed weak and tired, but the man is mad to go and join his troop now—wants to go right out with Ahorah in the morning, and Captain Cutler says no. Oh, they had quite a row!"

They had had rather more than quite a row, if truth were told. Doty had heard only a bit of it. Cutler had been taken by surprise when the Bugologist appeared, two strange, wiry Apaches at his heels, and at first had contented himself with reading Wren's dispatch, repeating it over the wires to Prescott. Then he turned on Blakely, silently, wearily waiting, seated at Doty's desk, and on the two Apaches, silently, stolidly waiting, squatted on the floor. Cutler wished to know how Blakely knew these couriers were coming, and how he came to leave the post without permission. For a moment the lieutenant simply gazed at him, unanswering, but when the senior somewhat sharply repeated the question, in part, Blakely almost as sharply answered: "I did not know they were coming nor that there was wrong in my going. Major Plume required nothing of the kind when we were merely going out for a ride."

This nettled Cutler. He had always said that Plume was lax, and here was proof of it. "I might have wanted you— I *did* want you, hours ago, Mr. Blakely, and even Major Plume would not countenance his officers spending the greater part of the night away from the post, especially on a government horse," and there had Cutler the whip hand of the scientist, and Blakely had sense enough to see it, yet not sense enough to accept. He was nervous and irritable, as well as tired. Graham had told him he was too weak to ride, yet he had gone, not thinking, of course, to be gone so long, but gone deliberately, and without asking the consent of the post commander. "My finding the runners was an accident," he said, with some little asperity of tone and manner. "In fact, I didn't find them. They found me. I had known them both at the reservation. Have I your permission, sir"—this with marked emphasis —"to take them for something to eat. They are very hungry,—have come far, and wish to start early and rejoin Captain Wren,—as I do, too."

"They will start when *I* am ready, Mr. Blakely," said Cutler, "and you certainly will not start before. In point of fact, sir, you may not be allowed to start at all."

It was now Blakely's turn to redden to the brows. "You surely will not prevent my going to join my troop, now that it is in contact with the enemy," said he. "All I need is a few hours' sleep. I can start at seven."

"You cannot, with my consent, Mr. Blakely," said the captain dryly. "There are reasons, in fact, why you can't leave here for any purpose unless the general himself give contrary orders. Matters have come up that—you'll probably have to explain."

And here Doty entered, hearing only the captain's last. At sight of his adjutant the captain stopped short in his reprimand. "See to it that these runners have a good supper, Mr. Doty," said Cutler. "Stir up my company cook, if need be, but take them with you now." Then, turning again on Blakely, "The doctor wishes you to go to bed at once, Mr. Blakely, and I will see you in the morning, but no more riding away without permission," he concluded, and thereby closed the interview. He had, indeed, other things to say to, and inquire of, Blakely, but not until he had further consulted Graham. He confidently expected the coming day would bring instructions from headquarters to hold both Blakely and Trooper Downs at the post, as a result of his dispatches, based on the revelation of poor Pat Mullins. But Downs, forewarned, perhaps, had slipped into hiding somewhere—an old trick of his, when punishment was imminent. It might be two or three days before Downs turned up again, if indeed he turned up at all, but Blakely was here and could be held. Hence the "horse order" of the earlier evening.

It was nearly two when Blakely reached his quarters, rebuffed and stung. He was so nervous, however, that, in spite of serious fatigue, he found it for over an hour impossible to sleep. He turned out his light and lay in the dark, and the atmosphere of the room seemed heavily charged with rank tobacco. His new "striker" had sat up, it seems, keeping faithful vigil against his master's return, but, as the hours wore on, had solaced himself with pipe after pipe, and wandering about to keep awake. Most of the time, he declared, he had spent in a big rocking chair on the porch at the side door, but the scent of the weed and of that veteran pipe permeated the entire premises, and the Bugologist hated dead tobacco. He got up and tore down the blanket screen at the side windows and opened all the doors wide and tried his couch again, and still he wooed the drowsy god in vain. "Nor poppy nor mandragora" had he to soothe him. Instead there were new and anxious thoughts to vex, and so another half hour he tossed and tumbled, and when at last he seemed dropping to the borderland, perhaps, of dreams, he thought he must be ailing again and in need of new bandages or cooling drink or something, for the muffled footfalls, betrayed by creaking pine rather than by other sound, told him drowsily that the attendant or somebody, cautioned not to disturb him, was moving slowly across the room. He might have been out on the side porch to get cool water from the *olla*, but he needn't be so confoundedly slow and cautious, though he couldn't help the creaking. Then, what could the attendant want in the front room, where were still so many of the precious glass cases unharmed, and the Bugologist's favorite books and his big desk, littered with papers, etc.? Blakely thought to hail and warn him against moving about among those brittle glass things, but reflected that he, the new man, had done the reshifting under his, Blakely's, supervision, and knew just where each item was placed and how to find the passage way between them. It really was a trifle intricate. How could he have gone into the spare room at Captain Wren's, and there made his home as—she—Mrs. Plume had first suggested? There would not have been room for half his plunder, to say nothing of himself. "What on earth can Nixon want?" he sleepily asked himself, "fumbling about there among those cases? Was that a crack or a snap?" It sounded like both, a splitting of glass, a wrenching of lock spring or something. "Be careful there!" he managed to call. No answer. Perhaps it was some one of the big hounds, then, wandering restlessly about at night. They often did, and—why, yes, that would account for it. Doors and windows were all wide open here, what was to prevent? Still, Blakely wished he hadn't extinguished his lamp. He might then have explored. The sound ceased entirely for a moment, and, now that he was quite awake, he remembered that the hospital attendant was no longer with him. Then the sounds must have been made by the striker or the hounds. Blakely had no dogs of his own. Indeed they were common property at the post, most of them handed down with the rest of the public goods and chattels by their predecessors of the—th. At all events, he felt far too languid, inert, weak, indifferent or something. If the striker, he had doubtless come down for cool water. If the hounds, they were in search of something to eat, and in either case why bother about it? The incident had so far distracted his thoughts from the worries of the night that now, at last and in good earnest, he was dropping to sleep.

But in less than twenty minutes he was broad awake again, with sudden start—gasping, suffocating, listening in amaze to a volley of snapping and cracking, half-smothered, from the adjoining room. He sprang from his bed with a cry of alarm and flung himself through a thick, hot veil of eddying, yet invisible, smoke, straight for the communicating doorway, and was brought up standing by banging his head against the resounding pine, tight shut instead of open as he had left it, and refusing to yield to furious battering. It was locked, bolted, or barred from the other side. Blindly he turned and rushed for the side porch and the open air, stumbling against the striker as the latter came clattering headlong down from aloft. Then together they rushed to the parlor window, now cracking and splitting from the furious heat within. A volume of black fume came belching forth, driven and lashed by ruddy tongues of flame within, and their shouts for aid went up on the wings of the dawn, and the infantry sentry on the eastward post came running to see; caught one glimpse of the glare at that southward window; bang went his rifle with a ring that came echoing back from the opposite cliffs, as all Camp Sandy sprang from its bed in answer to the stentorian shout "Fire! No. 5!"

Charles King

CHAPTER XIII

WHOSE LETTERS?

There is something about a night alarm of fire at a military post that borders on the thrilling. In the days whereof we write the buildings were not the substantial creations of brick and stone to be seen to-day, and those of the scattered "camps" and stations in that arid, sun-scorched land of Arizona were tinder boxes of the flimsiest and most inflammable kind.

It could hardly have been a minute from the warning shot and yell of No. 5—repeated right and left by other sentries and echoed by No. 1 at the guard-house—before bugle and trumpet were blaring their fierce alarm, and the hoarse roar of the drum was rousing the inmates of the infantry barracks. Out they came, tumbling pell-mell into the accustomed ranks, confronted by the sight of Blakely's quarters one broad sheet of flame. With incredible speed the blaze had burst forth from the front room on the lower floor; leaped from window to window, from ledge to ledge; fastened instantly on overhanging roof, and the shingled screen of the veranda; had darted up the dry wooden stairway, devouring banister, railing, and snapping pine floor, and then, billowing forth from every crack, crevice, and casement of the upper floor streamed hissing and crackling on the blackness that precedes the dawn, a magnificent glare that put to shame the feeble signal fires lately gleaming in the mountains. Luckily there was no wind—there never was a wind at Sandy—and the flames leaped straight for the zenith, lashing their way into the huge black pillar of smoke cloud sailing aloft to the stars.

Under their sergeants, running in disciplined order, one company had sped for the water wagon and were now slowly trundling that unwieldy vehicle, pushing, pulling, straining at the wheels, from its night berth close to the corrals. Rushing like mad, in no order at all, the men of the other company came tearing across the open parade, and were faced and halted far out in front of officers' row by Blakely himself, barefooted and clad only in his pyjamas, but all alive with vim and energy.

"Back, men! back for your blankets!" he cried. "Bring ladders and buckets! Back with you, lively!" They seemed to catch his meaning at the instant. His soldier home with everything it contained was doomed. Nothing could save it. But there stood the next quarters,—Truman's and Westervelt's double set,—and in the intense heat that must speedily develop, it might well be that the dry, resinous woodwork that framed the adobe would blaze forth on its own account and spread a conflagration down the line. Already Mrs. Truman, with Norah and the children, was being hurried down to the doctor's, while Truman himself, with the aid of two or three neighboring "strikers," had stripped the beds of their single blanket and, bucketing these with water, was slashing at the veranda roof and cornice along the northward side.

Somebody came with a short ladder, and in another moment three or four adventurous spirits, led by Blakely and Truman, were scrambling about the veranda roof, their hands and faces glowing in the gathering heat, spreading blankets over the shingling and cornice. In five minutes all that was left of Blakely's little homestead was gone up in smoke and fierce, furious heat and flame, but the daring and well-directed effort of the garrison had saved the rest of the line. In ten minutes nothing but a heap of glowing beams and embers, within four crumbling walls of adobe, remained of the "beetle shop." Bugs, butterflies, books, chests, desk, trunks, furniture, papers, and such martial paraphernalia as a subaltern might require in that desert land, had been reduced to ashes before their owner's eyes. He had not saved so much as a shoe. His watch, lying on the table by his bedside, a silk handkerchief, and a little scrap of a note, written in girlish hand and carried temporarily in the breast pocket, were the only items he had managed to bring with him into the open air. He was still gasping, gagging, half-strangling, when Captain Cutler accosted him to know if he could give the faintest explanation of the starting of so strange and perilous a fire, and Blakely, remembering the stealthy footsteps and that locked or bolted door, could not but say he believed it incendiary, yet could think of no possible motive.

It was daybreak as the little group of spectators, women and children of the garrison, began to break up and return to their homes, all talking excitedly, all intolerant of the experiences of others, and centered solely in the narrative of their own. Leaving a dozen men with buckets, readily filled from the acequia which turned the old water wheel just across the post of No. 4, and sending the big water wagon down to the stream for another liquid load, the infantry went back to their barracks and early coffee. The drenched blankets, one by one, were stripped from the gable end of Truman's quarters, every square inch of the paint thereon being now a patch of tiny blisters, and there, as the dawn broadened and the pallid light took on again a tinge of rose, the officers gathered about Blakely in his scorched and soaked pyjamas, extending both condolence and congratulation.

"The question is, Blakely," remarked Captain Westervelt dryly, "will you go to Frisco to refit now, or wait till Congress reimburses?" whereat the scientist was observed to smile somewhat ruefully. "The question is, Bugs," burst in young Doty irrepressibly, "will you wear this rig, or Apache full dress, when you ride after Wren? The runners start at six," whereat even the rueful smile was observed to vanish, and without answer Blakely turned away, stepping gingerly into the heated sand with his bare white feet.

"Don't bother about dousing anything else, sergeant," said he presently, to the soldier supervising the work of the bucket squad. "The iron box should be under what's left of my desk—about there," and he indicated a charred and steaming heap, visible through a gap in the doubly baked adobe that had once been the side window. "Lug that out as soon as you can cool things off. I'll probably be back by that time." Then, turning again to the group of officers, and ignoring Doty—Blakely addressed himself to the senior.

"Captain Cutler," said he, "I can fit myself out at the troop quarters with everything I need for the field, at least, and wire to San Francisco for what I shall need when we return. I shall be ready to go with Ahorah at six."

There was a moment of silence. Embarrassment showed plainly in almost every face. When Cutler spoke it was with obvious effort. Everybody realized that Blakely, despite severe personal losses, had been the directing head in checking the progress of the flames. Truman had borne admirable part, but Blakely was at once leader and actor. He deserved well of his commander. He was still far from strong. He was weak and weary. His hands and face were scorched and in places blistered, yet, turning his back on the ruins of his treasures, he desired to go at once to join his comrades in the presence of the enemy. He had missed every previous opportunity of sharing perils and battle with them. He could afford such loss as that no longer, in view of what he knew had been said. He had every right, so thought they all, to go, yet Cutler hesitated. When at last he spoke it was to temporize.

"You're in no condition for field work, Mr. Blakely," said he. "The doctor has so assured me, and just now things are taking such shape I—need you here."

"You will permit me to appeal by wire, sir?" queried Blakely, standing attention in his bedraggled night garb, and forcing himself to a semblance of respect that he was far from feeling.

"I—I will consult Dr. Graham and let you know," was the captain's awkward reply.

Two hours later Neil Blakely, in a motley dress made up of collections from the troop and trader's stores—a combination costume of blue flannel shirt, bandanna kerchief, cavalry trousers with machine-made saddle piece, Tonto moccasins and leggings, fringed gauntlets and a broad-brimmed white felt hat, strode into the messroom in quest of eggs and coffee. Doty had been there and vanished. Sick call was sounding and Graham was stalking across the parade in the direction of the hospital, too far away to be reached by human voice, unless uplifted to the pitch of attracting the whole garrison. The telegraph operator had just clicked off the last of half a dozen messages scrawled by the lieutenant— orders on San Francisco furnishers for the new outfit demanded by the occasion, etc., but Captain Cutler was still mured within his own quarters, declining to see Mr. Blakely until ready to come to the office. Ahorah and his swarthy partner were already gone, "started even before six," said the acting sergeant major, and Blakely was fuming with impatience and sense of something much amiss. Doty was obviously dodging him, there could be no doubt of that, for the youngster was between two fires, the post commander's positive orders on one hand and Blakely's urgent pleadings on the other.

Over at "C" Troop's quarters was the lieutenant's saddle, ready packed with blanket, greatcoat, and bulging saddle-bags. Over in "C" Troop's stables was Deltchay—the lieutenant's bronco charger, ready fed and groomed, wondering why he was kept in when the other horses were out at graze. With the saddle kit were the troop carbine and revolver, Blakely's personal arms being now but stockless tubes of seared and blistered steel. Back of "C" Troop's quarters lolled a half-breed Mexican packer, with a brace of mules, one girt with saddle, the other in shrouding aparejo—diamond-hitched, both borrowed from the post trader with whom Blakely's note of hand was good as a government four per cent.—all ready to follow the lieutenant to the field whither right and duty called him. There, too, was Nixon, the new "striker," new clad as was his master, and full panoplied for the field, yet bemoaning the loss of soldier treasures whose value was never fully realized until they were irrevocably gone. Six o'clock, six-thirty, six-forty-five and even seven sped by and still there came no summons to join the soldier master. There had come instead, when Nixon urged that he be permitted to lead forth both his own troop horse and Deltchay, the brief, but significant reply: "Shut yer gab, Nixon. There's no horse goes till the captain says so!"

At seven o'clock, at last, the post commander came forth from his doorway; saw across the glaring level of the parade the form of Mr. Blakely impatiently pacing the veranda at the adjutant's office, and, instead of going thither, as was his wont, Captain Cutler turned the other way and strode swiftly to the hospital, where Graham met him at the bedside of Trooper patient Patrick Mullins. "How is he?" queried Cutler.

"Sleeping—thank God—and not to be wakened," was the Scotchman's answer. "He had a bad time of it during the fire."

"What am I to tell Blakely?" demanded Cutler, seeking strength for his faltering hand. "You're bound to help me now, Graham."

"Let him go and you *may* make it worse," said the doctor, with a clamp of his grizzled jaws. "Hold him here and you're sure to."

"Can't you, as post surgeon, tell him he isn't fit to ride?"

"Not when he rides the first half of the night and puts out a nasty fire the last. Can't you, as post commander, tell him you forbid his going till you hear from Byrne and investigate the fire?" If Graham had no patience with a frail woman, he had nothing but contempt for a weak man. "If he's bound to be up and doing something, though," he added, "send him out with a squad of men and orders to hunt for Downs."

Cutler had never even thought of it. Downs was still missing. No one had seen him. His haunts had been searched to no purpose. His horse was still with the herd. One man, the sergeant of the guard, the previous day, had marked the brief farewell between the missing man and the parting maid—had seen the woman's gloved hand stealthily put forth and the little folded packet passed to the soldier's ready palm. What that paper contained no man ventured to conjecture. Cutler and Graham, notified by Sergeant Kenna of what he had seen, puzzled over it in vain. Norah Shaughnessy could perhaps unravel it, thought the doctor, but he did not say.

Cutler came forth from the shaded depths of the broad hallway to face the dazzling glare of the morning sunshine, and the pale, stern, reproachful features of the homeless lieutenant, who simply raised his hand in salute and said: "I've been ready two hours, sir, and the runners are long gone."

"Too long and too far for you to catch them now," said Cutler, catching at another straw. "And there is far more important matter here. Mr. Blakely, I want that man Downs followed, found, and brought back to this post, and you're the only man to do it. Take a dozen troopers, if necessary, and set about it, sir, at once."

A soldier was at the moment hurrying past the front of the hospital, a grimy-looking packet in his hand. Hearing the voice of Captain Cutler, he turned, saw Lieutenant Blakely standing there at attention, saw that, as the captain finished, Blakely still remained a moment as though about to speak—saw that he seemed a trifle dazed or stunned. Cutler marked it, too. "This is imperative and immediate, Mr. Blakely," said he, not unkindly. "Pull yourself together if you are fit to go at all, and lose no more time." With that he started away. Graham had come to the doorway, but Blakely never seemed to see him. Instead he suddenly roused and, turning sharp, sprang down the wooden steps as though to overtake the captain, when the soldier, saluting, held forth the dingy packet.

"It was warped out of all shape, sir," said he. "The blacksmith pried out the lid wid a crowbar. The books are singed and soaked and the packages charred—all but this."

It fell apart as it passed from hand to hand, and a lot of letters, smoke-stained, scorched at the edges, and some of them soaking wet, also two or three *carte de visite* photographs, were scattered on the sand. Both men bobbed in haste to gather them up, and Graham came hurriedly down to help. As Blakely straightened again he swayed and staggered slightly, and the doctor grasped him by the arm, a sudden clutch that perhaps shook loose some of the recovered papers from the long, slim fingers. At all events, a few went suddenly back to earth, and, as Cutler turned, wondering what was amiss, he saw Blakely, with almost ashen face, supported by the doctor's sturdy arm to a seat on the edge of the piazza; saw, as he quickly retraced his steps, a sweet and smiling woman's face looking up at him out of the trampled sands, and, even as he stooped to recover the pretty photograph, though it looked far younger, fairer, and more winsome than ever he had seen it, Cutler knew the face at once. It was that of Clarice, wife of Major Plume. Whose, then, were those scattered letters?

CHAPTER XIV

AUNT JANET BRAVED

Nightfall of a weary day had come. Camp Sandy, startled from sleep in the dark hour before the dawn, had found topic for much exciting talk, and was getting tired as the twilight waned. No word had come from the party sent in search of Downs, now deemed a deserter. No sign of him had been found about the post. No explanation had occurred to either Cutler or Graham of the parting between Elise and the late "striker." She had never been known to notice or favor him in any way before. Her smiles and coquetries had been lavished on the sergeants. In Downs there was nothing whatsoever to attract her. It was not likely she had given him money, said Cutler, because he was about the post all that day after the Plumes' departure and with never a sign of inebriety. He could not himself buy whisky, but among the ranchmen, packers, and prospectors forever hanging about the post there were plenty ready to play middleman for anyone who could supply the cash, and in this way were the orders of the post commander made sometimes abortive. Downs was gone, that was certain, and the question was, which way?

A sergeant and two men had taken the Prescott road;

followed it to Dick's Ranch, in the Cherry Creek Valley, and were assured the missing man had never gone that way. Dick was himself a veteran trooper of the—th. He had invested his savings in this little estate and settled thereon to grow up with the country—the Stannards' winsome Millie having accepted a life interest in him and his modest property. They knew every man riding that trail, from the daily mail messenger to the semi-occasional courier. Their own regiment had gone, but they had warm interest in its successors. They knew Downs, had known him ever since his younger days when, a trig young Irish-Englishman, some Londoner's discharged valet, he had 'listed in the cavalry, as he expressed it, to reform. A model of temperance, soberness, and chastity was Downs between times, and his gifts as groom of the chambers, as well as groom of the stables, made him, when a model, invaluable to bachelor officers in need of a competent soldier servant. In days just after the great war he had won fame and money as a light rider. It was then that Lieutenant Blake had dubbed him "Epsom" Downs, and well-nigh quarreled with his chum, Lieutenant Ray, over the question of proprietorship when the two were sent to separate stations and Downs was "striking" for both. Downs settled the matter by getting on a seven-days' drunk, squandering both fame and money, and, though forgiven the scriptural seventy times seven (during which term of years his name was changed to Ups and Downs), finally forfeited the favor of both these indulgent masters and became thereafter simply Downs, with no ups of sufficient length to restore the average—much less to redeem him. And yet, when eventually "bobtailed" out of the—th, he had turned up at the old arsenal recruiting depot at St. Louis, clean-shaven, neat, deft-handed, helpful, to the end that an optimistic troop commander "took him on again," in the belief that a reform had indeed been inaugurated. But, like most good soldiers, the commander referred to knew little of politics or potables, otherwise he would have set less store by the strength of the reform movement and more by that of the potations. Downs went so far on the highroad to heaven this time as to drink nothing until his first payday. Meantime, as his captain's mercury, messenger, and general utility man, moving much in polite society at the arsenal and in town, he was frequently to be seen about Headquarters of the Army, then established by General Sherman as far as possible from Washington and as close to the heart of St. Louis. He learned something of the ins and outs of social life in the gay city, heard much theory and little truth about the time that Lieutenant Blakely, returning suddenly thereto after an absence of two months, during which time frequent letters had passed between him and Clarice Latrobe, found that Major Plume had been her shadow for weeks, her escort to dance after dance, her companion riding, driving, dining day after day. Something of this Blakely had heard in letters from friends. Little or nothing thereof had he heard from her. The public never knew what passed between them (Elise, her maid, was better informed). But Blakely within the day left town again, and within the week there appeared the announcement of her forthcoming marriage, Plume the presumably happy man. Downs got full the first payday after his re-enlistment, as has been said, and drunk, as in duty bound, at the major's "swagger" wedding. It was after this episode he fell utterly from grace and went forth to the frontier irreclaimably "Downs." It was a seven-days' topic of talk at Sandy that Lieutenant Blakely, when acting Indian agent at the reservation, should have accepted the services of this unpromising specimen as "striker." It was a seven-weeks' wonder that Downs kept the pact, and sober as a judge, from the hour he joined the Bugologist to the night that self-contained young officer was sent crashing into his beetle show under the impact of Wren's furious fist. Then came the last pound that broke the back of Downs' wavering resolution, and now had come— what? The sergeant and party rode back from Dick's to tell Captain Cutler the deserter had not taken the Cherry Creek road. Another party just in reported similarly that he had not taken the old, abandoned Grief Hill trail. Still another returned from down-stream ranches to say he could not have taken that route without being seen—and he had not been seen. Ranchman Strom would swear to that because Downs was in his debt for value received in shape of whisky, and Strom was rabid at the idea of his getting away. In fine, as nothing but Downs was missing, it became a matter of speculation along toward tattoo as to whether Downs could have taken anything at all—except possibly his own life.

Cutler was now desirous of questioning Blakely at length, and obtaining his views and theories as to Downs, for Cutler believed that Blakely had certain well-defined views which he was keeping to himself. Between these two, however, had grown an unbridgeable gulf. Dr. Graham had declared at eight o'clock that morning that Mr. Blakely was still so weak that he ought not to go with the searching parties, and on receipt of this dictum Captain Cutler had issued his, to wit, that Blakely should not go either in search of Downs or in pursuit of Captain Wren. It stung Blakely and angered him even against Graham, steeling him against the post commander. Each of these gentlemen begged him to make his temporary home under his roof, and Blakely would not. "Major Plume's quarters are now vacant, then," said Cutler to Graham. "If he won't come to you or to me, let him take a room there." This, too, Blakely refused. He reddened, what is more, at the suggestion. He sent Nixon down to Mr. Hart's, the trader's, to ask if he could occupy a spare room there, and when Hart said, yes, most certainly,

Cutler reddened in turn when told of it, and sent Lieutenant Doty, the adjutant, to say that the post commander could not "consent to an officer's occupying quarters outside the garrison when there was abundant room within." Then came Truman and Westervelt to beg Blakely to come to them. Then came a note from Mrs. Sanders, reminding him that, as an officer of the cavalry, it would be casting reflections on his own corps to go and dwell with aliens. "Captain Sanders would never forgive me," said she, "if you did not take our spare room. Indeed, I shall feel far safer with a man in the house now that we are having fires and Indian out-breaks and prisoners escaping and all that sort of thing. *Do* come, Mr. Blakely." And in that blue flannel shirt and the trooper trousers and bandanna neckerchief, Blakely went and thanked her; sent for Nixon and his saddle-bags, and with such patience as was possible settled down forthwith. Truth to tell it was high time he settled somewhere, for excitement, exposure, physical ill, and mental torment had told upon him severely. At sunset, as he seemed too miserable to leave his room and come to the dining table, Mrs. Sanders sent for the doctor, and reluctantly Blakely let him in.

That evening, just after tattoo had sounded, Kate Sanders and Angela were having murmured conference on the Wrens' veranda. Aunt Janet had gone to hospital to carry unimpeachable jelly to the several patients and dubious words of cheer. Jelly they absorbed with much avidity and her words with meek resignation. Mullins, she thought, after his dreadful experience and close touch with death, must be in receptive mood and repentant of his sins. Of just what sins to repent poor Pat might still be unsettled in his mind. It was sufficient that he had them, as all soldiers must have, said Miss Wren, and now that his brain seemed clearing and the fever gone and he was too weak and helpless to resist, the time seemed ripe for the sowing of good seed, and Janet went to sow.

But there by Mullins's bed, all unabashed at Janet's marked disapprobation, sat Norah Shaughnessy. There, in flannel shirt and trooper trousers and bandanna neckerchief, pale, but collected, stood the objectionable Mr. Blakely. He was bending over, saying something to Mullins, as she halted in the open doorway, and Blakely, looking quickly up, went with much civility to greet and escort her within. To his courteous, "Good-evening, Miss Wren, may I relieve you of your basket?" she returned prompt negative and, honoring him with no further notice, stood and gazed with Miss Shaughnessy at the focus— Miss Shaughnessy who, after one brief glance, turned a broad Irish back on the intruder at the doorway and resumed her murmuring to Mullins.

"Is the doctor here—or Steward Griffin?" spoke the lady, to the room at large, looking beyond the lieutenant and toward the single soldier attendant present.

"The doctor and the steward are both at home just now, Miss Wren," said Blakely. "May I offer you a chair?"

Miss Wren preferred to stand.

"I wish to speak with Steward Griffin," said she again. "Can you go for him?" this time obviously limiting her language to the attendant himself, and carefully excluding Mr. Blakely from the field of her recognition. The attendant dumbly shook his head. So Aunt Janet tried again.

"Norah, *you* know where the steward lives, will you—" But Blakely saw rebellion awake again in Ireland

and interposed.

"The steward shall be here at once, Miss Wren," said he, and tiptoed away. The lady's doubtful eye turned and followed him a moment, then slowly she permitted herself to enter. Griffin, heading for the dispensary at the moment and apprised of her visit, came hurrying in. Blakely, pondering over the few words Mullins had faintly spoken, walked slowly over toward the line. His talk with Graham had in a measure stilled the spirit of rancor that had possessed him earlier in the day. Graham, at least, was stanch and steadfast, not a weathercock like Cutler. Graham had given him soothing medicine and advised his strolling a while in the open air—he had slept so much of the stifling afternoon—and now, hearing the sound of women's voices on the dark veranda nearest him, he veered to the left, passed around the blackened ruin of his own quarters and down along the rear of the line just as the musician of the guard was sounding "Lights Out"— "Taps."

And then a sudden thought occurred to him. Sentries began challenging at taps. He was close to the post of No. 5. He could even see the shadowy form of the sentry slowly pacing toward him, and here he stood in the garb of a private soldier instead of his official dress. It caused him quickly to veer again, to turn to his right, the west, and to enter the open space between the now deserted quarters of the permanent commander and those of Captain Wren adjoining them to the north. Another moment and he stopped short. Girlish voices, low and murmurous, fell upon his ear. In a moment he had recognized them. "It won't take me two minutes, Angela. I'll go and get it now," were the first words distinctly heard, and, with a rustle of skirts, Kate Sanders bounded lightly from the piazza to the sands and disappeared around the corner of the major's quarters, going in the direction of her home. For the first time in many eventful days Blakely stood almost within touch of the girl whose little note was even then nestling in an inner pocket, and they were alone.

"Miss Angela!"

Gently he spoke her name, but the effect was startling. She had been reclining in a hammock, and at sound of his voice struggled suddenly to a sitting posture, a low cry on her lips. In some strange way, in the darkness, the fright, confusion,—whatever it may have been,—she lost her balance and her seat. The hammock whirled from under her, and with exasperating thump, unharmed but wrathful, the girl was tumbled to the resounding floor. Blakely sprang to her aid, but she was up in the split of a second, scorning, or not seeing, his eager, outstretched hand.

"My—Miss Angela!" he began, all anxiety and distress, "I hope you're not hurt," and the outstretched hands were trembling.

"I *know* I'm not," was the uncompromising reply, "not in the least; startled—that's all! Gentlemen don't usually come upon one that way—in the dark." She was panting a bit, but striving bravely, angrily, to be calm and cool—icy cool.

"Nor would I have come that way," then, stupidly, "had I known you were—here. Forgive me."

How could she, after that? She had no wish to see him, so she had schooled herself. She would decline to see him, were he to ask for her at the door; but, not for an instant did she wish to hear that he did not wish to see her, yet he had haplessly, brusquely said he wouldn't have come had he known she was there. It was her duty to leave him, instantly. It was her desire first to punish him.

"My aunt is not at home," she began, the frost of the Sierras in her tone.

"I just left her, a moment ago, at the hospital," said he, steadfastly ignoring her repellent tone. Indeed, if anything, the tone rejoiced him, for it told a tale she would not have told for realms and empires. He was ten years older and had lived. "But—forgive me," he went on, "you are trembling, Miss Angela." She was, and loathed herself, and promptly denied it. He gravely placed a chair. "You fell heavily, and it must have jarred you. Please sit down," and stepping to the *olla*, "let me bring you some water."

She was weak. Her knees, her hands, were shaking as they never shook before. He had seen her aunt at the hospital. He had left her aunt there without a moment's delay that he might hasten to see her, Angela. He was here and bending over her, with brimming gourd of cool spring water. Nay, more, with one hand he pressed it to her lips, with the other he held his handkerchief so that the drops might not fall upon her gown. He was bending over her, so close she could hear, she thought, the swift beating of his heart. She knew that if what Aunt Janet had told, and her father had seen, of him were true, she would rather die than suffer a touch of his hand. Yet one hand had touched her, gently, yet firmly, as he helped her to the chair, and the touch she loathed was sweet to her in spite of herself. From the moment of their first meeting this man had done what no other man had done before— spoken to her and treated her as a grown woman, with a man's admiration in his fine blue eyes, with deference in word and chivalric grace in manner. And in spite of the mean things whispered about him—about him and— anybody, she had felt her young heart going out to him, her buoyant, joyous, healthful nature opening and expanding in the sunshine of his presence. And now he had come to seek her, after all the peril and excitement and trouble he had undergone, and now, all loverlike tenderness and concern, was bending over her and murmuring to her, his deep voice almost as tremulous as her hand. Oh, it couldn't be true that he—cared for—was interested in—that woman, the major's wife! Not that she *ought* to care one way or another, except that it was so despicable—so unlike him. Yet she had promised herself—had virtually promised her father—that she would hold far aloof from this man, and here he stood, so close that their heart-beats almost intermingled, and he was telling her that he wished she had kept and never returned the little butterfly net, for now, when it had won a value it never before had known, it was his fate to lose it. "And now," he said, "I hope to be sent to-morrow to join your father in the field, and I wish to tell you that, whenever I go, I shall first come to see what you may have to send to him. Will you—be here, Miss Angela?"

For a moment—silence. She was thinking of her duty to her father, of her implied promise, of all that Janet had told her, and so thinking could not for the moment answer—could not meet his earnest gaze. Dark as it was she felt, rather than saw, the glow of his deep blue eyes. She could not mistake the tenderness of his tone. She had so believed in him. He seemed so far above the callow, vapid, empty-headed youngsters the other girls were twittering about from morn till night. She felt that she believed in him now, no matter what had been said or who had said it. She felt that if he would but say it was all a mistake—that no woman had crossed his threshold, all

Camp Sandy might swear to the truth of the story, and she would laugh at it. But how could she ask such a thing of him? Her cheeks took fire at the thought. It was he who broke the silence.

"Something has happened to break your faith in me, Miss Angela," said he, with instant gravity. "I certainly had it— I *know* I had it—not a week ago"; and now he had dropped to a seat in the swaying hammock, and with calm strength and will bent toward her and compelled her attention. "I have a right to know, as matters stand. Will you tell me, or must I wait until I see your father?" With that Neil Blakely actually sought to take her hand. She whipped it behind her at the instant. "Will you tell me?" he repeated, bending closer.

From down the line, dancing along the wooden veranda, came the sound of swift footfalls—Kate Sanders hurrying back. Another moment and it would be too late. The denial she longed to hear from his lips might never be spoken. If spoken at all it must be here and now, yet how could she—how could *she* ask *him*?

"I will tell you, Mr. Blakely." The words came from the window of the darkened parlor, close at hand. The voice was that of Janet Wren, austere and uncompromising. "I got here in time to hear your question—I will answer for my niece—"

"Aunt Janet—No!"

"Be quiet, Angela. Mr. Blakely, it is because this child's father saw, and I heard of, that which makes you unworthy the faith of a young, pure-hearted girl. Who was the—the creature to whom you opened your door last Wednesday midnight?"

Kate Sanders, singing softly, blithely, came tripping along the major's deserted veranda, her fresh young voice, glad, yet subdued, caroling the words of a dear old song that Parepa had made loved and famous full ten years before:

"And as he lingered by her side,
In spite of his comrade's warning
The old, old story was told again
At five o'clock in the morning."

Then came sudden silence, as springing to the sandy ground, the singer reached the Wrens' veranda and saw the dim form of Mr. Blakely, standing silently confronting a still dimmer form, faintly visible at the side window against the soft, tempered light of the hanging lamp in the hall.

"Who was the creature?" I repeat, were the strange words, in Miss Wren's most telling tone, that brought Kate Sanders to a halt, startled, silent.

Then Blakely answered: "Some day I shall tell Miss Angela, madam, but never—you. Good-night."

CHAPTER XV

A CALL FOR HELP

That night the wire across the mountains to Prescott was long alive with news, and there was little rest for operator, adjutant, or commanding officer at Sandy. Colonel Byrne, it seems, had lost telegraphic touch with his chief, who, quitting Camp McDowell, had personally taken the field somewhere over in the Tonto Basin beyond the Matitzal Range, and Byrne had the cares of a continent on his hands. Three of the five commands out in the field had had sharp encounters with the foe. Official business itself was sufficiently engrossing, but there were other matters assuming grave proportions. Mrs. Plume had developed a feverish anxiety to hie on to the Pacific and out of Arizona just at a time when, as her husband had to tell her, it was impossible for him, and impolitic for her, to go. Matters at Sandy, he explained, were in tangled shape. Mullins partially restored, but still, as Plume assured her, utterly out of his head, had declared that his assailants were women; and other witnesses, Plume would not give names, had positively asserted that Elise had been seen along the sentry post just about the time the stabbing occurred. Everything now, said he, must depend on Captain Wren, who was known to have seen and spoken to Elise, and who could probably testify that she returned to their roof before the tragic affair of the night. But Wren was now away up in the mountains beyond Snow Lake and might be going far over through Sunset Pass to the Colorado Chiquito. Meantime he, Plume, was responsible for Elise, in duty bound to keep her there to face any accuser. In her nervous, semi-hysterical state the wife could not well be told how much she, too, was involved. It was not necessary. She knew—all Fort Whipple, as Prescott's military post was called, knew all about the fire that had destroyed the "beetle shop" and Blakely's belongings. Elise, in wild excitement, had rushed to her mistress with that news and the further information that Downs was gone and could not be found. This latter fact, indeed, they learned before Plume ever heard of it—and made no mention of it in his presence.

"I shall have to run down to Sandy again," said Byrne, to Plume. "Keep up your heart and—watch that French-woman. The jade!" And with the following day he was bounding and bumping down the stony road that led from the breezy, pine-crested heights about headquarters to the sandy flats and desert rocks and ravines fifty miles to the east and twenty-five hundred feet below. "Shall be with you after dark," he wired Cutler, who was having a bad quarter of an hour on his own account, and wishing all Sandy to the devil. It had transpired that Strom's rival ranchman, a little farther down the valley, was short just one horse and set of horse equipments. He had made no complaint. He had accused nobody. He had never failed in the past to appear at Sandy with charge of theft and demand for damages at the expense of the soldiery whenever he missed an item, big or little—and sometimes when he didn't miss a thing. But now he came not at all, and Cutler jumped at the explanation: he had sold that steed, and Downs, the deserter, was the purchaser. Downs must have had money to aid in his escape. Downs must have received it from someone eager to get him out of the way. It might well be Elise, for who else would trust him? and Downs must be striking for the south, after wide *detour*. No use now to chase him. The wire was the only thing with which to round him up, so the stage stations on the Gila route, and the scattered army posts, were all notified of the desertion, and Downs's description, with all his imperfections, was flashed far and wide over the Territory. He could no more hope to escape than fly on the wings of night. He would be cut off or run down long before he could reach Mexico; that is, he *would* be if only troopers got after him. The civil list of Arizona in 1875 was of peculiar constitution. It stood ready at any time to resolve itself into a modification of the old-day underground railways, and help spirit off soldier criminals, first thoughtfully relieving them of care and responsibility for any surplus funds in their possession.

And with Downs gone one way, Wren's troop gone another, and Blakely here clamoring to follow, Cutler was mentally torn out of shape. He believed it his duty to hold Blakely at least until the colonel came, and he lacked the "sand" to tell him so.

From Wren not another word had been received direct, but Bridger at the agency had sent word that the Indians there were constantly in receipt of news from the hostiles that filled them with excitement. Wren, at last accounts, had gone into the mountains south of Sunset Pass toward Chevlon's Fork, and his trail was doubtless watched to head off couriers or cut down stragglers. Blakely's appeal to be allowed to follow and join his troop had been declared foolish, and the attempt foolhardy, by Captain Cutler. This and not the real reason was given, coupled of course, with the doctor's dictum. But even Graham had begun to think Blakely would be the better for anything that would take him away from a station where life had been one swift succession of ills and mishaps.

And even Graham did not dream how sorely Blakely had been hit. Nor could he account for the access of nervous irritability that possessed his patient all the livelong day, while waiting, as they all were, for the coming of Colonel Byrne. Mrs. Sanders declared to Mrs. Graham her private impression that he was on the verge of prostration, although, making an effort, Blakely had appeared at breakfast after an early morning walk, had been most courteous, gentle, and attentive to her and to her whole-some, if not actually homely, Kate. How the mother's heart yearned over that sweet-natured, sallow-faced child! But after breakfast Blakely had wandered off again and was out on the *mesa*, peering through a pair of borrowed glasses over the dreary eastward landscape and up and down the deep valley. "How oddly are we constituted!" said Mrs. Sanders. "If I only had his money, I'd never be wearing my heart out in this desert land." She was not the only army wife and mother that should have married a stockbroker—anything rather than a soldier.

The whole post knew by noon that Byrne was coming, and waited with feverish impatience. Byrne was the power that would put an end to the doubts and distrac-tions, decide who stabbed Pat Mullins, who set fire to the "beetle shop," where Epsom Downs had gone, and could even settle, possibly, the long-doubtful question, "Who struck Billy Patterson?" Sandy believed in Byrne as it did in no one since the days of General Crook. With exceptions, all Sandy society was out on the parade, the porticoes, or the northward bluff, as the sun went down. These two were the Misses Wren. "Angela," said Miss Janet, "is keeping her room to-day, and pretending to keep her temper"—this to Kate Sanders, who had twice sought admission, despite a girlish awe of, if not aversion to, this same Aunt Janet.

"But don't you think she'd like to see me just a little while, Miss Wren?" the girl inquired, her hand caressing the sleek head of one of the big hounds as she spoke. Hounds were other objects of Miss Wren's disfavor. "Lazy, pilfering brutes," she called them, when after hours of almost incredible labor and ingenious effort they had managed to tear down, and to pieces, a haunch of venison she had slung to the rafters of the back porch. "You can come in, Kate, provided you keep out the dogs," was her ungracious answer, "and I'll go see. I think she's sleeping now, and ought not to be disturbed."

"Then I won't disturb her," was Miss Sanders's prompt reply, as she turned away and would have gone, but the elder restrained her. Janet did not wish the girl to go at all. She knew Angela had asked for her, and doubtless longed to see her; and now, having administered her feline scratch and made Kate feel the weight of her disapproval, she was quite ready to promote the very interview she had verbally condemned. Perhaps Miss Sanders saw and knew this and preferred to worry Miss Wren as much as possible. At all events, only with reluctance did she obey the summons to wait a minute, and stood with a pout on her lips as the spinster vanished in the gloom of the hallway. Angela could not have been asleep, for her voice was audible in an instant. "Come up, Kate," she feebly cried, just as Aunt Janet had begun her little sermon, and the sermon had to stop, for Kate Sanders came, and neither lass was in mood to listen to pious exhortation. Moreover, they made it manifest to Aunt Janet that there would be no interchange of confidences until she withdrew. "You are not to talk yourselves into a pitch of excitement," said she. "Angela must sleep to-night to make up for the hours she lost—thanks to the abominable remarks of that hardened young man." With that, after a pull at the curtain, a soothing thump or two at Angela's pillow, and the muttered wish that the coming colonel were empowered to arrest recalcitrant nieces as well as insubordinate subs, she left them to their own devices. They were still in eager, almost breathless chat when the crack of whip and sputter of hoofs and wheels through gravelly sands told that the inspector's ambulance had come. Was it likely that Angela could sleep until she heard the probable result of the inspector's coming?

He was closeted first with Cutler. Then Dr. Graham was sent for, and the three walked over to the hospital, just as the musicians were forming for tattoo. They were at Mullins's bedside, with the steward and attendants outside, when taps went wailing out upon the night. There were five minutes of talk with that still bewildered patient. Then Byrne desired to see Mr. Blakely at once and alone. Cutler surrendered his office to the department inspector, and thither the lieutenant was summoned. Mrs. Sanders, with Mrs. Truman, was keeping little Mrs. Bridger company at the moment, and Blakely bowed courteously to the three in passing by.

"Even in that rough dress," said Mrs. Sanders reflectively, as her eyes followed the tall, straight figure over the moonlit parade, "he is a most distinguished looking man."

"Yes," said Mrs. Bridger, still unappeased. "If he were a Sioux, I suppose they'd call him 'Man-In-Love-With-His-Legs.'" Blakely heard the bubble of laughter that followed him on his way, and wished that he, too, felt in mood as merry. The acting sergeant major, a clerk, and young Cassidy, the soldier telegraph operator, seated at the westward end of the rough board porch of the adjutant's office, arose and saluted as he entered. Byrne had sent every possible hearer out of the building.

Five minutes the conference lasted, no sound coming from within. Cutler and Graham, with Captain Westervelt, sat waiting on the porch of the doctor's quarters, Mrs. Graham being busy with her progeny aloft. Others of the officers and families were also on the piazzas, or strolling slowly up and down the pathway, but all eyes wandered from time to time toward the dim light at the office. All was dark at the barracks. All was hushed and still about the post. The sentry call for half-past ten was still some minutes' distant, when one of the three seated figures at the end of the office porch was seen to rise. Then the other two started to their feet. The first hastened to the door and began to knock. So breathless was the night that over on the verandas the imperative thumping could be distinctly heard, and everyone ceased talk and listened. Then, in answer to some query from within, the voice of young Cassidy was uplifted.

"I beg pardon, sir, but that's the agency calling me, and it's hurry."

They saw the door open from within; saw the soldier admitted and the door closed after him; saw the two men waiting standing and expectant, no longer content to resume their chat. For three minutes of suspense there came no further sound. Then the door was again thrown open, and both Byrne and Blakely came hurrying out. In the memory of the earliest inhabitant never had Sandy seen the colonel walk so fast. Together they came striding straight toward Cutler's, and the captain arose and went to meet them, foreboding in his soul. Graham and Westervelt, restrained by discipline, held back. The women and younger officers, hushed by anxiety, gazed at the swift-coming pair in dread and fascination. There was a moment of muttered conference with the commanding officer, some hurried words, then Blakely was seen to spring away, to be recalled by Cutler, to start a second time, only to be again recalled. Then Cutler, shouting, "Mr. Doty, I need you!" hurried away toward the office, and Blakely, fairly running, sped straight for the barracks of Wren's troop. Only Byrne was left to answer the storm of question that burst upon him all at once, women thronging about him from all along the line.

"We have news from the agency," said he. "It is from Indian runners, and may not be reliable—some rumor of a sharp fight near Sunset Pass."

"Are there particulars, colonel—anybody killed or wounded?" It was Mrs. Sanders who spoke, her face very pale.

"We cannot know—as yet. It is all an Indian story. Mr. Blakely is going at once to investigate," was the guarded answer. But Mrs. Sanders knew, as well as a dozen others, that there *were* particulars—that somebody had been killed or wounded, for Indian stories to that effect had been found singularly reliable. It was Wren's troop that had gone to Sunset Pass, and here was Wren's sister with question in her eye, and at sight of her the colonel turned and hurried back to headquarters, following the post commander.

Another moment and Blakely, in the broad light streaming suddenly from the office room of Wren's troop, came speeding straight across the parade again in the direction of Sanders's quarters, next to the last at the southward end of the row. They sought, of course, to intercept him, and saw that his face was pale, though his manner was as composed as ever. To every question he had but one thing to say: "Colonel Byrne and the captain know all that I do—and more. Ask them." But this he said with obvious wish to be questioned no further,—said it gently, but most firmly,—and then, with scant apology, passed on. Five minutes more and Nixon was lugging out the lieutenant's field kit on the Sanders's porch, and Blakely, reappearing, went straight up the row to Wren's. It was now after 10.30, but he never hesitated. Miss Janet, watching him from the midst of her friends, saw him stride, unhesitatingly, straight to the door and knock. She followed instantly, but, before she could reach the steps, Kate Sanders, with wonder in her eyes, stood faltering before him.

"Will you say to Miss Angela that I have come as I promised? I am going at once to—join the troop. Can I see her?" he asked.

"She isn't well, Mr. Blakely. She hasn't left her room to-day." And Miss Sanders began herself to tremble, for up the steps came the resolute lady of the house, whom seeing, Mr. Blakely honored with a civil bow, but with not a word.

"I will hear your message, Mr. Blakely," said Miss Wren, pallid, too, and filled with wordless anxiety, but determined none the less.

"Miss Sanders has heard it, madam," was the uncompromising answer. "Will you see Miss Angela, please?" This again to Kate—and, without another word, she went.

"Mr. Blakely," began the lady impressively, "almost the last thing my brother said to me before leaving the post was that he wished no meetings between you and Angela.

Why do you pursue her? Do you wish to compel me to take her away?"

For a moment he was silent. Then, "It is I who must go, Miss Wren," was the answer, and she, who expected resentment, looked at him in surprise, so gentle, so sorrowing was his tone. "I had hoped to bear her message, but shall intrude no more. If the news that came to-night should be confirmed—and only in that event—say to her, if you please, that I shall do my best to find her father."

CHAPTER XVI

A RETURN TO COMMAND

With but a single orderly at his back, Mr. Blakely had left Camp Sandy late at night; had reached the agency, twenty miles up stream, two hours before the dawn and found young Bridger waiting for him. They had not even a reliable interpreter now. Arahawa, "Washington Charley," had been sent to the general at Camp McDowell. Lola's father, with others of her kin, had taken Apache leave and gone in search of the missing girl. But between the sign language and the *patois* of the mountains, a strange mixture of Spanish, English, and Tonto Apache, the officers had managed, with the aid of their men, to gather explanation of the fierce excitement prevailing all that previous day among the Indians at the agency. There had been another fight, a chase, a scattering of both pursuers and pursued. Most of the troops were at last accounts camping in the rocks near Sunset Pass. Two had been killed, several were wounded, three were missing, lost to everybody. Even the Apaches swore they knew not where they were—a sergeant, a trumpeter, and "Gran Capitan" himself—Captain Wren.

In the paling starlight of the coming day Blakely and Bridger plied the reluctant Indians with questions in every

　　　　　Charles King

form possible with their limited knowledge of the sign language. Blakely, having spent so many years on staff duty, had too little knowledge of practical service in the field. Bridger was but a beginner at best. Together they had decided on their course. A wire was sent to Sandy saying that from all they could gather the rumors were probably true, but urging that couriers be sent for Dick, the Cherry Creek settler, and Wales Arnold, another pioneer who had lived long in Apache land and owned a ranch on the little Beaver. They could get more out of the Indians than could these soldiers. It would be hours after dawn before either Dick or his fellow frontiersman could arrive. Meanwhile Sandy must bear the suspense as well as it might. The next wire came from Bridger at nine o'clock:

Arnold arrived hour ago. Examined six. Says stories probably true. Confident Wren not killed.

For answer Byrne wired that a detachment of a dozen men with three packers had marched at five o'clock to report to Blakely for such duty as he might require, and the answer came within the minute:

Blakely gone. Started for Snow Lake 4.30. Left orders detachment follow. Took orderly and two Apache Yuma scouts.

Byrne, Cutler, and Graham read with grave and anxious faces, but said very little. It was Blakely's way.

And that was the last heard of the Bugologist for as much as a week.

Meantime there was a painful situation at Fort Whipple, away up in "the hills." Major Plume, eager on his wife's account to get her to the seashore—"Monterey or Santa Barbara," said the sapient medical director—and ceaselessly importuned by her and viciously nagged by Elise, found himself bound to the spot. So long as Mullins stuck to his story Plume knew it would never do for him to leave. "A day or two more and he may abate or amend his statement," wrote Graham. Indeed, if Norah Shaughnessy were not there to prompt—to prop—his memory, Graham thought it like enough that even now the soldier would have wavered. But never a jot or tittle had Mullins been shaken from the original statement.

"There was two women," he said, "wid their shawls over their heads," and those two, refusing to halt at his demand, had been overtaken and one of them seized, to his bitter cost, for the other had driven a keen-bladed knife through his ribs, even as he sought to examine his captive. "They wouldn't spake," said he, "so what could I do but pull the shawl from the face of her to see could she be recognized?" Then came the fierce, cat-like spring of the taller of the two. Then the well-nigh fatal thrust. What afterwards became of the women he could say no more than the dead. Norah might rave about its being the Frenchwoman that did it to protect the major's lady—this he spoke in whispered confidence and only in reply to direct question—but it wouldn't be for the likes of him to preshume. Mullins, it seems, was a soldier of the old school.

Then came fresh and dire anxiety at Sandy. Four days after Blakely's start there appeared two swarthy runners from the way of Beaver Creek. They bore a missive scrawled on the paper lining of a cracker box, and it read about as follows:

CAMP IN SUNSET PASS, November 3d.

COMMANDING OFFICER, CAMP SANDY:

Scouting parties returning find no trace of Captain
Wren and Sergeant Carmody, but we shall persevere.
Indians lurking all about us make it difficult. Shall be
needing rations in four days. All wounded except
Flynn doing fairly well. Hope couriers sent you on
30th and 31st reached you safely.

The dispatch was in the handwriting of Benson, a trooper
of good education, often detailed for clerical work. It was
signed "Brewster, Sergeant."

Who then were the couriers, and what had become of
them? What fate had attended Blakely in his lonely and
perilous ride? What man or pair of men could pierce that
cordon of Indians lurking all around them and reach the
beleaguered command? What need to speculate on the
fate of the earlier couriers anyway? Only Indians could
hope to outwit Indians in such a case. It was madness to
expect white men to get through. It was madness for
Blakely to attempt it. Yet Blakely was gone beyond
recall, perhaps beyond redemption. From him, and from
the detachment that was sent by Bridger to follow his
trail, not a word had come of any kind. Asked if they had
seen or heard anything of such parties, the Indian couriers
stolidly shook their heads. They had followed the old
Wingate road all the way until in sight of the valley.
Then, scrambling through a rocky labyrinth, impossible
for hoof or wheel, had made a short cut to the head waters
of the Beaver. Now Blakely, riding from the agency
eastward slowly, should have found that Wingate trail
before the setting of the first day's sun, and his followers
could not have been far behind. It began to look as though
the Bugologist had never reached the road. It began to be
whispered about the post that Wren and his luckless

companions might never be found at all. Kate Sanders had ceased her song. She was now with Angela day and night.

One hope, a vague one, remained beside that of hearing from the baker's dozen that rode on Blakely's trail. Just as soon as Byrne received the Indian story concerning Wren's disappearance, he sent runners eastward on the track of Sanders's troop, with written advice to that officer to drop anything he might be doing along the Black Mesa and, turning northward, to make his way through a country hitherto untrod by white man, between Baker's Butte at the south and the Sunset Mountains at the north. He was ordered to scout the canon of Chevlon's Fork, and to look for sign on every side until, somewhere among the "tanks" in the solid rock about the mountain gateway known as Sunset Pass, he should join hands with the survivors of Webb's troop, nursing their wounded and guarding the new-made graves of their dead. Under such energetic supervision as that of Captain Sanders it was believed that even Apache Yuma scouts could be made to accomplish something, and that new heart would be given Wren's dispirited men. By this time, too, if Blakely had not fallen into the hands of the Apaches, he should have been joined by the intended escort, and, thus strengthened, could either push on to the pass, or, if surrounded, take up some strong position among the rocks and stand off his assailants until found by his fellow-soldiers under Sanders. Moreover, Byrne had caused report of the situation to be sent to the general via Camp McDowell, and felt sure he would lose no time in directing the scouting columns to head for the Sunset country. Scattered as were the hostile Apaches, it was apparent that they were in greater force northward, opposite the old reservation, than along the Mogollon Range southeast of it. There was hope, activity, animation, among the little camps and garrisons toward the broad valley of the Gila as the early days of November wore away. Only here at Sandy was there suspense as well as deep despond.

It was a starlit Sunday morning that Blakely rode away eastward from the agency. It was Wednesday night when Sergeant Brewster's runners came, and never a wink of sleep had they or their inquisitors until Thursday was ushered in. It was Saturday night again, a week from the night Neil Blakely strove to see and say good-by to Angela Wren. It was high time other runners came from Brewster, unless they, too, had been cut off, as must have been the fate of their forerunners. All drills had been suspended at Sandy; all duty subordinated to guard. Cutler had practically abolished the daily details, had doubled his sentries, had established outlying pickets, and was even bent on throwing up intrenchments or at least digging rifle pits, lest the Apaches should feel so "cocky" over their temporary successes as to essay an attack on the post. Byrne smiled and said they would hardly try that, but he approved the pickets. It was noted that for nearly a week,—not since Blakely's start from the agency,—no signal fires had been seen in the Red Rock country or about the reservation. Mr. Truman, acting as post quartermaster, had asked for additional men to protect his little herd, for the sergeant in charge declared that, twice, long-distance shots had come from far away up the bouldered heights to the west. The daily mail service had been abandoned, so nervous had the carrier become, and now, twice each week, a corporal and two men rode the rugged trail, thus far without seeing a sign of Apaches. The wire, too, was undisturbed, but an atmosphere of alarm and dread clung about the scattered ranches even as far as the Agua Fria to the west, and the few officials left at Prescott found it impossible to reassure the settlers, who, quitting their new homes, had either clustered about some favored ranch for general defense or, "packing" to

Fort Whipple, were clamoring there for protection with which to return to and occupy their abandoned roofs.

And all this, said Byrne, between his set teeth, because a bumptious agent sought to lay forceful hands upon the daughter of a chief. Poor Daly! He had paid dearly for that essay. As for Natzie, and her shadow Lola, neither one had been again seen. They might indeed have dropped back from Montezuma Well after the first wild stampede, but only fruitless search had the soldiers made for them. Even their own people, said Bridger, at the agency, were either the biggest liars that ever lived or the poorest trailers. The Apaches swore the girls could not be found. "I'll bet Sergeant Shannon could nail them," said Hart, the trader, when told of the general denial among the Indians. But Shannon was far away from the field column, leading his moccasined comrades afoot and in single file long, wearisome climbs up jagged cliffs or through deep canons, where unquestionably the foe had been in numbers but the day before, yet now they were gone. Shannon might well be needed at the far front, now that most of the Apache scouts had proved timid or worthless, but Byrne wished he had him closer home.

It was the Saturday night following the coming of the runners with confirmation of the grewsome Indian stories. Colonel Byrne, with Graham, Cutler, and Westervelt, had been at the office half an hour in consultation when, to the surprise of every soul at Sandy, a four-mule team and Concord wagon came bowling briskly into the post, and Major Plume, dust-covered and grave, marched into the midst of the conference and briefly said: "Gentlemen, I return to resume command."

Nobody had a word to say beyond that of welcome. It was manifestly the proper thing for him to do. Unable, in face of the stories afloat, to take his wife away, his proper place in the pressing emergency was at his post in command.

To Colonel Byrne, who guardedly and somewhat dubiously asked, "How about Mrs. Plume and that—French thing?" the major's answer was prompt:

"Both at Fort Whipple and in—good hands," said he. "My wife realizes that my duty is here, and, though her recovery may be retarded, she declares she will remain there or even join me. She, in fact, was so insistent that I should bring her back with me that it embarrassed me somewhat. I vetoed it, however."

Byrne gazed at him from under his shaggy eyebrows. "H'm," said he, "I fancied she had shaken the dust of Sandy from her shoes for good and all—that she hoped never to come back."

"I, too," answered Plume ingenuously. "She hated the very mention of it,—this is between ourselves,—until this week. Now she says her place is here with me, no matter how she may suffer," and the major seemed to dwell with pride on this new evidence of his wife's devotion. It was, indeed, an unusual symptom, and Byrne had to try hard to look credulous, which Plume appreciated and hurried on:

"Elise, of course, seemed bent on talking her out of it, but, with Wren and Blakely both missing, I could not hesitate. I had to come. Oh, captain, is Truman still acting quartermaster?" this to Cutler. "He has the keys of my house, I suppose."

And so by tattoo the major was once more harbored under his old roof and full of business. From Byrne and his associates he quickly gathered all particulars in their possession. He agreed with them that another day must bring tidings from the east or prove that the Apaches had surrounded and perhaps cut down every man of the command. He listened eagerly to the details Byrne and others were able to give him. He believed, by the time "taps" came, he had already settled on a plan for another relief column, and he sent for Truman, the quartermaster.

"Truman," said he, "how much of a pack train have you got left?"

"Hardly a mule, sir. Two expeditions out from this post swallows up pretty much everything."

"Very true; yet I may have to find a dozen packs before we get half through this business. The ammunition is in your hands, too, isn't it? Where do you keep it?" and the major turned and gazed out in the starlight.

"Only place I got, sir—quartermaster's storehouse," and Truman eyed his commander doubtfully.

"Well, I'm squeamish about such things as that," said the major, looking even graver, "especially since this fire here. By the way, was much of Blakely's property—er—rescued—or recovered?"

"Very little, sir. Blakely lost pretty much everything, except some papers in an iron box—the box that was warped all out of shape."

"Where is it now?" asked Plume, tugging at the strap of a dressing case and laying it open on the broad window-seat.

"In my quarters, under my bed, sir."

"Isn't that rather—unsafe?" asked Plume. "Think how quick *he* was burned out."

"Best I can do, sir. But he said it contained little of value, mainly letters and memoranda. No valuables at all, in fact. The lock wouldn't work, so the blacksmith strap-ironed it for him. That prevents it being opened by anyone, you know, who hasn't the proper tools."

"I see," said Plume reflectively. "It seems rather unusual to take such precaution with things of no value. I suppose Blakely knows his own business, however. Thank you very much Truman. Good-night."

"I suppose he did, at least, when he had the blacksmith iron that box," thought Truman, as he trudged away. "He did, at any rate, when he made me promise to keep it with the utmost care. Not even you can have it, Major Plume, although you are the post commander."

CHAPTER XVII

A STRANGE COMING

With one orderly and a pair of Apache Yuma scouts, Neil Blakely had set forth in hopes of making his way to Snow Lake, far up in the range to the east. The orderly was all very well,—like most of his fellows, game, true, and tried,—but few were the leaders who had any faith in Apache Yumas. Of those Indians whom General Crook had successively conquered, then turned to valuable use, the Hualpais had done well and proved reliable; the Apache Mohaves had served since '73, and in scout after scout and many a skirmish had proved loyal and worthy allies against the fierce, intractable Tontos, many of whom had never yet come in to an agency or accepted the bounty of the government. Even a certain few of these Tontos had proffered fealty and been made useful as runners and trailers against the recalcitrants of their own band. But the Apache Yumas, their mountain blood tainted by the cross with the slothful bands of the arid, desert flats of the lower Colorado, had won a bad name from the start, and deserved it. They feared the Tontos, who had thrashed them again and again, despoiled them of their plunder, walked away with their young women, insulted and jeered at their young men. Except when backed by the braves of other bands, therefore, the

Apache Yumas were fearful and timorous on the trail. Once they had broken and run before a mere handful of Tontos, leaving a wounded officer to his fate. Once, when scaling the Black Mesa toward this very Snow Lake, they had whimpered and begged to be sent home, declaring no enemy was there in hiding, when the peaks were found alive with Tontos. The Red Rock country and the northward spurs of the Mogollon seemed fraught with some strange, superstitious terror in their eyes, and if the "nerve" of a dozen would desert them when ordered east of the Verde, what could be expected of Blakely's two? No wonder, then, the elders at Sandy were sorely troubled!

But the Bugologist had nothing else to choose from. All the reliable, seasoned scouts were already gone with the various field columns. Only Apache Yumas remained, and only the least promising of the Apache Yumas at that. Bridger remembered how reluctantly these two had obeyed the summons to go. "If they don't sneak away and come back swearing they have lost the lieutenant, I'm a gopher," said he, and gave orders accordingly to have them hauled before him should they reappear. Confidently he looked to see or hear of them as again lurking about the commissary storehouse after the manner of their people, beggars to the backbone. But the week went by without a sign of them. "There's only one thing to explain that," said he. "They've either deserted to the enemy or been cut off and killed." What, then, had become of Blakely? What fate had befallen Wren?

By this time, late Saturday night, acting for the department commander now lost somewhere in the mountains, Byrne had re-enforced the guards at the agency and the garrison at Sandy with infantry drawn from Fort Whipple at Prescott, for thither the Apaches would never venture.

The untrammeled and sovereign citizen had his own way of treating the obnoxious native to the soil.

By this time, too, further word should have come from some of the field columns, Sanders's especially. But though runners had reached the post bearing brief dispatches from the general, showing that he and the troops from the more southerly posts were closing in on the wild haunts of the Tontos about Chevlon's Fork, not a sign had come from this energetic troop commander, not another line from Sergeant Brewster or his men, and there were women at Camp Sandy now nearly mad with sleepless dread and watching. "It means," said Byrne, "that the hostiles are between us and those commands. It means that couriers can't get through, that's all. I'm betting the commands are safe enough. They are too strong to be attacked." But Byrne was silent as to Blakely; he was dumb as to Wren. He was growing haggard with anxiety and care and inability to assure or comfort. The belated rations needed by Brewster's party, packed on mules hurried down from Prescott, were to start at dawn for Sunset Pass under stout infantry guard, and they, too, would probably be swallowed up in the mountains. The ranch people down the valley, fearful of raiding Apaches, had abandoned their homes, and, driving their stock before them, had taken refuge in the emptied corrals of the cavalry. Even Hart, the veteran trader, seemed losing his nerve under the strain, for when such intrepid frontiersmen as Wales Arnold declared it reckless to venture across the Sandy, and little scouting parties were greeted with long-range shots from hidden foe, it boded ill for all dwellers without the walls of the fort. For the first time in the annals of Camp Sandy, Hart had sandbagged his lower story, and he and his retainers practically slept upon their arms.

It was after midnight. Lights still burned dimly at the guard-house, the adjutant's office, and over at the quarters of the commanding officer, where Byrne and Plume were in consultation. There were sleepless eyes in every house along the line. Truman had not turned in at all. Pondering over his brief talk with the returned commander, he had gone to the storehouse to expedite the packing of Brewster's rations, and then it occurred to him to drop in a moment at the hospital. In all the dread and excitement of the past two days, Pat Mullins had been well-nigh forgotten. The attendant greeted him at the entrance. Truman, as he approached, could see him standing at the broad open doorway, apparently staring out through the starlight toward the black and distant outlines of the eastward mountains. Mullins at least was sleeping and seemed rapidly recovering, said he, in answer to Truman's muttered query. "Major Plume," he added, "was over to see him a while ago, but I told the major Pat was asleep." Truman listened without comment, but noted none the less and lingered. "You were looking out to the east," he said. "Seen any lights or fire?"

"Not I, sir. But the sentry there on No. 4 had the corporal out just now. He's seen or heard something, and they've moved over toward No. 5's post."

Truman followed. How happened it that when Byrne and Plume had so much to talk of the latter could find time to come away over to the hospital to inquire for a patient? And there! the call for half-past twelve had started at the guard-house and rung out from the stables and corrals. It was Four's turn to take it up now. Presently he did, but neither promptly nor with confidence. There were new men on the relief just down from Fort Whipple and strange to Sandy and its surroundings; but surely, said Truman, they should not have been assigned to Four and

Five, the exposed or dangerous posts, so long as there were other men, old-timers at Sandy, to take these stations. No. 4's "A-all's well" sounded more like a wail of remonstrance at his loneliness and isolation. It was a new voice, too, for in those days officers knew not only the face, but the voice, of every man in the little command, and—could Truman be mistaken—he thought he heard a subdued titter from the black shadows of his own quarters, and turned his course thither to investigate. Five's shout went up at the instant, loud, confident, almost boastful, as though in rebuke of Four's timidity, and, as Truman half expected, there was the corporal of the guard leaning on his rifle, close to the veranda steps, and so absorbed he never heard the officer approach until the lieutenant sharply hailed:

"Who's that on No. 4?"

"One of 'C' Company's fellers, sir," answered the watcher, coming to his senses and attention at the instant. "Just down from Prescott, and thinks he sees ghosts or Indians every minute. Nearly shot one of the hounds a moment ago."

"You shouldn't put him on that post—"

"I didn't sir," was the prompt rejoinder. "'Twas the sergeant. He said 'twould do him good, but the man's really scared, lieutenant. Thought I'd better stay near him a bit."

Across the black and desolate ruin of Blakely's quarters, and well out on the northward *mesa*, they could dimly discern the form of the unhappy sentry pacing uneasily along his lonely beat, pausing and turning every moment as though fearful of crouching assailant. Even among these veteran infantrymen left at Sandy, that northeast corner had had an uncanny name ever since the night of Pat Mullins's mysterious stabbing. Many a man would gladly have shunned sentry duty at that point, but none dare confess to it. Partly as a precaution, partly as protection to his sentries, the temporary commander had early in the week sent out a big "fatigue" detail, with knives and hatchets to slice away every clump of sage or greasewood that could shelter a prowling Apache for a hundred yards out from the line. But the man now on No. 4 was palpably nervous and distressed, in spite of this fact. Truman watched him a moment in mingled compassion and amusement, and was just turning aside to enter his open doorway when the corporal held up a warning hand.

Through the muffling sand of the roadway in rear of the quarters, a tall, dark figure was moving straight and swift toward the post of No. 4, and so far within that of No. 5 as to escape the latter's challenge. The corporal sprung his rifle to the hollow of his arm and started the next instant, sped noiselessly a few yards in pursuit, then abruptly halted. "It's the major, sir," said he, embarrassed, as Truman joined him again. "Gad, I hope No. 4 won't fire!"

Fire he did not, but his challenge came with a yell. "W-whocomesthere?"—three words as one and that through chattering teeth.

"Commanding officer," they heard Plume clearly answer, then in lower tone, but distinctly rebukeful. "What on earth's the matter, No. 4? You called off very badly. Anything disturbing you out here?"

The sentry's answer was a mumble of mingled confusion and distress. How could he own to his post commander that he was scared? No. 5 now was to be seen swiftly coming up the eastward front so as to be within supporting or hearing distance—curiosity, not sympathy, impelling; and so there were no less than five men, four of them old and tried soldiers, all within fifty yards of the angle made by the two sentry beats, all wide awake, yet not one of their number could later tell just what started it. All on a sudden, down in Sudsville, down among the southward quarters of the line, the hounds went rushing forth, barking and baying excitedly, one and all heading for the brink of the eastward *mesa*, yet halting short as though afraid to approach it nearer, and then, darting up and down, barking, sniffing, challenging angrily, they kept up their fierce alarm. Somebody or something was out there in the darkness, perhaps at the very edge of the bluff, and the dogs dare go no further. Even when the corporal, followed by No. 5, came running down the post, the hounds hung back, bristling and savage, yet fearful. Corporal Foote cocked his rifle and went crouching forward through the gloom, but the voice of the major was heard:

"Don't go out there, corporal. Call for the guard," as he hurried in to his quarters in search of his revolver. Truman by this time had run for his own arms and together they reappeared on the post of No. 5, as a sergeant, with half a dozen men, came panting from across the parade, swift running to the scene.

"No. 4 would have it that there were Indians, or somebody skulking about him when I was examining him a moment ago," said Plume hurriedly. "Shut up, you brutes!" he yelled angrily at the nearest hounds. "Scatter your men forward there, sergeant, and see if we can find anything." Other men were coming, too, by this time, and a lantern was dancing out from Doty's quarters. Byrne, pyjama-clad and in slippered feet, shuffled out to join the party as the guard, with rifles at ready, bored their way out to the front, the dogs still suspiciously sniffing and growling. For a moment or two no explanation offered. The noise was gradually quieting down. Then from far out to the right front rose the shout: "Come here with that lantern!" and all hands started at the sound.

Old Shaughnessy, saddler sergeant, was the first on the spot with a light. All Sudsville seemed up and astir. Some of the women, even, had begun to show at the narrow doorways. Corporal Foote and two of the guard were bending over some object huddled in the sand. Together they turned it over and tugged it into semblance of human shape, for the thing had been shrouded in what proved to be a ragged cavalry blanket. Senseless, yet feebly breathing and moaning, half-clad in tattered skirt and a coarsely made *camisa* such as was worn by peon women of the humblest class, with blood-stained bandages concealing much of the face and head, a young Indian woman was lifted toward the light. A soldier started on the run for Dr. Graham; another to the laundresses' homes for water. Others, still, with the lanterns now coming flitting down the low bluff, began searching through the sands for further sign, and found it within the minute— sign of a shod horse and of moccasined feet,—moccasins not of Tonto, but of Yuma make, said Byrne, after a moment's survey.

Rough, yet tender, hands bore the poor creature to the nearest shelter—Shaughnessy's quarters. Keen, eager eyes and bending forms followed hoof and foot prints to the ford. Two Indians, evidently, had lately issued, dripping, from the stream; one leading an eager horse, for it had been dancing sidewise as they neared the post, the other, probably sustaining the helpless burden on its back. Two

Indians had then re-entered the swift waters, almost at the point of emergence, one leading a reluctant, resisting animal, for it had struggled and plunged and set its fore feet against the effort. The other Indian had probably mounted as they neared the brink. Already they must be a good distance away on the other side, rendering pursuit probably useless. Already the explanation of their coming was apparent. The woman had been hurt or wounded when far from her tribe, and the Indians with her were those who had learned the white man's ways, knew that he warred not on women and would give this stricken creature care and comfort, food and raiment and relieve them of all such trouble. It was easy to account for their bringing her to Sandy and dropping her at the white man's door, but how came they by a shod horse that knew the spot and strove to break from them at the stables—strove hard against again being driven away? Mrs. Shaughnessy, volubly haranguing all within hearing as the searchers returned from the ford, was telling how she was lying awake, worrin' about Norah and Pat Mullins and the boys that had gone afield (owing her six weeks' wash) when she heard a dull trampin' like and what sounded like horses' stifled squeal (doubtless the leading Indian had gripped the nostrils to prevent the eager neigh), and then, said she, all the dogs roused up and rushed out, howling.

And then came a cry from within the humble doorway, where merciful hands were ministering to the suffering savage, and Plume started at the sound and glared at Byrne, and men stood hushed and startled and amazed, for the voice was that of Norah and the words were strange indeed:

"Fur the love of hivin, look what she had in her girdle! Shure it's Leese's own scarf, I tell ye—the Frenchwoman at the major's!"

And Byrne thought it high time to enter and take possession.

CHAPTER XVIII

A STRANGER GOING

At the first faint flush of dawn the little train of pack mules, with the rations for the beleaguered command at Sunset Pass, was started on its stony path. Once out of the valley of the Beaver it must clamber over range after range and stumble through deep and tortuous canons. A road there was—the old trail by Snow Lake, thence through the famous Pass and the Sunset crossing of the Colorado Chiquito to old Fort Wingate. It wormed its way out of the valley of the broader stream some miles further to the north and in face of the Red Rock country to the northeast, but it had not been traveled in safety for a year. Both Byrne and Plume believed it beset with peril, watched from ambush by invisible foes who could be relied upon to lurk in hiding until the train was within easy range, then, with sudden volley, to pick off the officers and prominent sergeants and, in the inevitable confusion, aided by their goatlike agility, to make good their escape. Thirty sturdy soldiers of the infantry under a veteran captain marched as escort, with Plume's orders to push through to the relief of Sergeant Brewster's command, and to send back Indian runners with full account of the situation. The relief of Wren's company accomplished, the next thing was to be a search for Wren himself, then a determined effort to find Blakely, and all the time to keep a lookout for Sanders's troop that must be somewhere north of Chevlon's Fork, as well as for the two or three little columns that should be breaking their way through the unblazed wilderness, under the personal direction of the general himself. Captain Stout and his party were out of sight up the Beaver before the red eye of the morning came peering over the jagged heights to the east, and looking in upon a garrison whose eyes were equally red and bleary through lack of sleep—a garrison worn and haggard through anxiety and distress gravely augmented by the events of the night. All Sandy had been up and astir within five minutes after Norah Shaughnessy's startling cry, and all Sandy asked with bated breath the same question: How on earth happened it that this wounded waif of the Apaches, this unknown Indian girl, dropped senseless at their doorway in the dead hours of the night, should have in her possession the very scarf worn by Mrs. Plume's nurse-companion, the Frenchwoman Elise, as she came forth with her mistress to drive away from Sandy, as was her hope, forever.

Prominent among those who had hastened down to Sudsville, after the news of this discovery had gone buzzing through the line of officers' quarters, was Janet Wren. Kate Sanders was staying with Angela, for the girls seemed to find comfort in each other's presence and society. Both had roused at sound of the clamor and were up and half dressed when a passing hospital attendant hurriedly shouted to Miss Wren the tidings. The girls, too, would have gone, but Aunt Janet sternly bade them remain indoors. She would investigate, she said, and bring them all information.

Dozens of the men were still hovering about old Shaughnessy's quarters as the tall, gaunt form of the captain's sister came stalking through the crowd, making straight for the doorway. The two senior officers, Byrne and Plume, were, in low tones, interrogating Norah. Plume had been shown the scarf and promptly seconded Norah. He knew it at once—knew that, as Elise came forth that dismal morning and passed under the light in the hall, she had this very scarf round her throat—this that had been found upon the person of a wounded and senseless girl. He remembered now that as the sun climbed higher and the air grew warmer the day of their swift flight to Prescott, Elise had thrown open her traveling sack, and he noticed that the scarf had been discarded. He did not see it anywhere about the Concord, but that proved nothing. She might easily have slipped it into her bag or under the cushions of the seat. Both he and Byrne, therefore, watched with no little interest when, after a brief glance at the feverish and wounded Indian girl, moaning in the cot in Mrs. Shaughnessy's room, Miss Wren returned to the open air, bearing the scarf with her. One moment she studied it, under the dull gleam of the lantern of the sergeant of the guard, and then slowly spoke:

"Gentlemen, I have seen this worn by Elise and I believe I know how it came to find its way back here—and it does not brighten the situation. From our piazza, the morning of Major Plume's start for Prescott, I could plainly see Downs hanging about the wagon. It started suddenly, as perhaps you remember, and as it rolled away something went fluttering to the ground behind. Everybody was looking after the Concord at the moment—everybody but Downs, who quickly stooped, picked up the thing, and turned hurriedly away. I believe he had this scarf when he deserted and that he has fallen into the hands of the Apaches."

Byrne looked at the post commander without speaking. The color had mounted one moment to the major's face, then left him pallid as before. The hunted, haggard, weary look about his eyes had deepened. That was all. The longer he lived, the longer he served about this woebegone spot in mid Arizona, the more he realized the influence for evil that handmaid of Shaitan seemed to exert over his vain, shallow, yet beautiful and beloved wife. Against it he had wrought and pleaded in vain. Elise had been with them since her babyhood, was his wife's almost indignant reply. Elise had been faithful to her— devoted to her all her life. Elise was indispensable; the only being that kept her from going mad with home-sickness and misery in that God-forsaken clime. Sobs and tears wound up each interview and, like many a stronger man, Plume had succumbed. It might, indeed, be cruel to rob her of Elise, the last living link that bound her to the blessed memories of her childhood, and he only mildly strove to point out to her how oddly, yet persistently, her good name had suffered through the words and deeds of this flighty, melodramatic Frenchwoman. Something of her baleful influence he had seen and suspected before ever they came to their exile, but here at Sandy, with full force he realized the extent of her machinations. Clarice was not the woman to go prowling about the quarters in the dead hours of the night, no matter how nervous and sleepless at home. Clarice was not the woman to be having back-door conferences with the servants of other households, much less the "striker" of an officer with whose name hers, as a maiden, had once been linked. He recalled with a shudder the events of the night that sent the soldier Mullins to hospital, robbed of his wits, if not of his life. He recalled with dread the reluctant admissions of the doctor and of Captain Wren. Sleep-walking, indeed! Clarice never elsewhere at any time had shown somnambulistic symptoms. It was Elise beyond doubt who had lured her forth for some purpose he could neither foil nor fathom. It was Elise who kept up this discreditable and mysterious commerce with Downs,—something that had culminated in the burning of Blakely's home, with who knows what evidence,—something that had terminated only with Downs's mad desertion and probable death. All this and more went flashing through his mind as Miss Wren finished her brief and significant story, and it dawned upon him that, whatever it might be to others, the death of Downs—to him, and to her whom he loved and whose honor he cherished—was anything but a calamity, a thing to mourn. Too generous to say the words, he yet turned with lightened heart and met Byrne's searching eyes, then those of Miss Wren now fixed upon him with austere challenge, as though she would say the flight and fate of this friendless soldier were crimes to be laid only at his door.

Byrne saw the instant distress in his comrade's face, and, glancing from him to her, almost in the same instant saw the inciting cause. Byrne had one article of faith if he lacked the needful thirty-nine. Women had no place in official affairs, no right to meddle in official matters, and what he said on the spur of his rising resentment was intended for her, though spoken to him. "So Downs skipped eastward, did he, and the Apaches got him! Well, Plume, that saves us a hanging." And Miss Wren turned away in wrath unspeakable.

That Downs had "skipped eastward" received further confirmation with the coming day, when Wales Arnold rode into the fort from a personally conducted scout up the Beaver. Riding out with Captain Stout's party, he had paid a brief visit to his, for the time, abandoned ranch, and was surprised to find there, unmolested, the two persons and all the property he had left the day he hurried wife and household to the shelter of the garrison. The two persons were half-breed Jose and his Hualpai squaw. They had been with the Arnolds five long years, were known to all the Apaches, and had ever been in highest favor with them because of the liberality with which they dispensed the *largesse* of their employer. Never went an Indian empty-stomached from their door. All the stock Wales had time to gather he had driven in to Sandy. All that was left Jose had found and corraled. Just one quadruped was missing—Arnold's old mustang saddler, Dobbin. Jose said he had been gone from the first and with him an old bridle and saddle. No Indian took him, said he. It was a soldier. He had found "government boot tracks" in the sand. Then Downs and Dobbin had gone together, but only Dobbin might they ever look to see again.

It had been arranged between Byrne and Captain Stout that the little relief column should rest in a deep canon beyond the springs from which the Beaver took its source, and, later in the afternoon, push on again on the long, stony climb toward the plateau of the upper Mogollon. There stood, about twenty-five miles out from the post on a bee line to the northeast, a sharp, rocky peak just high enough above the fringing pines and cedars to be distinctly visible by day from the crest of the nearest foothills west of the flagstaff. Along the sunset face of this gleaming *picacho* there was a shelf or ledge that had often been used by the Apaches for signaling purposes; the renegades communicating with their kindred about the agency up the valley. Invisible from the level of Camp Sandy, these fires by night, or smoke and flashes by day, reached only those for whom they were intended—the Apaches at the reservation; but Stout, who had known the neighborhood since '65, had suggested that lookouts equipped with binoculars be placed on the high ground back of the post. Inferior to the savage in the craft, we had no code of smoke, fire, or, at that time, even sun-flash signal, but it was arranged that one blaze was to mean "Unmolested thus far." Two blazes, a few yards apart, would mean "Important news by runner." In the latter event Plume was to push out forty or fifty men in dispersed order to meet and protect the runner in case he should be followed, or possibly headed off, by hostile tribesmen. Only six Indian allies had gone with Stout and he had eyed them with marked suspicion and disfavor. They, too, were Apache Yumas. The day wore on slowly, somberly. All sound of life, melody, or merriment had died out at Camp Sandy. Even the hounds seemed to feel that a cloud of disaster hung over the garrison. Only at rare intervals some feminine shape flitted along the line of deserted verandas—some woman on a mission of mercy to some mourning, sore-troubled sister among the scattered households. For several hours before high noon the wires from Prescott had been hot with demand for news, and with messages from Byrne or Plume to department headquarters. At meridian, however, there came a lull, and at 2 P. M. a break. Somewhere to the west the line was snapped and down. At 2.15 two linesmen galloped forth to find and repair damages, half a dozen "doughboys" on a buckboard going as guard. Otherwise, all day long, no soldier left the post, and when darkness settled down, the anxious operator, seated at his keyboard, was still unable to wake the spirit of the gleaming copper thread that spanned the westward wilderness.

All Sandy was wakeful, out on the broad parade, or the officers' verandas, and gazing as one man or woman at the bold, black upheaval a mile behind the post, at whose summit twinkled a tiny star, a single lantern, telling of the vigil of Plume's watchers. If Stout made even fair time he should have reached the *picacho* at dusk, and now it was nearly nine and not a glimmer of fire had been seen at the appointed rendezvous. Nine passed and 9.15, and at 9.30 the fifes and drums of the Eighth turned out and began the long, weird complaint of the tattoo. Nobody wished to go to bed. Why not sound reveille and let them sit up all night, if they chose? It was far better than tossing sleepless through the long hours to the dawn. It was nearly time for "taps"—lights out—when a yell went up from the parade and all Sandy started to its feet. All on a sudden the spark at the lookout bluff began violently to dance, and a dozen men tore out of garrison, eager to hear the news. They were met halfway by a sprinting corporal, whom they halted with eager demand for his news. "*Two* blazes!" he panted, "two! I must get in to the major at once!" Five minutes more the Assembly, not Taps, was sounding. Plume was sending forth his fifty rescuers, and with them, impatient for tidings from the far front, went Byrne, the major himself following as soon as he could change to riding dress. The last seen of the little command was the glinting of the starlight on the gun barrels as they forded the rippling stream and took the trail up the narrow, winding valley of the Beaver.

It was then a little after ten o'clock. The wire to Prescott was still unresponsive. Nothing had been heard from the linesmen and their escort, indicating that the break was probably far over as the Agua Fria. Not a sign, except Stout's signal blazes at the *picacho*, had been gathered from the front. Camp Sandy was cut off from the world, and the actual garrison left to guard the post and protect the women, children and the sick as eleven o'clock drew nigh, was exactly forty men of the fighting force. It was believed that Stout's couriers would make the homeward run, very nearly, by the route the pack-train took throughout the day, and if they succeeded in evading hostile scouts or parties, would soon appear about some of the breaks of the upper Beaver. Thither, therefore, with all possible speed Plume had directed his men, promising Mrs. Sanders, as he rode away, that the moment a runner was encountered he would send a light rider at the gallop, on his own good horse—that not a moment should be lost in bearing them the news.

But midnight came without a sign. Long before that hour, as though by common impulse, almost all the women of the garrison had gathered about Truman's quarters, now the northernmost of the row and in plain view of the confluence of the Sandy and the Beaver. Dr. Graham, who had been swinging to and fro between the limits of the Shaughnessys' and the hospital, stopped to speak with them a moment and gently drew Angela to one side. His grave and rugged face was sweet in its tenderness as he looked down into her brimming eyes. "Can you not be content at home, my child?" he murmured. "You seem like one of my own bairns, Angela, now that your brave father is afield, and I want to have his bonnie daughter looking her best against the home-coming. Surely Aunt Janet will bring you the news the moment any comes, and I'll bid Kate Sanders bide with you!"

No, she would not—she could not go home. Like every other soul in all Camp Sandy she seemed to long to be just there. Some few had even gone out further, beyond the sentries, to the point of the low bluff, and there, chatting only in whispers, huddled together, listening in anxiety inexpressible for the muffled sound of galloping hoofs on soft and sandy shore. No, she *dare* not, for within the four walls of that little white room what dreams and visions had the girl not seen? and, wakening shuddering, had clung to faithful Kate and sobbed her heart out in those clasping, tender, loyal arms. No beauty, indeed, was Kate, as even her fond mother ruefully admitted, but there was that in her great, gentle, unselfish heart that made her beloved by one and all. Yet Kate had pleaded with Angela in vain. Some strange, forceful mood had seized the girl and steeled and strengthened her against even Janet Wren's authority. She would not leave the little band of watchers. She was there when, toward half-past twelve, at last the message came. Plume's own horse came tearing through the flood, and panting, reeking, trembling into their midst, and his rider, little Fifer Lanigan, of Company "C," sprang from saddle and thrust his dispatch into Truman's outstretched hand.

With women and children crowding about him, and men running to the scene from every side, by the light of a lantern held in a soldier's shaking hand, he read aloud the contents:

"BIVOUAC AT PICACHO, 9 P. M.

"C. O. CAMP SANDY:

"Reached this point after hard march, but no active opposition, at 8 P. M. First party sent to build fire on ledge driven in by hostiles. Corporal Welch shot through left side—serious. Threw out skirmishers and drove them off after some firing, and about 9.20 came suddenly upon Indian boy crouching among rocks, who held up folded paper which I have read and forward herewith. We shall, of course, turn toward Snow Lake, taking boy as guide. March at 3 A. M. Will do everything possible to reach Wren on time.

(Signed) "STOUT, Commanding."

Within was another slip, grimy and with dark stains. And

Truman's voice well-nigh failed him as he read:

"November —th.

"C. O. CAMP SANDY:

"Through a friendly Apache who was with me at the reservation I learned that Captain Wren was lying wounded, cut off from his troop and with only four of his men, in a canon southwest of Snow Lake. With Indian for guide we succeeded reaching him second night, but are now surrounded, nearly out of ammunition and rations. Three more of our party are wounded and one, Trooper Kent, killed. If not rushed can hold out perhaps three days more, but Wren sorely needs surgical aid.

(Signed) "BLAKELY."

That was all. The Bugologist with his one orderly, and apparently without the Apache Yuma scouts, had gone straightway to the rescue of Wren. Now all were cut off and surrounded by a wily foe that counted on, sooner or later, overcoming and annihilating them, and even by the time the Indian runner slipped out (some faithful spirit won by Blakely's kindness and humanity when acting agent), the defense had been reduced just one-half. Thank God that Stout with his supplies and stalwart followers was not more than two days' march away, and was going straightway to the rescue!

It was nearly two when Plume and his half-hundred came drifting back to the garrison, and even then some few of the watchers were along the bluff. Janet Wren, having at last seen pale-faced, silent Angela to her room and bed, with Kate Sanders on guard, had again gone forth to extract such further information as Major Plume might have. Even at that hour men were at work in the corrals, fitting saddles to half a dozen spare horses,—about all that were left at the post,—and Miss Wren learned that Colonel Byrne, with an orderly or two, had remained at Arnold's ranch,—that Arnold himself, with six horsemen from the post, was to set forth at four, join the colonel at dawn, and together all were to push forward on the trail of Stout's command, hoping to overtake them by nightfall. She whispered this to sleepless Kate on her return to the house, for Angela, exhausted with grief and long suspense, had fallen, apparently, into deep and dreamless slumber.

But the end of that eventful night was not yet. Arnold and his sextette slipped away soon after four o'clock, and about 4.50 there came a banging at the major's door. It was the telegraph operator. The wire was patched at last, and the first message was to the effect that the guard had been fired on in Cherry Creek canon—that Private Forrest was sorely wounded and lying at Dick's deserted ranch, with two of their number to care for him. Could they possibly send a surgeon at once?

There was no one to go but Graham. His patients at the post were doing fairly well, but there wasn't a horse for him to ride. "No matter," said he, "I'll borrow Punch. He's needing exercise these days." So Punch was ordered man-saddled and brought forthwith. The orderly came back in ten minutes. "Punch aint there, sir," said he. "He's been gone over half an hour."

"Gone? Gone where? Gone how?" asked Graham in amaze.

"Gone with Miss Angela, sir. She saddled him herself and

rode away not twenty minutes after Arnold's party left. The sentries say she followed up the Beaver."

CHAPTER XIX

BESIEGED

Deep down in a ragged cleft of the desert, with shelving rock and giant bowlder on every side, without a sign of leaf, or sprig of grass, or tendril of tiny creeping plant, a little party of haggard, hunted men lay in hiding and in the silence of exhaustion and despond, awaiting the inevitable. Bulging outward overhead, like the counter of some huge battleship, a great mass of solid granite heaved unbroken above them, forming a recess or cave, in which they were secure against arrow, shot, or stone from the crest of the lofty, almost vertical walls of the vast and gloomy canon. Well back under this natural shelter, basined in the hollowed rock, a blessed pool of fair water lay unwrinkled by even a flutter of breeze. Relic of the early springtime and the melting snows, it had been caught and imprisoned here after the gradually failing stream had trickled itself into nothingness. One essential, one comfort then had not been denied the beleaguered few, but it was about the only one. Water for drink, for fevered wounds and burning throats, they had in abundance; but the last "hardtack" had been shared, the last scrap of bacon long since devoured. Of the once-abundant rations only coffee grains were left. Of the cartridge-crammed "thimble belts," with which they had entered the canon and the Apache trap, only three contained so much as a single copper cylinder, stopped by its forceful lead. These three belonged to troopers, two of whom, at least, would never have use for them again. One of these, poor Jerry Kent, lay buried beneath the little cairn of rocks in still another cavelike recess a dozen yards away, hidden there by night, when prowling Apaches could not see the sorrowing burial party and crush them with bowlders heaved over the precipice above, or shoot them down with whistling lead or steel-tipped arrow from some safe covert in the rocky walls.

Cut off from their comrades while scouting a side ravine, Captain Wren and his quartette of troopers had made stiff and valiant fight against such of the Indians as permitted hand or head to show from behind the rocks. They had felt confident that Sergeant Brewster and the main body would speedily miss them, or hear the sound of firing and turn back *au secours*, but sounds are queerly carried in such a maze of deep and tortuous clefts as seamed the surface in every conceivable direction through the wild basin of the Colorado. Brewster's rearmost files declared long after that never the faintest whisper of affray had reached their ears, already half deadened by fatigue and the ceaseless crash of iron-shod hoofs on shingly rock. As for Brewster himself, he was able to establish that Wren's own orders were to "push ahead" and try to make Sunset Pass by nightfall, while the captain, with such horses as seemed freshest, scouted right and left wherever possible. The last seen of Jerry Kent, it later transpired, was when he came riding after them to say the captain had gone into the mouth of the gorge opening to the west, and the last message borne from the commander to the troop came through Jerry Kent to Sergeant Dusold, who brought up the rear. They had passed the mouths of half a dozen ravines within the hour, some on one side, some on the other, and Dusold "passed the word" by sending Corporal Slater clattering up the canon, skirting the long drawn-out column of files until, far in the lead, he could overtake the senior sergeant and deliver his message. Later, when Brewster rode back with all but the little guard left over his few broken-down men and mounts in Sunset Pass, Dusold could confidently locate in his own mind the exact spot where Kent overtook him; but Dusold was a drill-book dragoon of the Prussian school, consummately at home on review or parade, but all at sea, so to speak, in the mountains. They never found a trace of their loved leader. The clefts they scouted were all on the wrong side.

And so it happened that relief came not, that one after another the five horses fell, pierced with missiles or crushed and stunned by rocks crashing down from above, that Kent himself was shot through the brain, and Wren skewered through the arm by a Tonto shaft, and plugged with a round rifle ball in the shoulder. Sergeant Carmody bound up his captain's wound as best he could, and by rare good luck, keeping up a bold front, and answering every shot, they fought their way to this little refuge in the rocks, and there, behind improvised barricades or bowlders, "stood off" their savage foe, hoping rescue might soon reach them.

But Wren was nearly wild from wounds and fever when the third day came and no sign of the troop. Another man had been hit and stung, and though not seriously wounded, like a burnt child, he now shunned the fire and became, perforce, an ineffective. Their scanty store of rations was gone entirely. Sergeant Carmody and his alternate watchers were worn out from lack of sleep when, in the darkness of midnight, a low hail in their own tongue came softly through the dead silence,—the voice of Lieutenant Blakely cautioning, "Don't fire, Wren. It's the Bugologist," and in another moment he and his orderly afoot, in worn Apache moccasins, but equipped with crammed haversacks and ammunition belts, were being welcomed by the besieged. There was little of the emotional and nothing of the melodramatic about it. It was, if anything, rather commonplace. Wren was flighty and disposed to give orders for an immediate attack in force on the enemy's works, to which the sergeant, his lips trembling just a bit, responded with prompt salute: "Very good, sir, just as quick as the men can finish supper. Loot'nent Blakely's compliments, sir, and he'll be ready in ten minutes," for Blakely and his man, seeing instantly the condition of things, had freshened the little fire and begun unloading supplies. Solalay, their Indian guide, after piloting them through the woodland southwest of Snow Lake, had pointed out the canon, bidden them follow it and, partly in the sign language, partly in Spanish, partly in the few Apache terms that Blakely had learned during his agency days, managed to make them understand that Wren was to be found some five miles further on, and that most of the besieging Tontos were on the heights above or in the canon below. Few would be encountered, if any, on the up-stream side. Then, promising to take the horses and the mules to Camp Sandy, he had left them. He dared go no farther toward the warring Apaches. They would suspect and butcher him without mercy.

But Solalay had not gone without promise of further aid. Natzie's younger brother, Alchisay, had recently come to him with a message from her, and should be coming with another. Solalay thought he could find the boy and send him to them to be used as a courier. Blakely's opportune coming had cheered not a little the flagging defense, but, not until forty-eight hours thereafter, by which time their condition had become almost desperate and the foe almost daring, did the lithe, big-eyed, swarthy little Apache reach them. Blakely knew him instantly, wrote his dispatch and bade the boy go with all speed, with the result we know. "Three more of our party are wounded," he had written, but had not chosen to say that one of them was himself.

A solemn sight was this that met the eyes of the Bugologist, as Carmody roused him from a fitful sleep, with the murmured words, "Almost light, sir. They'll be on us soon as they can see." Deep in under the overhang and close to the pool lay one poor fellow whose swift, gasping breath told all too surely that the Indian bullet had found fatal billet in his wasting form. It was Chalmers, a young Southerner, driven by poverty at home and prospect of adventure abroad to seek service in the cavalry. It was practically his first campaign, and in all human probability his last. Consciousness had left him hours ago, and his vagrant spirit was fast loosing every earthly bond, and already, in fierce dreamings, at war with unseen and savage foe over their happy hunting grounds in the great Beyond. Near him, equally sheltered, yet further toward the dim and pallid light, lay Wren, his strong Scotch features pinched and drawn with pain and loss of blood and lack of food. Fever there was little left, there was so little left for it to live upon. Weak and helpless as a child in arms he lay, inert and silent. There was nothing he could do. Never a quarter hour had passed since he had been forced to lie there that some one of his devoted men had not bathed his forehead and cooled his burning wounds with abundant flow of blessed water. Twice since his gradual return to consciousness had he asked for Blakely, and had bidden him sit and tell him of Sandy, asking for tidings of Angela, and faltering painfully as he bethought himself of the last instructions he had given. How could Blakely be supposed to know aught of her or of the household bidden to treat him practically as a stranger? Now, he thought it grand that the Bugologist had thrown all consideration of peril to the wind and had hastened to their aid to share their desperate fortunes. But Wren knew not how to tell of it. He took courage and hope when Blakely spoke of Solalay's loyalty, of young Alchisay's daring visit and his present mission. Apaches of his band had been known to traverse sixty miles a day over favorable ground, and Alchisay, even through such a labyrinth of rock, ravine, and precipice, should not make less than thirty. Within forty-eight hours of his start the boy ought to reach the Sandy valley, and surely no moment would then be lost in sending troops to find and rescue them. But four days and nights, said Blakely to himself, was the least time in which they could reasonably hope for help, and now only the third night had gone,—gone with their supplies of every kind. A few hours more and the sun would be blazing in upon even the dank depths of the canon for his midday stare. A few minutes more and the Apaches, too, would be up and blazing on their own account. "Keep well under shelter," were Blakely's murmured orders to the few men, even as the first, faint breath of the dawn came floating from the broader reaches far down the rocky gorge.

In front of their cavelike refuge, just under the shelving mass overhead, heaped in a regular semicircle, a rude parapet of rocks gave shelter to the troopers guarding the approaches. Little loopholes had been left, three looking down and two northward up the dark and tortuous rift. In each of these a loaded carbine lay in readiness. So well chosen was the spot that for one hundred yards southeastward—down stream—the narrow gorge was commanded by the fire of the defense, while above, for nearly eighty, from wall to wall, the approach was similarly swept. No rush was therefore possible on part of the Apaches without every probability of their losing two or three of the foremost. The Apache lacks the magnificent daring of the Sioux or Cheyenne. He is a fighter from ambush; he risks nothing for glory's sake; he is a monarch in craft and guile, but no hero in open battle. For nearly a week now, day after day, the position of the defenders had been made almost terrible by the fierce bombardment to which it had been subjected, of huge stones or bowlders sent thundering down the almost precipitous walls, then bounding from ledge to ledge, or glancing from solid, sloping face diving, finally, with fearful crash into the rocky bed at the bottom, sending a shower of fragments hurtling in every direction, oft dislodging some section of parapet, yet never reaching the depths of the cave. Add to this nerve-racking siege work the instant, spiteful flash of barbed arrow or zip and crack of bullet when hat or hand of one of the defenders was for a second exposed, and it is not difficult to fancy the wear and tear on even the stoutest heart in the depleted little band.

And still they set their watch and steeled their nerves, and in dogged silence took their station as the pallid light grew roseate on the cliffs above them. And with dull and wearied, yet wary, eyes, each soldier scanned every projecting rock or point that could give shelter to lurking foe, and all the time the brown muzzles of the carbines were trained low along the stream bed. No shot could now be thrown away at frowsy turban or flaunting rag along the cliffs. The rush was the one thing they had to dread and drive back. It was God's mercy the Apache dared not charge in the dark.

Lighter grew the deep gorge and lighter still, and soon in glorious radiance the morning sunshine blazed on the lofty battlements far overhead, and every moment the black shadow on the westward wall, visible to the defense long rifle-shot southeastward, gave gradual way before the rising day god, and from the broader open reaches beyond the huge granite shoulder, around which wound the canon, and from the sun-kissed heights, a blessed warmth stole softly in, grateful inexpressibly to their chilled and stiffened limbs. And still, despite the growing hours, neither shot nor sign came from the accustomed haunts of the surrounding foe. Six o'clock was marked by Blakely's watch. Six o'clock and seven, and the low moan from the lips of poor young Chalmers, or the rattle of some pebble dislodged by the foot of crouching guardian, or some murmured word from man to man,—some word of wonderment at the unlooked for lull in Apache siege operations,—was the only sound to break the almost deathlike silence of the morning. There was one other, far up among the stunted, shriveled pines and cedars that jutted from the opposite heights. They could hear at intervals a weird, mournful note, a single whistling call in dismal minor, but it brought no new significance. Every day of their undesired and enforced sojourn, every hour of the interminable day, that raven-like, hermit bird of the Sierras had piped his unmelodious signal to some distant feathered fellow, and sent a chill to the heart of more than one war-tried soldier. There was never a man in Arizona wilds that did not hate the sound of it. And yet, as eight o'clock was noted and still no sight or sound of assailant came, Sergeant Carmody turned a wearied, aching eye from his loophole and muttered to the officer crouching close beside him: "I could wring the neck of the lot of those infernal cat crows, sir, but I'll thank God if we hear no worse sound this day."

Blakely rose to his feet and wearily leaned upon the breastworks, peering cautiously over. Yesterday the sight of a scouting hat would have brought instant whiz of arrow, but not a missile saluted him now. One arm, his left, was rudely bandaged and held in a sling, a rifle ball from up the cliff, glancing from the inner face of the parapet, had torn savagely through muscle and sinew, but mercifully scored neither artery nor bone. An arrow, whizzing blindly through a southward loophole, had grazed his cheek, ripping a straight red seam far back as the lobe of the ear, which had been badly torn. Blakely had little the look of a squire of dames as, thus maimed and scarred and swathed in blood-stained cotton, he peered down the deep and shadowy cleft and searched with eyes keen, if yet unskilled, every visible section of the opposite wall. What could their silence mean? Had they found other game, pitifully small in numbers as these besieged, and gone to butcher them, knowing well that, hampered by their wounded, these, their earlier victims, could not hope to escape? Had they got warning of the approach of some strong force of soldiery—Brewster scouting in search of them, or may be Sanders himself? Had they slipped away, therefore, and could the besieged dare to creep forth and shout, signal, or even fire away two or three of these last precious cartridges in hopes of catching the ear of searching comrades?

Wren, exhausted, had apparently dropped into a fitful doze. His eyes were shut, his lips were parted, his long, lean fingers twitched at times as a tremor seemed to shoot through his entire frame. Another day like the last or at worst like this, without food or nourishment, and even such rugged strength as had been his would be taxed to the utmost. There might be no to-morrow for the sturdy soldier who had so gallantly served his adopted country, his chosen flag. As for Chalmers, the summons was already come. Far from home and those who most loved and would sorely grieve for him, the brave lad was dying. Carmody, kneeling by his side, but the moment before had looked up mutely in his young commander's face, and his swimming, sorrowing eyes had told the story.

Nine o'clock had come without a symptom of alarm or enemy from without, yet death had invaded the lonely refuge in the rocks, claiming one victim as his tribute for the day and setting his seal upon still another, the prospective sacrifice for the dismal morrow, and Blakely could stand the awful strain no longer.

"Sergeant," said he, "I must know what this means. We must have help for the captain before this sun goes down, or he may be gone before we know it."

And Carmody looked him in the face and answered: "I am strong yet and unhurt. Let me make the try, sir. Some of our fellows must be scouting near us, or these beggars wouldn't have quit. I can find the boys, if anyone can."

Blakely turned and gazed one moment into the deep and dark recess where lay his wounded and the dying. The morning wind had freshened a bit, and a low, murmurous song, nature's AEolian, came softly from the swaying pine and stunted oak and juniper far on high. The whiff that swept to their nostrils from the lower depths of the canon told its own grewsome tale. There, scattered along the stream bed, lay the festering remains of their four-footed comrades, first victims of the ambuscade. Death lurked about their refuge then on every side, and was even invading their little fortress. Was this to be the end, after all? Was there neither help nor hope from any source?

Turning once again, a murmured prayer upon his lips, Blakely started at sight of Carmody. With one hand uplifted, as though to caution silence, the other concaved at his ear, the sergeant was bending eagerly forward, his eyes dilating, his frame fairly quivering. Then, on a sudden, up he sprang and swung his hat about his head. "Firing, sir! Firing, sure!" he cried. Another second, and with a gasp and moan he sank to earth transfixed; a barbed arrow, whizzing from unseen space, had pierced him through and through.

CHAPTER XX

WHERE IS ANGELA?

For a moment as they drew under shelter the stricken form of the soldier, there was nothing the defense could do but dodge. Then, leaving him at the edge of the pool, and kicking before them the one cowed and cowering shirker of the little band, Blakely and the single trooper still unhit, crept back to the rocky parapet, secured a carbine each and knelt, staring up the opposite wall in search of the foe. And not a sign of Apache could they see.

Yet the very slant of the arrow as it pierced the young soldier, the new angle at which the bullets bounded from the stony crest, the lower, flatter flight of the barbed missiles that struck fire from the flinty rampart, all told the same story. The Indians during the hours of darkness, even while dreading to charge, had managed to crawl, snake-like, to lower levels along the cliff and to creep closer up the stream bed, and with stealthy, noiseless hands to rear little shelters of stone, behind which they were now crouching invisible and secure. With the illimitable patience of their savage training they had then waited, minute after minute, hour after hour, until, lulled at last into partial belief that their deadly foe had slipped away, some of the defenders should be emboldened to venture into view, and then one well-aimed volley at the signal from the leader's rifle, and the vengeful shafts of those who had as yet only the native weapon, would fall like lightning stroke upon the rash ones, and that would end it. Catlike they had crouched and watched since early dawn. Catlike they had played the old game of apparent weariness of the sport, of forgetfulness of their prey and tricked their guileless victims into hope and self-exposure, then swooped again, and the gallant lad whose last offer and effort had been to set forth in desperate hope of bringing relief to the suffering, had paid for his valor with his life. One arrow at least had gone swift and true, one shaft that, launched, perhaps, two seconds too soon for entire success, had barely anticipated the leader's signal and spoiled the scheme of bagging all the game. Blakely's dive to save his fallen comrade had just saved his own head, for rock chips and spattering lead flew on every side, scratching, but not seriously wounding him.

And then, when they "thought on vengeance" and the three brown muzzles swept the opposite wall, there followed a moment of utter silence, broken only by the faint gasping of the dying man. "Creep back to Carmody, you," muttered Blakely to the trembling lad beside him. "You are of no account here unless they try to charge. Give him water, quick." Then to Stern, his one unhurt man, "You heard what he said about distant firing. Did you hear it?"

"Not I, sir, but I believe *they* did—an' be damned to them!" And Stern's eyes never left the opposite cliff, though his ears were strained to catch the faintest sound from the lower canon. It was there they last had seen the troop. It was from that direction help should come. "Watch them, but don't waste a shot, man. I must speak to

Carmody," said Blakely, under his breath, as he backed on hands and knees, a painful process when one is sore wounded. Trembling, whimpering like whipped child, the poor, spiritless lad sent to the aid of the stricken and heroic, crouched by the sergeant's side, vainly striving to pour water from a clumsy canteen between the sufferer's pallid lips. Carmody presently sucked eagerly at the cooling water, and even in his hour of dissolution seemed far the stronger, sturdier of the two—seemed to feel so infinite a pity for his shaken comrade. Bleeding internally, as was evident, transfixed by the cruel shaft they did not dare attempt to withdraw, even if the barbed steel would permit, and drooping fainter with each swift moment, he was still conscious, still brave and uncomplaining. His dimmed and mournful eyes looked up in mute appeal to his young commander. He knew that he was going fast, and that whatever rescue might come to these, his surviving fellow-soldiers, there would be none for him; and yet in his supreme moment he seemed to read the question on Blakely's lips, and his words, feeble and broken, were framed to answer.

"Couldn't—you hear 'em, lieutenant?" he gasped. "I can't be—mistaken. I know—the old—Springfield *sure*! I heard 'em way off—south—a dozen shots," and then a spasm of agony choked him, and he turned, writhing, to hide the anguish on his face. Blakely grasped the dying soldier's hand, already cold and limp and nerveless, and then his own voice seemed, too, to break and falter.

"Don't try to talk, Carmody; don't try! Of course you are right. It must be some of our people. They'll reach us soon. Then we'll have the doctor and can help you. Those saddle-bags!" he said, turning sharply to the whimpering creature kneeling by them, and the lad drew hand across his streaming eyes and passed the worn leather pouches.

From one of them Blakely drew forth a flask, poured some brandy into its cup and held it to the soldier's lips. Carmody swallowed almost eagerly. He seemed to crave a little longer lease of life. There was something tugging at his heartstrings, and presently he turned slowly, painfully again. "Lieutenant," he gasped, "I'm not scared to die—this way anyhow. There's no one to care—but the boys—but there's one thing"—and now the stimulant seemed to reach the failing heart and give him faint, fluttering strength—"there's one thing I ought—I ought to tell. You've been solid with the boys—you're square, and I'm not—I haven't always been. Lieutenant—I was on guard—the night of the fire—and Elise, you know—the French girl—she—she's got most all I saved—most all I—won, but she was trickin' me—all the time, lieutenant—me and Downs that's gone—and others. She didn't care. You—you aint the only one I—I—"

"Lieutenant!" came in excited whisper, the voice of Stern, and there at his post in front of the cave he knelt, signaling urgently. "Lieutenant, quick!"

"One minute, Carmody! I've got to go. Tell me a little later." But with dying strength Carmody clung to his hand.

"I must tell you, lieutenant—now. It wasn't Downs's fault. She—she made—"

"Lieutenant, quick! for God's sake! They're coming!" cried the voice of the German soldier at the wall, and wrenching his wrist from the clasp of the dying man, Blakely sprang recklessly to his feet and to the mouth of the cave just as Stern's carbine broke the stillness with resounding roar. Half a dozen rifles barked their instant echo among the rocks. From up the hillside rose a yell of savage hate and another of warning. Then from behind their curtaining rocks half a dozen dusky forms, their dirty white breechclouts streaming behind them, sprang suddenly into view and darted, with goatlike ease and agility, zigzagging up the eastward wall. It was a foolish thing to do, but Blakely followed with a wasted shot, aimed one handed from the shoulder, before he could regain command of his judgment. In thirty seconds the cliff was as bare of Apaches as but the moment before it had been dotted. Something, in the moment when their savage plans and triumph seemed secure, had happened to alarm the entire party. With warning shouts and signals they were scurrying out of the deep ravine, scattering, apparently, northward. But even as they fled to higher ground there was order and method in their retreat. While several of their number clambered up the steep, an equal number lurked in their covert, and Blakely's single shot was answered instantly by half a dozen, the bullets striking and splashing on the rocks, the arrows bounding or glancing furiously. Stern ducked within, out of the storm. Blakely, flattening like hunted squirrel close to the parapet, flung down his empty carbine and strove to reach another, lying loaded at the southward loophole, and at the outstretched hand there whizzed an arrow from aloft whose guiding feather fairly seared the skin, so close came the barbed messenger. Then up the height rang out a shrill cry, some word of command in a voice that had a familiar tang to it, and that was almost instantly obeyed, for, under cover of sharp, well-aimed fire from aloft, from the shelter of projecting rock or stranded bowlder, again there leaped into sight a few scattered, sinewy forms that rushed in bewildering zigzag up the steep, until safe beyond their supports, when they, too, vanished, and again the cliff stood barren of Apache foemen as the level of the garrison parade. It was science in savage warfare against which the drill book of the cavalry taught no method whatsoever. Another minute and even the shots had ceased. One glimpse more had Blakely of dingy, trailing breechclouts, fluttering in the breeze now stirring the fringing pines and cedars, and all that was left of the late besiegers came clattering down the rocks in the shape of an Indian shield. Stern would have scrambled out to nab it, but was ordered down. "Back, you idiot, or they'll have you next!" And then they heard the feeble voice of Wren, pleading for water and demanding to be lifted to the light. The uproar of the final volley had roused him from an almost deathlike stupor, and he lay staring, uncomprehending, at Carmody, whose glazing eyes were closed, whose broken words had ceased. The poor fellow was drifting away into the shadows with his story still untold.

"Watch here, Stern, but keep under cover," cried Blakely. "I'll see to the captain. Listen for any shot or sound, but hold your fire," and then he turned to his barely conscious senior and spoke to him as he would to a helpless child. Again he poured a little brandy in his cup. Again he held it to ashen lips and presently saw the faint flutter of reviving strength. "Lie still just a moment or two, Wren," he murmured soothingly. "Lie still. Somebody's coming. The troop is not far off. You'll soon have help and home and—Angela"—even then his tongue faltered at her name. And Wren heard and with eager eyes questioned imploringly. The quivering lips repeated huskily the name of the child he loved. "Angela—where?"

"Home—safe—where you shall be soon, old fellow, only—brace up now. I must speak one moment with Carmody," and to Carmody eagerly he turned. "You were speaking of Elise and the fire—of Downs, sergeant—" His words were slow and clear and distinct, for the soldier had drifted far away and must be recalled. "Tell me again.

What was it?"

But only faint, swift gasping answered him. Carmody either heard not, or, hearing, was already past all possibility of reply. "Speak to me, Carmody. Tell me what I can do for you?" he repeated. "What word to Elise?" He thought the name might rouse him, and it did. A feeble hand was uplifted, just an inch or two. The eyelids slowly fluttered, and the dim, almost lifeless eyes looked pathetically up into those of the young commander. There was a moment of almost breathless silence, broken only by a faint moan from Wren's tortured lips and the childish whimpering of that other—the half-crazed, terror-stricken soldier.

"Elise," came the whisper, barely audible, as Carmody strove to lift his head, "she—promised"—but the head sank back on Blakely's knee. Stern was shouting at the stone gate—shouting and springing to his feet and swinging his old scouting hat and gazing wildly down the canon. "For God's sake hush, man!" cried the lieutenant. "I must hear Carmody." But Stern was past further shouting now. Sinking on his knees, he was sobbing aloud. Scrambling out into the daylight of the opening, but still shrinking within its shelter, the half-crazed, half-broken soldier stood stretching forth his arms and calling wild words down the echoing gorge, where sounds of shouting, lusty-lunged, and a ringing order or two, and then the clamor of carbine shots, told of the coming of rescue and new life and hope, and food and friends, and still Blakely knelt and circled that dying head with the one arm left him, and pleaded and besought—even commanded. But never again would word or order stir the soldier's willing pulse. The sergeant and his story had drifted together beyond the veil, and Blakely, slowly rising, found the lighted entrance swimming dizzily about him, first level and then up-ended; found himself sinking, whither he neither knew nor cared; found the canon filling with many voices, the sound of hurrying feet and then of many rushing waters, and then—how was it that all was dark without the cave, and lighted—lantern-lighted—here within? They had had no lantern, no candle. Here were both, and here was a familiar face—old Heartburn's—bending reassuringly over Wren, and someone was—. Why, where was Carmody? Gone! And but a moment ago that dying head was there on his knee, and then it was daylight, too, and now—why, it must be after nightfall, else why these lanterns? And then old Heartburn came bending over him in turn, and then came a rejoiceful word:

"Hello, Bugs! Well, it *is* high time you woke up! Here, take a swig of this!"

Blakely drank and sat up presently, dazed, and Heartburn went on with his cheery talk. "One of you men out there call Captain Stout. Tell him Mr. Blakely's up and asking for him," and, feeling presently a glow of warmth coursing in his veins, the Bugologist roused to a sitting posture and began to mumble questions. And then a burly shadow appeared at the entrance, black against the ruddy firelight in the canon without, where other forms began to appear. Down on his knee came Stout to clasp his one available hand and even clap him on the back and send unwelcome jar through his fevered, swollen arm. "Good boy, Bugs! You're coming round famously. We'll start you back to Sandy in the morning, you and Wren, for nursing, petting, and all that sort of thing. They are lashing the saplings now for your litters, and we've sent for Graham, too, and he'll meet you on the the way, while we shove on after Shield's people."

"Shield—Raven Shield?" queried Blakely, still half dazed. "Shield was killed—at Sandy," and yet there was the memory of the voice he knew and heard in this very canon.

"Shield, yes; and now his brother heads them. Didn't he send his card down to you, after the donicks, and be damned to him? You foregathered with both of them at the agency. Oh, they're all alike, Bugs, once they're started on the warpath. Now we must get you out into the open for a while. The air's better."

And so, an hour later, his arm carefully dressed and bandaged, comforted by needed food and fragrant tea and the news that Wren was reviving under the doctor's ministrations, and would surely mend and recover, Blakely lay propped by the fire and heard the story of Stout's rush through the wilderness to their succor. Never waiting for the dawn, after a few hours' rest at Beaver Spring, the sturdy doughboys had eagerly followed their skilled and trusted leader all the hours from eleven, stumbling, but never halting even for rest or rations, and at last had found the trail four miles below in the depths of the canon. There some scattering shots had met them, arrow and rifle both, from up the heights, and an effort was made to delay their progress. Wearied and footsore though were his men, they had driven the scurrying foe from rock to rock and then, in a lull that followed, had heard the distant sound of firing that told them whither to follow on. Only one man, Stern, was able to give them coherent word or welcome when at last they came, for Chalmers and Carmody lay dead, Wren in a stupor, Blakely in a deathlike swoon, and "that poor chap yonder" loony and hysterical as a crazy man. Thank God they had not, as they had first intended, waited for the break of day.

Another dawn and Stout and most of his men had pushed on after the Apaches and in quest of the troop at Sunset Pass. By short stages the soldiers left in charge were to move the wounded homeward. By noon these latter were halted under the willows by a little stream. The guards were busy filling canteens and watering pack mules, when the single sentry threw his rifle to the position of "ready" and the gun lock clicked loud. Over the stony ridge to the west, full a thousand yards away, came a little band of riders in single file, four men in all. Wren was sleeping the sleep of exhaustion. Blakely, feverish and excited, was wide awake. Mercifully the former never heard the first question asked by the leading rider—Arnold, the ranchman—as he came jogging into the noonday bivouac. Stone, sergeant commanding, had run forward to meet and acquaint him with the condition of the rescued men. "Got there in time then, thank God!" he cried, as wearily he flung himself out of saddle and glanced quickly about him. There lay Wren, senseless and still between the lashed ribs of his litter. There lay Blakely, smiling feebly and striving to hold forth a wasted hand, but Arnold saw it not. Swiftly his eyes flitted from face to face, from man to man, then searched the little knot of mules, sidelined and nibbling at the stunted herbage in the glen. "I don't see Punch," he faltered. "Wh-where's Miss Angela?"

CHAPTER XXI

OUR VANISHED PRINCESS

Then came a story told in fierce and excited whisperings, Arnold the speaker, prompted sometimes by his companions; Stone, and the few soldiers grouped about him, awe-stricken and dismayed. Blakely had started up from his litter, his face white with an awful dread, listening in wordless agony.

At six the previous morning, loping easily out from Sandy, Arnold's people had reached the ranch and found the veteran colonel with his orderlies impatiently waiting for them. These latter had had abundant food and coffee and the colonel was fuming with impatience to move, but Arnold's people had started on empty stomachs, counting on a hearty breakfast at the ranch. Jose could have it ready in short order. So Byrne, with his men, mounted and rode ahead on the trail of the infantry, saying the rest could overtake him before he reached the rocky and dangerous path over the first range. For a few miles the Beaver Valley was fairly wide and open. Not twenty minutes later, as Arnold's comrades sat on the porch on the north side of the house, they heard swift hoof-beats, and wondered who could be coming now. But, without an instant's pause, the rider had galloped by, and one of the men, hurrying to the corner of the ranch, was amazed to see the lithe, slender form of Angela Wren speeding her pet pony like the wind up the sandy trail. Arnold refused to believe at first, but his eyes speedily told him the same story. He had barely a glimpse of her before she was out of sight around a grove of willows up the stream. "Galloping to catch the colonel," said he, and such was his belief. Angela, he reasoned, had hastened after them to send some message of love to her wounded father, and had perhaps caught sight of the trio far out in the lead. Arnold felt sure that they would meet her coming back, sure that there was no danger for her, with Byrne and his fellows well out to the front. They finished their breakfast, therefore, reset their saddles, mounted and rode for an hour toward the Mogollon and still the pony tracks led them on, overlying those of the colonel's party. Then they got among the rocks and only at intervals found hoof-prints; but, far up along the range, caught sight of the three horsemen, and so, kept on. It was after ten when at last they overtook the leaders, and then, to their consternation, Angela Wren was not with them. They had neither seen nor heard of her, and Byrne was aghast when told that, alone and without a guide, she had ridden in among the foothills of those desolate, pathless mountains. "The girl is mad," said he, "and yet it's like her to seek to reach her father."

Instantly they divided forces to search for her. Gorges and canons innumerable seamed the westward face of this wild spur of the Sierras, and, by the merest luck in the world, one of Arnold's men, spurring along a stony ridge, caught sight of a girlish form far across a deep ravine, and quickly fired two shots in signal that he had "sighted" the chase. It brought Arnold and two of his men to the spot and, threading their way, sometimes afoot and leading their steeds, sometimes in saddle and urging them through the labyrinth of bowlders, they followed on. At noon they had lost not only all sight of her, but of their comrades, nor had they seen the latter since. Byrne and his orderlies, with three of the party that "pulled out" from Sandy with Arnold in the morning, had disappeared. Again and again they fired their Henrys, hoping for answering signal, or perhaps to attract Angela's attention. All doubt as to her purpose was now ended. Mad she might be, but determined she was, and had deliberately dodged past them at the Beaver, fearing opposition to her project. At two, moreover, they found that she could "trail" as well as they, for among the stunted cedars at the crest of a steep divide, they found the print of the stout brogans worn by their infantry comrades, and, down among the rocks of the next ravine, crushed bits of hardtack by a "tank" in the hillside. She had stopped there long enough at least to water Punch, then pushed on again.

Once more they saw her, not three miles ahead at four o'clock, just entering a little clump of pines at the top of a steep acclivity. They fired their rifles and shouted loud in hopes of halting her, but all to no purpose. Night came down and compelled them to bivouac. They built a big fire to guide the wanderers, but morning broke without sign of them; so on they went, for now, away from the rocks the trail was often distinct, and once again they found the pony hoof-prints and thanked God. At seven by Arnold's watch, among the breaks across a steep divide they found another tank, more crumbs, a grain sack with some scattered barley, more hardtack and the last trace of Angela. Arnold's hand shook, as did his voice, as he drew forth a little fluttering ribbon—the "snood" poor Wren so loved to see binding his child's luxuriant hair.

They reasoned she had stopped here to feed and water her pony, and had probably bathed her face and flung loose her hair and forgotten later the binding ribbon. They believed she had followed on after Stout's hard-marching company. It was easy to trail. They counted on finding her when they found her father, and now here lay Wren unconscious of her loss, and Blakely, realizing it all—cruelly, feverishly realizing it—yet so weakened by his wounds as to be almost powerless to march or mount and go in search of her.

No question now as to the duty immediately before them. In twenty minutes the pack mules were again strapped between the saplings, the little command was slowly climbing toward the westward heights, with Arnold and two of his friends scouting the rough trail and hillsides, firing at long intervals and listening in suspense almost intolerable for some answering signal. The other of their number had volunteered to follow Stout over the plateau toward the Pass and acquaint him with the latest news.

While the sun was still high in the heavens, far to the northward, they faintly heard or thought they heard two rifle shots. At four o'clock, as they toiled through a tangle of rock and stunted pine, Arnold, riding well to the front, came suddenly out upon a bare ledge from which he could look over a wild, wide sweep of mountain side, stretching leagues to north and south, and there his keen and practiced eye was greeted by a sight that thrilled him with dread unspeakable. Dread, not for himself or his convoy of wounded, but dread for Angela. Jutting, from the dark fringe of pines along a projecting bluff, perhaps four miles away, little puffs or clouds of smoke, each separate and distinct, were sailing straight aloft in the pulseless air—Indian signals beyond possibility of doubt. Some Apaches, then, were still hovering about the range overlooking the broad valley of the Sandy, some of the bands then were prowling in the mountains between the scouting troops and the garrisoned post. Some must have been watching this very trail, in hopes of intercepting couriers or stragglers, some *must* have seen and seized poor Angela.

He had sprung from saddle and leveled his old field glass at the distant promontory, so absorbed in his search he did not note the coming of the little column. The litter bearing Blakely foremost of the four had halted close beside him, and Blakely's voice, weak and strained, yet commanding, suddenly startled him with demand to be told what he saw, and Arnold merely handed him the glass and pointed. The last of the faint smoke puffs was just soaring into space, making four still in sight. Blakely never even took the binocular. He had seen enough by the unaided eye.

With uplifted hand the sergeant had checked the coming of the next litter, Wren's, and those that followed it. One of the wounded men, the poor lad crazed by the perils of the siege, was alert and begging for more water, but Wren was happily lost to the world in swoon or slumber. To the soldier bending over him he seemed scarcely breathing. Presently they were joined by two of Arnold's party who had been searching out on the left flank. They, too, had seen, and the three were now in low-toned conference. Blakely for the moment was unnoted, forgotten.

"That tank—where we found the ribbon—was just about two miles yonder," said Arnold, pointing well down the rugged slope toward the southwest, where other rocky, pine-fringed heights barred the view to the distant Sandy. "Surely the colonel or some of his fellows must be along here. Ride ahead a hundred yards or so and fire a couple of shots," this to one of his men, who silently reined his tired bronco into the rude trail among the pine cones and disappeared. The others waited. Presently came the half-smothered sound of a shot and a half-stifled cry from the rearmost litter. Every such shock meant new terror to that poor lad, but Wren never stirred. Half a minute passed without another sound than faint and distant echo; then faint, and not so distant, came another sound, a prolonged shout, and presently another, and then a horseman hove in sight among the trees across a nearly mile-wide dip. Arnold and his friends rode on to meet him, leaving the litters at the crest. In five minutes one of the riders reappeared and called: "It's Horn, of the orderlies. He reports Colonel Byrne just ahead. Come on!" and turning, dove back down the twisted trail.

The colonel might have been just ahead when last seen, but when they reached the tank he was far aloft again, scouting from another height to the northward, and while the orderly went on to find and tell him, Arnold and his grave-faced comrade dismounted there to await the coming of the litters. Graver were the faces even than before. The news that had met them was most ominous. Two of those who searched with Colonel Byrne had found pony tracks leading northward—leading in the very direction in which they had seen the smoke. There was no other pony shoe in the Sandy valley. It could be none other than Angela's little friend and comrade—Punch.

And this news they told to Blakely as the foremost litter came. He listened with hardly a word of comment; then asked for his scouting notebook. He was sitting up now. They helped him from his springy couch to a seat on the rocks, and gave him a cup of the cold water. One by one the other litters were led into the little amphitheater and unlashed. Everyone seemed to know that here must be the bivouac for the night, their abiding place for another day, perhaps, unless they should find the captain's daughter.

They spoke, when they spoke at all, in muffled tones, these rough, war-worn men of the desert and the mountain. They bent over the wounded with sorrowing eyes, and wondered why no surgeon had come out to meet them. Heartburn, of course, had done his best, dressing and rebandaging the wounds at dawn, but then he had to go on with Stout and the company, while one of the Apache Yumas was ordered to dodge his way in to Sandy, with a letter urging that Graham be sent out to follow the trail and meet the returning party.

Meanwhile the sun had dropped behind the westward heights; the night would soon be coming down, chill and overcast. Byrne was still away, but he couldn't miss the tank, said one of the troopers who had ridden with him. Twice during the morning they had all met there and then gone forth again, searching—searching. Punch's little hoof-tracks, cutting through a sandy bit in the northward ravine, had drawn them all that way, but nothing further had been found. His horse, too, said the orderly, was lame and failing, so he had been bidden to wait by the water and watch for couriers either from the front or out from the post. Byrne was one of those never-give-up men, and they all knew him.

Barley was served out to the animals, a little fire lighted, lookouts were stationed, and presently their soldier supper was ready, and still Blakely said nothing. He had written three notes or letters, one of which seemed to give him no little trouble, for one after another he thrust two leaves into the fire and started afresh. At length they were ready, and he signaled to Arnold. "You can count, I think, on Graham's getting here within a few hours," said he. "Meantime you're as good a surgeon as I need. Help me on with this sling." And still they did not fathom his purpose. He was deathly pale, and his eyes were eloquent of dread unspeakable, but he seemed to have forgotten pain, fever, and prostration. Arnold, in the silent admiration of the frontier, untied the support, unloosed the bandages, and together they redressed the ugly wound. Then presently the Bugologist stood feebly upon his feet and looked about him. It was growing darker, and not another sound had come from Byrne.

"Start one of your men into Sandy at once," said Blakely, to the sergeant, and handed him a letter addressed to Major Plume. "He will probably meet the doctor before reaching the Beaver. These other two I'll tell you what to do with later. Now, who has the best horse?"

Arnold stared. Sergeant Stone quickly turned and saluted. "The lieutenant is not thinking of mounting, I hope," said he.

Blakely did not even answer. He was studying the orderly's bay. Stiff and a little lame he might be, but, refreshed and strengthened by abundant barley, he was a better weight-carrier than the other, and Blakely had weight. "Saddle your horse, Horn," said he, "and fasten on those saddle-bags of mine."

"But, lieutenant," ventured Arnold, "you are in no shape to ride anything but that litter. Whatever you think of doing, let me do."

"What I am thinking of doing nobody else can do," said Blakely. "What you can do is, keep these two letters till I call for them. If at the end of a week I fail to call, deliver them as addressed and to nobody else. Now, before dark I must reach that point younder," and he indicated the spot where in the blaze of the westering sun a mass of rock towered high above the fringing pine and mournful shadows at its base, a glistening landmark above the general gloom at the lower level and at that hour of the afternoon. "Now," he added quietly, "you can help me into saddle."

"But for God's sake, lieutenant, let some of us ride with you," pleaded Arnold. "If Colonel Byrne was here he'd never let you go."

"Colonel Byrne is not here, and I command, I believe," was the brief, uncompromising answer. "And no man rides with me because, with another man, I'd never find what I'm in search of." For a moment he bent over Wren, a world of wordless care, dread, and yet determination in his pale face. Arnold saw his wearied eyes close a moment, his lips move as though in petition, then he suddenly turned. "Let me have that ribbon," said he bluntly, and without a word Arnold surrendered it. Stone held the reluctant horse, Arnold helped the wounded soldier into the saddle. "Don't worry about me—any of you," said Blakely, in brief farewell. "Good-night," and with that he rode away.

Arnold and the men stood gazing after him. "Grit clean through," said the ranchman, through his set teeth, for a light was dawning on him, as he pondered over Blakely's words. "May the Lord grant I don't have to deliver these!" Then he looked at the superscriptions. One letter was addressed to Captain, or Miss Janet, Wren—the other to Mrs. Plume.

CHAPTER XXII

SUSPENSE

Sandy again. Four of the days stipulated by Lieutenant Blakely had run their course. The fifth was ushered in, and from the moment he rode away from the bivouac at the tanks no word had come from the Bugologist, no further trace of Angela. In all its history the garrison had known no gloom like this. The hospital was filled with wounded. An extra surgeon and attendants had come down from Prescott, but Graham was sturdily in charge. Of his several patients Wren probably was now causing him the sorest anxiety, for the captain had been grievously wounded and was pitiably weak. Now, when aroused at times from the lassitude and despond in which he lay, Wren would persist in asking for Angela, and, not daring to tell him the truth, Janet, Calvinist that she was to the very core, had to do fearful violence to her feelings and lie. By the advice of bluff old Byrne and the active connivance of the post commander, they had actually, these stern Scotch Presbyterians, settled on this as the deception to be practiced—that Angela had been drooping so sadly from anxiety and dread she had been taken quite ill, and Dr. Graham had declared she must be sent up to Prescott, or some equally high mountain resort, there to rest and recuperate. She was in good hands, said these arch-conspirators. She might be coming home any day. As for the troop and the campaign, he mustn't talk or worry or think about them. The general, with his big field columns, had had no personal contact with the Indians. They had scattered before him into the wild country toward the great Colorado, where Stout, with his hickory-built footmen, and Brewster, with most of Wren's troop, were stirring up Apaches night and day, while Sanders and others were steadily driving on toward the old Wingate road. Stout had found Brewster beleaguered, but safe and sound, with no more men killed and few seriously wounded. They had communicated with Sanders's side scouts, and were finding and following fresh trails with every day, when Stout was surprised to receive orders to drop pursuit and start with Brewster's fellows and to scout the west face of the mountains from the Beaver to the heights opposite the old Indian reservation. There was a stirring scene at bivouac when that order came, and with it the explanation that Angela Wren had vanished and was probably captured; that Blakely had followed and was probably killed. "They might shoot Blakely in fair fight," said Stout, who knew him, and knew the veneration that lived for him in the hearts of the Indian leaders, "but they at least would never butcher him in cold blood. Their unrestrained young men might do it." Stout's awful dread, like that of every man and woman at Sandy, and every soldier in the field, was for Angela. The news, too, had been rushed to the general, and his orders were instant. "Find the chiefs in the field," said he to his interpreter and guide. "Find Shield's people, and say that if a hair of her head is injured I shall hunt them down, braves, women, and children—I shall hunt them anyhow until they surrender her unharmed."

But the Apaches were used to being hunted, and some of them really liked the game. It was full of exhilaration and excitement, and not a few chances to hunt and hit back. The threat conveyed no terror to the renegades. It was to the Indians at the reservation that the tidings brought dismay, yet even there, so said young Bridger, leaders and followers swore they had no idea where the white maiden could be, much less the young chief. They, the peaceable and the poor servants of the great Father at Washington, had no dealings with these others, his foes.

About the post, where gloom and dread unspeakable prevailed, there was no longer the fear of possible attack. The Indian prisoners in the guard-house had dropped their truculent, defiant manner, and become again sullen and apathetic. The down-stream settlers had returned to their ranches and reported things undisturbed. Even the horse that had been missing and charged to Downs had been accounted for. They found him grazing placidly about the old pasture, with the rope halter trailing, Indian-knotted, from his neck, and his gray hide still showing stains of blood about the mane and withers. They wondered was it on this old stager the Apaches had borne the wounded girl to the garrison—she who still lay under the roof of Mother Shaughnessy, timidly visited at times by big-eyed, shy little Indian maids from the reservation, who would speak no word that Sudsville could understand, and few that even Wales Arnold could interpret. All they would or could divulge was that she was the daughter of old Eskiminzin, who was out in the mountains, and that she had been wounded "over there," and they pointed eastward. By whom and under what circumstances they swore they knew not, much less did they know of Downs, or of how she chanced to have the scarf once worn by the Frenchwoman Elise.

Then Arnold's wife and brood had gone back to their home up the Beaver, while he himself returned to the search for Angela and for Blakely. But those four days had passed without a word of hope. In little squads a dozen parties were scouring the rugged canons and cliffs for signs, and finding nothing. Hours each day Plume would come to the watchers on the bluff to ask if no courier had been sighted. Hours each night the sentries strained their eyes for signal fires. Graham, slaving with his sick and wounded, saw how haggard and worn the commander was growing, and spoke a word of caution. Something told him it was not all on account of those woeful conditions at the front. From several sources came the word that Mrs. Plume was in a state bordering on hysteric at department headquarters, where sympathetic women strove vainly to comfort and soothe her. It was then that Elise became a center of interest, for Elise was snapping with electric force and energy. "It is that they will assassinate madame—these monsters," she declared. "It is imperative, it is of absolute need, that madame be taken to the sea, and these wretches, unfeeling, they forbid her to depart." Madame herself, it would seem, so said those who had speech with her, declared she longed to be again with her husband at Sandy. Then it was Elise who demanded that they should move. Elise was mad to go—Elise, who took a turn of her own, a screaming fit, when the news came of the relief of Wren's little force, of the death of their brave sergeant, of the strange tale that, before dying, Carmody had breathed a confession to Lieutenant Blakely, which Blakely had reduced to writing before he set forth on his own hapless mission. It was Mrs. Plume's turn now to have to play nurse and comforter, and to strive to soothe, even to the extent of promising that Elise should be permitted to start by the very next stage to the distant sea, but when it came to securing passage, and in feverish, nervous haste the Frenchwoman had packed her chosen belongings into the one little trunk the stage people would consent to carry, lo! there came to her a messenger from headquarters where Colonel Byrne, grim, silent, saturnine, was again in charge. Any attempt on her part to leave would result in her being turned over at once to the civil authorities, and Elise understood and raved, but risked not going to jail. Mullins, nursed by his devoted Norah, was sitting up each day now, and had been seen by Colonel Byrne as that veteran passed through, ten pounds lighter of frame and heavier of heart than when he set forth, and Mullins had persisted in the story that he had been set upon and stabbed by two women opposite Lieutenant Blakely's quarters. What two had been seen out there that night but Clarice Plume and her Gallic shadow, Elise?

Meantime Aunt Janet was "looking ghastly," said the ladies along that somber line of quarters, and something really ought to be done. Just what that something should be no two could unite in deciding, but really Major Plume or Dr. Graham ought to see that, if something wasn't done, she would break down under the awful strain. She had grown ten years older in five days, they declared— was turning fearfully gray, and they were sure she never slept a wink. Spoken to on this score, poor Miss Wren was understood to say she not only could not sleep, but she did not wish to. Had she kept awake and watched Angela, as was her duty, the child could never have succeeded in her wild escapade. The "child," by the way, had displayed rare generalship, as speedily became known. She must have made her few preparations without a betraying sound, for even Kate Sanders, in the same room, was never aroused—Kate, who was now well-night heartbroken. They found that Angela had crept downstairs in her stockings, and had put on her riding moccasins and leggings at the kitchen steps. There, in the sand, were the tracks of her long, slender feet. They found that she had taken with her a roomy hunting-pouch that hung usually in her father's den. She had filled it, apparently, with food,—tea, sugar, even lemons, for half a dozen of this precious and hoarded fruit had disappeared. Punch, too, had been provided for. She had "packed" a half-bushel of barley from the stables. There was no one to say Miss Angela nay. She might have ridden off with the flag itself and no sentry would more than think of stopping her. Just what fate had befallen her no one dare suggest. The one thing, the only one, that roused a vestige of hope was that Lieutenant Blakely had gone *alone* on what was thought to be her trail.

Now here was a curious condition of things. If anyone had been asked to name the most popular officer at Sandy, there would have been no end of discussion. Perhaps the choice would have lain between Sanders, Cutler, and old Westervelt—good and genial men. Asked to name the least popular officer, and, though men, and women, too, would have shrunk from saying it, the name that would have occurred to almost all was that of Blakely. And why? Simply because he stood alone, self-poised, self-reliant, said his few friends, "self-centered and sel*fish*," said more than Mrs. Bridger, whereas a more generous man had never served at Sandy. That, however, they had yet to learn. But when a man goes his way in the world, meddling with no one else's business, and never mentioning his own, courteous and civil, but never intimate, studying a good deal but saying little, asking no favors and granting few, perhaps because seldom asked, the chances are he will win the name of being cold, indifferent, even repellent, "too high, mighty, and superior." His very virtues become a fault, for men and women love best those who are human like themselves, however they may respect. Among the troopers Blakely was as yet something of an enigma. His manner of speaking to them was unlike that of most of his fellows—it was grave, courteous, dignified, never petulant or irritable. In those old cavalry days most men better fancied something more demonstrative. "I like to see an officer flare up and—say things," said a veteran sergeant. "This here bug-catcher is too damned cold-blooded." They respected him, yes; yet they little understood and less loved him. They had known him too short a time.

But among the Indians Blakely was a demi-god. Grave, unruffled, scrupulously exact in word and deed, he made them trust him. Brave, calm, quick in moments of peril, he made them admire him. How fearlessly he had stepped into the midst of that half-frenzied sextette, *tiswin* drunk, and disarmed Kwonagietah and two of his fellow-revelers! How instant had been his punishment of that raging, rampant, mutinous old medicine man, 'Skiminzin, who dared to threaten him and the agency! (That episode only long years after reached the ears of the Indian Advancement Association in the imaginative East.) How gently and skillfully he had ministered to Shield's younger brother, and to the children of old Chief Toyah! It was this, in fact, that won the hate and envy of 'Skiminzin. How lavish was Blakely's bounty to the aged and to the little ones, and Indians love their children infinitely! The hatred or distrust of Indian man or woman, once incurred, is venomous and lasting. The trust, above all the gratitude, of the wild race, once fairly won, is to the full as stable. Nothing will shake it. There are those who say the love of an Indian girl, once given, surpasses that of her Circassian sister, and Bridger now was learning new stories of the Bugologist with every day of his progress in Apache lore. He had even dared to bid his impulsive little wife "go slow," should she ever again be tempted to say spiteful things of Blakely. "If what old Toyah tells me is true," said he, "and I believe him, Hualpai or Apache Mohave, there isn't a decent Indian in this part of Arizona that wouldn't give his own scalp to save Blakely." Mrs. Bridger did not tell this at the time, for she had said too much the other way; but, on this fifth day of our hero's absence, there came tidings that unloosed her lips.

Just at sunset an Indian runner rode in on one of Arnold's horses, and bearing a dispatch for Major Plume. It was from that sturdy campaigner, Captain Stout, who knew every mile of the old trail through Sunset Pass long years before even the—th Cavalry,—the predecessors of Plume, and Wren, and Sanders,—and what Stout said no man along the Sandy ever bade him swear to.

"Surprised small band, Tontos, at dawn to-day. They had saddle blanket marked 'W. A.' [Wales Arnold], and hat and underclothing marked 'Downs.' Indian boy prisoner says Downs was caught just after the 'big burning' at Camp Sandy [Lieutenant Blakely's quarters]. He says that Alchisay, Blakely's boy courier, was with them two days before, and told him Apache Mohaves had more of Downs's things, and that a white chief's daughter was over there in the Red Rocks. Sanders, with three troops, is east of us and searching that way now. This boy says Alchisay knew that Natzie and Lola had been hiding not far from Willow Tank on the Beaver trail—our route—but had fled from there same time Angela disappeared. Against her own people Natzie would protect Blakely, even were they demanding his life in turn for her Indian lover, Shield's. If these girls can be tracked and found, I believe you will have found Blakely and will find Angela."

That night, after being fed and comforted until even an Indian could eat no more, the messenger, a young Apache

Mohave, wanted *papel* to go to the agency, but Plume had other plans. "Take him down to Shaughnessy's," said he to Truman, "and see if he knows that girl." So take him they did, and at sight of his swarthy face the girl had given a low cry of sudden, eager joy; then, as though reading warning in his glance, turned her face away and would not talk. It was the play of almost every Apache to understand no English whatever, yet Truman could have sworn she understood when he asked her if she could guess where Angela was in hiding. The Indian lad had shaken his head and declared he knew nothing. The girl was dumb. Mrs. Bridger happened in a moment later, coming down with Mrs. Sanders to see how the strange patient was progressing. They stood in silence a moment, listening to Truman's murmured words. Then Mrs. Bridger suddenly spoke. "Ask her if she knows Natzie's cave," said she. "Natzie's cave," she repeated, with emphasis, and the Indian girl guilelessly shook her head, and then turned and covered her face with her hands.

CHAPTER XXIII

AN APACHE QUEEN

In the slant of the evening sunshine a young girl, an Indian, was crouching among the bare rocks at the edge of a steep and rugged descent. One tawny little hand, shapely in spite of scratches, was uplifted to her brows, shading her keen and restless eyes against the glare. In the other hand, the right, she held a little, circular pocket-mirror, cased in brass, and held it well down in the shade. Only the tangle of her thick, black hair and the top of her head could be seen from the westward side. Her slim young body was clothed in a dark-blue, well-made garment, half sack, half skirt, with long, loose trousers of the same material. There was fanciful embroidery of bead and thread about the throat. There was something un-Indian about the cut and fashion of the garments that suggested civilized and feminine supervision. The very way she wore her hair, parted and rolling back, instead of tumbling in thick, barbaric "bang" into her eyes, spoke of other than savage teaching; and the dainty make of her moccasins; the soft, pliant folds of the leggins that fell, Apache fashion, about her ankles, all told, with their beadwork and finish, that this was no unsought girl of the tribespeople. Even the sudden gesture with which, never looking back, she cautioned some follower to keep down, spoke significantly of rank and authority. It was a chief's daughter that knelt peering intently over the ledge of rocks toward the black shadows of the opposite slope. It was Natzie, child of a warrior leader revered among his people, though no longer spared to guide them—Natzie, who eagerly, anxiously searched the length of the dark gorge for sign or signal, and warned her companion to come no further.

Over the gloomy depths, a mile away about a jutting point, three or four buzzards were slowly circling, disturbed, yet determined. Over the broad valley that extended for miles toward the westward range of heights, the mantle of twilight was slowly creeping, as in his expressive sign language the Indian spreads his extended hands, palms down, drawing and smoothing imaginary blanket, the robe of night, over the face of nature. Far to the northward, from some point along the face of the heights, a fringe of smoke was drifting in the soft breeze sweeping down the valley from the farther Sierras. Wild, untrodden, undesired of man, the wilderness lay outspread—miles and miles of gloom and desolation, save where some lofty scarp of glistening rock, jutting from among the scattered growth of dark-hued pine and cedar, caught the brilliant rays of the declining sun.

Behind the spot where Natzie knelt, the general slope was broken by a narrow ledge or platform, bowlder-strewn— from which, almost vertically, rose the rocky scarp again. Among the sturdy, stunted fir trees, bearding the rugged face, frowned a deep fissure, dark as a wolf den, and, just in front of it, wide-eyed, open-mouthed, crouched Lola— Natzie's shadow. Rarely in reservation days, until after Blakely came as agent, were they ever seen apart, and now, in these days of exile and alarm, they were not divided. Under a spreading cedar, close to the opening, a tiny fire glowed in a crevice of the rocks, sending forth no betraying smoke. About it were some rude utensils, a pot or two, a skillet, an earthen *olla*, big enough to hold perhaps three gallons, two bowls of woven grass, close plaited, almost, as the famous fiber of Panama. In one of these was heaped a store of *pinons*, in the other a handful or two of wild plums. Sign of civilization, except a battered tin teapot, there was none, yet presently was there heard a sound that told of Anglo-Saxon presence— the soft voice of a girl in low-toned, sweet-worded song— song so murmurous it might have been inaudible save in the intense stillness of that almost breathless evening— song so low that the Indian girl, intent in her watch at the edge of the cliff, seemed not to hear at all. It was Lola who heard and turned impatiently, a black frown in her snapping eyes, and a lithe young Indian lad, hitherto unseen, dropped noiselessly from a perch somewhere above them and, filling a gourd at the *olla*, bent and disappeared in the narrow crevice back of the curtain of firs. The low song ceased gradually, softly, as a mother ceases her crooning lullaby, lest the very lack of the love-notes stir the drowsing baby brain to sudden waking.

With the last words barely whispered the low voice died away. The Indian lad came forth into the light again, empty-handed; plucked at Lola's gown, pointed to Natzie, for the moment forgotten, now urgently beckoning. Bending low, they ran to her. She was pointing across the deep gorge that opened a way to the southward. Something far down toward its yawning mouth had caught her eager eye, and grasping the arm of the lad with fingers that twitched and burned, she whispered in the Apache tongue:

"They're coming."

One long look the boy gave in the direction pointed, then, backing away from the edge, he quickly swept away a Navajo blanket that hung from the protruding branches of a low cedar, letting the broad light into the cavelike space beyond. There, on a hard couch of rock, skin, and blanket, lay a fevered form in rough scouting dress. There, with pinched cheeks, and eyes that heavily opened, dull and suffused, lay the soldier officer who had ridden forth to rescue and to save, himself now a crippled and helpless captive. Beside him, wringing out a wet handkerchief and spreading it on the burning forehead, knelt Angela. The girls who faced each other for the first time at the pool—the daughter of the Scotch-American captain—the daughter of the Apache Mohave chief—were again brought into strange companionship over the unconscious form of the soldier Blakely.

Resentful of the sudden glare that caused her patient to shrink and toss complainingly, Angela glanced up almost in rebuke, but was stilled by the look and attitude of the young savage. He stood with forefinger on his closed lips, bending excitedly toward her. He was cautioning her to make no sound, even while his very coming brought disturbance to her first thought—her fevered patient. Then, seeing both rebuke and question in her big, troubled eyes, the young Indian removed his finger and spoke two words: "Patchie come," and, rising, she followed him out to the flat in front.

Natzie at the moment was still crouching close to the edge, gazing intently over, one little brown hand nervously grasping the branch of a stunted cedar, the other as nervously clutching the mirror. So utterly absorbed was she that the hiss of warning, or perhaps of hatred, with which Lola greeted the sudden coming of Angela, seemed to fall unnoted on her ears. Lola, her black eyes snapping and her lips compressed, glanced up at the white girl almost in fury. Natzie, paying no heed whatever to what was occurring about her, knelt breathless at her post, watching, eagerly watching. Then, slowly, they saw her raise her right hand, still cautiously holding the little mirror, face downward, and at sight of this the Apache boy could scarcely control his trembling, and Lola, turning about, spoke some furious words, in low, intense tone, that made him shrink back toward the screen. Then the wild girl glared again at Angela, as though the sight of her were unbearable, and, with as furious a gesture, sought to drive her, too, again to the refuge of the dark cleft, but Angela never stirred. Paying no heed to Lola, the daughter of the soldier gazed only at the daughter of the chief, at Natzie, whose hand was now level with the surface of the rock. The next instant, far to the northwest flashed a slender beam of dazzling light, another— another. An interval of a second or two, and still another flash. Angela could see the tiny, nebulous dot, like will-'o-the-wisp, dancing far over among the rocks across a gloomy gorge. She had never seen it before, but knew it at a glance. The Indian girl was signaling to some of her father's people far over toward the great reservation, and the tale she told was that danger menaced. Angela could not know that it told still more,—that danger menaced not only Natzie, daughter of one warrior chief, and the chosen of another now among their heroic dead—it threatened those whom she was pledged to protect, even against her own people.

Somewhere down that deep and frowning rift to the southwest, Indian guides were leading their brethren on the trail of these refugees among the upper rocks. Somewhere, far over among the uplands to the northwest, other tribesfolk, her own kith and kin, were lurking, and these the Indian girl was summoning with all speed to her aid.

And in the slant of that same glaring sunshine, not four miles away, toiling upward along a rocky slope, following the faint sign here and there of Apache moccasin, a little command of hardy, war-worn men had nearly reached the crest when their leader signaled backward to the long column of files, and, obedient to the excited gestures of the young Hualpai guide, climbed to his side and gazed intently over. What he saw on a lofty point of rocks, well away from the tortuous "breaks" through which they had made most of their wearying marches from the upper Beaver, brought the light of hope, the fire of battle, to his somber eyes. "Send Arnold up here," he shouted to the men below, and Arnold came, clambering past rock and bowlder until he reached the captain's side, took one look in the direction indicated, and brought his brown hand down with resounding swat on the butt of his rifle. "Treed 'em!" said he exultantly; then, with doubtful, backward glance along the crouching file of weary men, some sitting now and fanning with their broad-brimmed hats, he turned again to the captain and anxiously inquired: "Can we make it before dark?"

"We must make it!" simply answered Stout.

And then, far over among the heights between them and the reservation, there went suddenly aloft—one, two, three—compact little puffs of bluish smoke. Someone was answering signals flashed from the rocky point—someone who, though far away, was promising aid.

"Let's be the first to reach them, lads," said Stout, himself a wearied man. And with that they slowly rose and went stumbling upward. The prize was worth their every effort, and hope was leading on.

An hour later, with barely half the distance traversed, so steep and rocky, so wild and winding, was the way, with the sun now tangent to the distant range afar across the valley, they faintly heard a sound that spurred them on— two shots in quick succession from unseen depths below the lofty point. And now they took the Indian jog trot. There was business ahead.

Between them and that gleaming promontory now lay a comparatively open valley, less cumbered with bowlders than were the ridges and ravines through which they had come, less obstructed, too, with stunted trees. Here was opportunity for horsemen, hitherto denied, and Stout called on Brewster and his score of troopers, who for hours had been towing their tired steeds at the rear of column. "Mount and push ahead!" said he. "You are Wren's own men. It is fitting you should get there first."

"Won't the captain ride with us—now?" asked the nearest sergeant.

"Not if it robs a man of his mount," was the answer. Yet there was longing in his eye and all men saw it. He had led them day after day, trudging afoot, because his own lads could not ride. Indeed, there had been few hours when any horse could safely bear a rider. There came half a dozen offers now. "I'll tramp afoot if the captain 'll only take my horse," said more than one man.

And so the captain was with them, as with darkness settling down they neared the great cliff towering against the southeastward sky. Then suddenly they realized they were guided thither only just in time to raise a well-nigh fatal siege. Thundering down the mountain side a big bowlder came tearing its way, launched from the very point that had been the landmark of their eager coming,

and with the downward crashing of the rock there burst a
yell of fury.

Midway up the steep incline, among the straggling timber,
two lithe young Indians were seen bounding out of a little
gully, only just in time to escape. Two or three others,
farther aloft, darted around a shoulder of cliff as though
scurrying out of sight. From the edge of the precipice the
crack of a revolver was followed by a second, and then by
a scream. "Dismount!" cried Brewster, as he saw the
captain throw himself from his horse; then, leaving only
two or three to gather in their now excited steeds,
snapping their carbines to full cock, with blazing eyes and
firm-set lips, the chosen band began their final climb.
"Don't bunch. Spread out right and left," were the only
cautions, and then in long, irregular line, up the mountain
steep they clambered, hope and duty still leading on, the
last faint light of the November evening showing them
their rocky way. Now, renegadoes, it is fight or flee for
your lives!

Perhaps a hundred yards farther up the jagged face the
leaders came upon an incline so steep that, like the Tontos
above them, they were forced to edge around to the
southward, whither their comrades followed. Presently,
issuing from the shelter of the pines, they came upon a
bare and bowlder-dotted patch to cross which brought
them plainly into view of the heights above, and almost
instantly under fire. Shot after shot, to which they could
make no reply, spat and flattened on the rocks about them,
but, dodging and ducking instinctively, they pressed
swiftly on. Once more within the partial shelter of the
pines across the open, they again resumed the climb,
coming suddenly upon a sight that fairly spurred them.
There, feet upward among the bowlders, stiff and swollen
in death, lay all that the lynxes had left of a cavalry horse.

Close at hand was the battered troop saddle. Caught in the bushes a few rods above was the folded blanket, and, lodged in a crevice, still higher, lay the felt-covered canteen, stenciled with the number and letter of Wren's own troop. It was the horse of the orderly, Horn—the horse on which the Bugologist had ridden away in search of Angela Wren. It was all the rescuers needed to tell them they were now on the trail of both, and now the carbines barked in earnest at every flitting glimpse of the foe, sending the wary Tontos skipping and scurrying southward. And, at last, breathless, panting, well-nigh exhausted, the active leaders found themselves halting at a narrow, twisting little game trail, winding diagonally up the slope, with that gray scarp of granite jutting from the mountain side barely one hundred yards farther; and, waving from its crest, swung by unseen hands, some white, fluttering object, faintly seen in the gathering dusk, beckoned them on. The last shots fired at the last Indians seen gleamed red in the autumn gloaming. They, the rescuers, had reached their tryst only just as night and darkness shrouded the westward valley. The last man up had to grope his way, and long before that last man reached the ledge the cheering word was passed from the foremost climber: "Both here, boys, and safe!"

An hour later brought old Heartburn to the scene, scrambling up with the other footmen, and speedily was he kneeling by the fevered officer's side. The troopers had been sent back to their horses. Only Stout, the doctor, Wales Arnold, and one or two sergeants remained at the ledge, with rescued Angela, the barely conscious patient, and their protectors, the Indian girls. Already the boy had been hurried off with a dispatch to Sandy, and now dull, apathetic, and sullen, Lola sat shrouded in her blanket, while Arnold, with the little Apache dialect he knew, was striving to get from Natzie some explanation of her daring and devotion.

Between tears and laughter, Angela told her story. It was much as they had conjectured. Mad with anxiety on her father's account, she said, she had determined to reach him and nurse him. She felt sure that, with so many troops out between the post and the scene of action, there was less danger of her being caught by Indians than of being turned back by her own people. She had purposely dashed by the ranch, fearing opposition, had purposely kept behind Colonel Byrne's party until she found a way of slipping round and past them where she could feel sure of speedily regaining the trail. She had encountered neither friend nor foe until, just as she would have ridden away from the Willow Tanks, she was suddenly confronted by Natzie, Lola, and two young Apaches. Natzie eagerly gesticulated, exclaiming, "Apaches, Apaches," and pointing ahead up the trail, and, though she could speak no English, convincing Angela that she was in desperate danger. The others were scowling and hateful, but completely under Natzie's control, and between them they hustled her pony into a ravine leading to the north and led him along for hours, Angela, powerless to prevent, riding helplessly on. At last they made her dismount, and then came a long, fearful climb afoot, up the steepest trail she had ever known, until it brought her here. And here, she could not tell how many nights afterwards—it seemed weeks, so had the days and hours dragged—here, while she slept at last the sleep of exhaustion, they had brought Mr. Blakely. He lay there in raging fever when she was awakened that very morning by Natzie's crying in her ear some words that sounded like: *"Hermano viene! Hermano viene!"*

Stout had listened with absorbing interest and to the very last word. Then, as one who heard at length full explanation of what he had deemed incredible, his hand went out and clutched that of Arnold, while his deep eyes, full of infinite pity, turned to where poor Natzie crouched, watching silently and in utter self-forgetfulness the doctor's ministrations.

"Wales," he muttered, "that settles the whole business. Whatever you do,—don't let that poor girl know that— they"—and now he warily glanced toward Angela— "they—are *not* brother and sister."

CHAPTER XXIV

THE MEETING AT SANDY

December, and the noonday sun at Sandy still beat hotly on the barren level of the parade. The fierce and sudden campaign seemed ended, for the time, at least, as only in scattered remnants could the renegade Indians be found. Eastward from the Agua Fria to the Chiquito, and northward from the Salado to the very cliffs of the grand canon, the hard-worked troopers had scoured the wild and mountainous country, striking hard whenever they found a hostile band, striving ever, through interpreters and runners, to bring the nervous and suspicious tribes to listen to reason and to return to their reservations. This for long days, however, seemed impossible. The tragic death of Raven Shield, most popular of the young chiefs, struck down, as they claimed, when he was striving only to defend Natzie, daughter of a revered leader, had stirred the savages to furious reprisals, and nothing but the instant action of the troops in covering the valley had saved the scattered settlers from universal massacre. Enough had been done by one band alone to thrill the West with horror, but these had fled southward into Mexico and were safe beyond the border. The settlers were slowly creeping back now to their abandoned homes, and one after another the little field detachments were marching to their accustomed stations. Sandy was filling up again with something besides the broken down and wounded.

First to come in was Stout's triumphant half hundred, the happiest family of horse and foot, commingled, ever seen upon the Pacific slope, for their proud lot it had been to reach and rescue Angela, beloved daughter of the regiment, and Blakely, who had well-nigh sacrificed himself in the effort to find and save her. Stout and his thirty "doughboys," Brewster, the sergeant, with his twenty troopers, had been welcomed by the entire community as the heroes of the brief campaign, but Stout would none of their adulation.

"There is the one you should thank and bless," said he, his eyes turning to where stood Natzie, sad and silent, watching the attendants who were lifting Neil Blakely from the litter to the porch of the commanding officer.

They had brought her in with them, Lola and Alchisay as well—the last two scowling and sullen, but ruled by the chieftain's daughter. They had loaded her with praise and thanks, but she paid no heed. Two hours after Stout and his troopers had reached the cliff and driven away the murderous band of renegades—Tontos and Apache Yumas—bent on stealing her captives, there had come a little party of her own kindred in answer to her signals, but these would have been much too late. Blakely would have been butchered. Angela and her benefactors, too, would probably have been the victims of their captors. Natzie could look for no mercy from them now. Through Wales Arnold, the captain and his men had little by little learned the story of Natzie's devotion. In the eyes of her father, her brother, her people, Blakely was greater even than the famous big chief, Crook, the Gray Fox, who had left them, ordered to other duties but the year gone by. Blakely had quickly righted the wrongs done them by a thieving agent. Blakely had given fair trial to and saved the life of Mariano, that fiery brother, who, ironed by the former agent's orders, had with his shackled hands struck down his persecutor and then escaped. Blakely had won their undying gratitude, and Stout and Arnold saw now why it was that one young brave, at least, could not share the love his people bore for *Gran Capitan Blanco*—that one was Quonothay—the Chief Raven Shield. They saw now why poor Natzie had no heart to give her Indian lover. They saw now why it was that Natzie wandered from the agency and hovered for some days before the outbreak there around the post. It was to be near the young white chief whom she well-nigh worshiped, whom she had been accustomed to see every day of her life during his duties at the agency. They saw now why it was the savage girl had dared the vengeance of the Apaches by the rescue of Angela. She believed her to be Blakely's sister, yet they could not give the reason why. They knew very little of Neil Blakely, but what they did know made them doubt that he could ever have been the one at fault. Over this problem both ranchman and soldier, Arnold and Stout, looked grave indeed. It was not like Blakely that he should make a victim of this young Indian girl. She was barely sixteen, said Arnold, who knew her people well. She had never been alone with Blakely, said her kinsfolk, who came that night in answer to her signals. She had saved Angela, believing her to be Blakely's own blood, had led her to her own mountain refuge, and then, confident that Blakely would make search for it and for his sister, had gone forth and found him, already half-dazed with fever and exhaustion, and had striven to lead his staggering horse up that precipitous trail. It was the poor brute's last climb. Blakely she managed to bring in safety to her lofty eerie. The horse had fallen, worn out in the effort, and died on the rocks below. She had roused Angela with what she thought would be joyful tidings, even though she saw that her hero was desperately ill. She thought, of course, the white girl knew the few words of Spanish that she could speak. All this was made evident to Arnold and Stout, partly through Natzie's young brother, who had helped to find and support the white chief, partly through the girl herself. It was evident to Arnold, too, that up to the time of their coming nothing had happened to undeceive Natzie as to that relationship. They tried to induce her to return to the agency, although her father and brother were still somewhere with the hostile bands, but she would not, she would go with them to Sandy, and they could not deny her. More than once on that rough march of three days they found themselves asking what would the waking be. Angela, daughter of civilization, under safe escort, had been sent on ahead, close following the courier who scurried homeward with the news. Natzie, daughter of the wilderness, could not be driven from the sight of Blakely's litter. The dumb, patient, pathetic appeal of her great soft eyes, as she watched every look in the doctor's face, was something wonderful to see. But now, at last, the fevered sufferer was home, still only semi-conscious, being borne within the walls of the major's quarters, and she who had saved him, slaved for him, dared for him, could only mutely gaze after his prostrate and wasted form as it disappeared within the darkened hallway in the arms of his men. Then came a light step bounding along the veranda—then came Angela, no longer clad in the riding garb in which hitherto Natzie had seen her, but in cool and shimmering white, with gladness and gratitude in her beautiful eyes, with welcome and protection in her extended hand, and the Indian girl looked strangely from her to the dark hallway within which her white hero had disappeared, and shrank back from the proffered touch. If this was the soldier's sister should not she now be at the soldier's side? Had she other lodge than that which gave him shelter, now that his own was burned? Angela saw for the first time aversion, question, suspicion in the great black eyes from which the softness and the pleading had suddenly fled. Then, rebuffed, disturbed, and troubled, she turned to Arnold, who would gladly have slipped away.

"Can't *you* make her understand, Mr. Arnold?" she pleaded. "I don't know a word of her language, and I so want to be her friend—so want to take her to my home!"

And then the frontiersman did a thing for which, when she heard of it one sunset later, his better half said words of him and to him that overstepped all bounds of parliamentary usage, and that only a wife would dare to employ. With the blundering stupidity of his sex, poor Arnold "settled things" for many a day and well-nigh ruined the sweetest romance that Sandy had ever seen the birth of.

"Ah, Miss Angela! only one place will ever be home to Natzie now. Her eyes will tell you that."

And already, regardless of anything these women of the white chiefs might think or say, unafraid save of seeing him no more, unashamed save of being where she could not heed his every look or call or gesture, the daughter of the mountain and the desert stood gazing again after the vanished form her eyes long months had worshiped, and the daughter of the schools and civilization stood flushing one-half moment, then slowly paling, as, without another glance or effort, she turned silently away. Kate Sanders it was who sprang quickly after her and encircled the slender waist with her fond and clasping arm.

That night the powers of all Camp Sandy were exhausted in effort to suitably provide for Natzie and her two companions. Mrs. Sanders, Mrs. Bridger, even Mother Shaughnessy and Norah pleaded successively with this princess of the wilderness, and pleaded in vain. Food and shelter elsewhere they proffered in abundance. Natzie sat stubbornly at the major's steps, and sadly at first, and angrily later, shook her head to every proposition. Then they brought food, and Lola and Alchisay ate greedily. Natzie would hardly taste a morsel. Every time Plume or Graham or a soldier nurse came forth her mournful eyes would study his face as though imploring news of the sufferer, who lay unconscious of her vigil, if not of her existence. Graham's treatment was beginning to tell, and Blakely was sleeping the sleep of the just. They had not let him know of the poor girl's presence at the door. They would not let her in for fear he might awake and see her, and ask the reason of her coming. They would not send or take her away, for all Sandy was alive with the strange story of her devotion. The question on almost every lip was "How is this to end?"

At tattoo there came a Mexican woman from one of the down-stream ranches, sent in by the post trader, who said she could speak the Apache-Mohave language sufficiently well to make Natzie understand the situation, and this frontier linguist strove earnestly. Natzie understood every word she said, was her report, but could not be made to understand that she ought to go. In the continued absence of Mrs. Plume, both the major and the post surgeon had requested of Mrs. Graham that she should come over for a while and "see what she could do," and, leaving her own sturdy bairnies, the good, motherly soul had come and presided over this diplomatic interview, proposing various plans for Natzie's disposition for the night. And other ladies hovering about had been sympathetically suggestive, but the Indian girl had turned deaf ear to everything that would even temporarily take her from her self-appointed station. At ten o'clock Mother Shaughnessy, after hanging uneasily about the porch a moment or two, gave muttered voice to a suggestion that other women had shrunk from mentioning:

"Has she been tould Miss Angela and—him—is no kin at all, at all?"

"I don't want her told," said Mrs. Graham briefly.

And so Natzie was still there, sitting sleepless in the soft and radiant moonlight, when toward twelve o'clock Graham came forth from his last visit for the night, and she lifted up her head and looked him dumbly in the face,—dumbly, yet imploring a word of hope or comfort,—and it was more than the soft-hearted Scot could bear. "Major," said he, as he gently laid a big hand upon the black and tangled wealth of hair, "that lad in yonder would have been beyond the ken of civilization days ago if it hadn't been for this little savage. I'm thinking he'll sleep none the worse for her watching over him. Todd's there for the night, the same that attended him before, and she won't be strange with him—or I'm mistaken."

"Why?" asked Plume, mystified.

"I'm not saying, until Blakely talks for himself. For one reason I don't *know*. For another, *he's* the man to tell, if anybody," and a toss of the head toward the dark doorway told who was meant by "he."

"D'you mean you'd have this girl squatting there by Blakely's bedside the rest of the night?" asked the commander, ruffled in spirit. "What's to prevent her singing their confounded death song, or invoking heathen spirits, or knifing us all, for that matter?"

"What was to prevent her from knifing the Bugologist and Angela both, when she had 'em?" was the sturdy reply. "The girl's a theoretical heathen, but a practical Christian. Come with us, Natzie," he finished, one hand extended to aid her to rise, the other pointing to the open doorway. She was on her feet in an instant, and, silently signing her companions to stay, followed the doctor into the house.

And so it happened that when Blakely wakened, hours later, the sight that met him, dimly comprehending, was that of a blue-coated soldier snoozing in a reclining chair, a blue-blanketed Indian girl seated on the floor near the foot of his bed, looking with all her soul in her gaze straight into his wondering eyes. At his low whisper, "Natzie," she sprang to her feet without word or sound; seized the thin white hand tremulously extended toward her, and, pillowing her cheek upon it, knelt humbly by the bedside, her black hair streaming to the floor. A pathetic picture it made in the dim light of the newborn day, forcing itself through the shrouded windows, and Major Plume, restless and astir the hour before reveille, stood unnoted a moment at the doorway, then strode back through the hall and summoned from the adjoining veranda another sleepless watcher, gratefully breathing the fragrance of the cool, morning air; and presently two dim forms had softly tiptoed to that open portal, and now stood gazing within until their eyes should triumph over the uncertain light—the post commander in his trim-fitting undress uniform, the tall and angular shape of Wren's elderly sister—the "austere vestal" herself. It may have been a mere twitch of the slim fingers under her tawny cheek that caused Natzie to lift her eyes in search of those of her hero and her protector. Instantly her own gaze, startled, was turned straight to the door. Then in another second she had sprung to her feet, and with fury in her face and attitude confronted the intruders. As she did so the sudden movement detached some object that hung within the breast of her loose-fitting sack— something bright and gleaming that clattered to the floor, falling close to the feet of the drowsing attendant, while another—a thin, circular case of soft leather, half-rolled, half-bounded toward the unwelcome visitors at the door.

Todd, roused to instant action at sight of the post commander, bent quickly and nabbed the first. The girl herself darted after the second, whereat the attendant, misjudging her motive, dreading danger to his betters or rebuke to himself, sprang upon her as she stooped, and dropping his first prize, dared to seize the Apache girl with both hands at the throat. There was a warning cry from the bed, a flash of steel through one slanting ray of sunshine, a shriek from the lips of Janet Wren, and with a stifled moan the luckless soldier sank in his tracks, while Natzie, the chieftain's daughter, a dripping blade in her uplifted hand, a veritable picture of fury, stood in savage triumph over him, her flashing eyes fixed upon the amazed commander, as though daring him, too, to lay hostile hands upon her.

CHAPTER XXV

RESCUE REQUITED

A change had come over the spirit of Camp Sandy's dream. The garrison that had gone to bed the previous night, leaving Natzie silent, watchful, wistful at the post commander's door, had hardly a thought that was not full of sympathy and admiration for her. Even women who could not find it possible to speak of her probable relations with Neil Blakely dwelt much in thought and word upon her superb devotion and her generosity. That he had encouraged her passionate and almost savage love for him there were few to doubt, whatsoever they might find it possible to say. That men and women both regarded her as, beyond compare, the heroic figure of the campaign there was none to gainsay. Even those who could not or did not talk of her at all felt that such was the garrison verdict. There were no men, and but few women, who would have condemned the doctor's act in leading her to Blakely's bedside. Sandy had spoken of her all that wonderful evening only to praise. It woke to hear the first tidings of the new day, and to ask only What was the cause?—What had led to her wild, swift vengeance? for Todd had in turn been carried to hospital, a sore-stricken man. The night before Natzie was held a queen: now she was held a captive.

248   Charles King

It all happened so suddenly that even Plume, who witnessed the entire incident, could not coherently explain it. Reveille was just over and the men were going to breakfast when the major's voice was heard shouting for the guard. Graham, first man to reach the scene, had collided with Janet Wren, whimpering and unnerved, as he bounded into the hallway. His first thought was that Plume's prophecy about the knifing had come true, and that Blakely was the victim. His first sight, when his eyes could do their office in that darkened room, was of Blakely wresting something from the grasp of the Indian girl, whose gaze was now riveted on that writhing object on the floor.

"See to him, doctor," he heard Blakely say, in feeble, but commanding tone. "I will see to her." But Blakely was soon in no condition to see to her or to anybody. The flicker of strength that came to him for a second or two at sight of the tragedy, left him as suddenly—left him feebler than before. He had no voice with which to protest when the stretchermen, who bore away poor Todd, were followed instantly by stout guardsmen who bore away Natzie. The dignity of the chieftain's daughter had vanished now. She had no knife with which to deal death to these new and most reluctant assailants—Graham found it under Blakely's pillow, long hours later. But, with all her savage, lissome strength she scratched and struck and struggled. It took three of their burliest to carry her away, and they did it with shame-hidden faces, while rude comrades chaffed and jeered and even shouted laughing encouragement to the girl, whose screams of rage had drawn all Camp Sandy to the scene. One doctor, two men, and the steward went with their groaning burden one way to the hospital. One officer, one sergeant, and half a dozen men had all they could do to take their raging charge another way to the guard-house. Ah, Plume, you might have spared that brave girl such indignity! But, where one face followed the wounded man with sympathetic eyes, there were twenty that never turned from the Indian girl until her screams were deadened by the prison doors.

"She stabbed a soldier who meant her no harm," was Plume's sullen and stubborn answer to all appeals, for good and gentle women went to him, begging permission to go to her. It angered him presently to the extent of repeating his words with needless emphasis and additions when Mother Shaughnessy came to make her special appeal. Shure she had learned how to care for these poor creatures, was her claim, along o' having little Paquita on her hands so many days, "and now that poor girl beyant will be screaming herself into fits!"

"Let her scream," said Plume, unstrung and shaken, "but hold you your tongue or I'll find a separate cell for you. No woman shall be knifing my men, and go unpunished, if I can help it," and so saying he turned wrathfully from her.

"Heard you that now?" stormed Mother Shaughnessy, as he strode away. "Who but he has helped his women to go unpunished—" and the words were out and heard before the sergeant major could spring and silence her. Before another day they were echoing all over the post—were on their way to Prescott, even, and meeting, almost at the northward gateway, the very women the raging laundress meant. Of her own free will Clarice Plume was once again at Sandy, bringing with her, sorely against the will of either, but because a stronger will would have it so— and sent his guards to see to it—a cowed and scared and semi-silent companion of whom much ill was spoken now about the garrison—Elise Lebrun.

The news threw Norah Shaughnessy nearly into spasms. "'Twas she that knifed Pat Mullins!" she cried. "'Twas she drove poor Downs to dhrink and desartion. 'Twas she set Carmody and Shannon to cuttin' each other's throats"— which was news to a garrison that had seen the process extend no further than to each other's acquaintance. And more and stormier words the girl went on to say concerning the commander's household until Mullins himself mildly interposed. But all these things were being told about the garrison, from which Lola and Alchisay had fled in terror to spread the tidings that their princess was a prisoner behind the bars. These were things that were being told, too, to the men of Sanders's returning troop before they were fairly unsaddled at the stables; and that night, before ever he sought his soldier pillow, Shannon had been to "C" Troop's quarters in search of Trooper Stern and had wrung from him all that he could tell of Carmody's last fight on earth—of his last words to Lieutenant Blakely.

Meantime a sorely troubled man was Major Plume. That his wife would have to return to Sandy he had learned from the lips of Colonel Byrne himself. Her own good name had been involved, and could only be completely cleared when Wren and Blakely were sufficiently recovered to testify, and when Mullins should be so thoroughly restored as to be fit for close cross-examination. Plume could in no wise connect his beloved wife with either the murderous assault on Mullins or the mysterious firing of Blakely's quarters, but he knew that Sandy could not so readily acquit her, even though it might saddle the actual deed upon her instrument—Elise. He had ordered that Blakely should be brought to his own quarters because there he could not be reached by any who were unacceptable to himself, the post commander. There were many things he wished to know about and from Blakely's lips alone. He could not stoop to talk with other men about the foibles of his wife. He knew that iron box in Truman's care contained papers, letters, or *something* of deep interest to her. He knew full well now that, at some time in the not far distant past, Blakely himself had been of deep interest to her and she to Blakely. He had Blakely's last letter to himself, written just before the lonely start in quest of Angela, but that letter made no reference to the contents of the box or to anything concerning their past. He had heard that Wales Arnold had been intrusted with letters for Blakely to Clarice, his wife, and to Captain, or Miss Janet Wren. Arnold had not been entirely silent on the subject. He did not too much like the major, and rather rejoiced in this opportunity to show his independence of him. Plume had gone so far as to ask Arnold whether such letters had been intrusted to him, and Wales said, yes; but, now that Blakely was safely back and probably going to pull through, he should return the letters to the writer as soon as the writer was well enough to appreciate what was being done. Last, but not least, Plume had picked up near the door in Blakely's room the circular, nearly flat, leather-covered case which had dropped, apparently, from Natzie's gown, and, as it had neither lock nor latch, Plume had opened it to examine its contents.

To his surprise it contained a beautifully executed miniature, a likeness of a fair young girl, with soft blue eyes and heavy, arching brows, a delicately molded face and mouth and chin, all framed in a tumbling mass of tawny hair. It was the face of a child of twelve or thirteen, one that he had never seen and of whom he knew nothing. Neither cover, backing, nor case of the miniature gave the faintest clew as to its original or as to its ownership. What was Natzie doing with this?—and to whom did it belong? A little study satisfied him there was something familiar in the face, yet he could not place it.

The very night of her coming, therefore, he told his wife the story and handed her the portrait. One glance was enough. "I know it, yes," said Mrs. Plume, "though I, too, have never seen her. She died the winter after it was taken. It is Mr. Blakely's sister, Ethel," and Mrs. Plume sat gazing at the sweet girl features, with strange emotion in her aging face. There was something—some story—behind all this that Plume could not fathom, and it nettled him. Perhaps he, too, was yielding to a fit of nerves. Elise, the maid, had been remanded to her room, and could be heard moving about with heavy, yet uncertain tread. "She is right over Blakely," quoth the major impatiently. "Why can't the girl be quiet?"

"Why did you bring him *here*, then?" was the weary answer. "I cannot control Elise. They have treated her most cruelly."

"There are things you cannot explain and that she must," said he, and then, to change the subject, stretched forth his hand to take again the picture. She drew it back one moment, then, remembering, surrendered it.

"You saw this in—St. Louis, I suppose," said he awkwardly. He never could bear to refer to those days—the days before he had come into her life.

"Not that perhaps, but the photograph from which it was probably painted. She was his only sister. He was educating her in the East." And again her thoughts were drifting back to those St. Louis days, when, but for the girl sister he so loved, she and Neil Blakely had been well-nigh inseparable. Someone had said then, she remembered, that she was jealous even of that love.

And now again her husband was gazing fixedly at the portrait, a light coming into his lined and anxious face. Blakely had always carried this miniature with him, for he now remembered that the agent, Daly, had spoken of it. Natzie and others might well have seen it at the reservation. The agent's wife had often seen it and had spoken of his sorrow for the sister he had lost. The picture, she said, stood often on his little camp table. Every Indian who entered his tent knew it and saw it. Why, surely; Natzie, too, mused the major, and then aloud:

"I can see now what we have all been puzzling over. Angela Wren might well have looked like this—four years ago."

"There is not the faintest resemblance," said Clarice, promptly rising and quitting the room.

It developed with another day that Mrs. Plume had no desire to see Miss Wren, the younger. She expressed none, indeed, when policy and the manners of good society really required it. Miss Janet had come in with Mrs. Graham and Mrs. Sanders to call upon the wife of the commanding officer and say what words of welcome were possible as appropriate to her return. "And Angela," said Janet, for reasons of her own, "will be coming later." There was no response, nor was there to the next tentative. The ladies thought Mrs. Plume should join forces with them and take Natzie out of the single cell she occupied. "Can she not be locked at the hospital, under the eye of the matron, with double sentries? It is hard to think of her barred in that hideous place with Apache prisoners and rude men all about her." But again was Mrs. Plume unresponsive. She would say no word of interest in either Angela or Natzie. At the moment when her husband was in melting mood and when a hint from her lips would have secured the partial release of the Indian girl, the hint was withheld. It would have been better for her, for her husband, for more than one brave lad on guard, had the major's wife seen fit to speak, but she would not.

So that evening brought release that, in itself, brought much relief to the commanding officer and the friends who still stood by him.

Thirty-six hours now had Natzie been a prisoner behind the bars, and no one of those we know had seen her face. At tattoo the drums and fifes began their sweet, old-fashioned soldier tunes. The guard turned out; the officer of the day buckled his belt with a sigh and started forth to inspect, just as the foremost soldiers appeared on the porch in front, buttoning their coats and adjusting their belts and slings. Half their number began to form ranks; the other half "stood by," within the main room, to pass out the prisoners, many of whom wore a clanking chain. All on a sudden there arose a wild clamor—shouts, scuffling, the thunder of iron upon resounding woodwork, hoarse orders, curses, shrieks, a yell for help, a shot, a mad scurry of many feet, furious cries of "Head 'em off!" "Shoot!" "No, no, don't shoot! You'll kill our own!" A dim cloud of ghostly, shadowy forms went tearing away down the slope toward the south. There followed a tremendous rush of troop after troop, company after company,—the whole force of Camp Sandy in uproarious pursuit,—until in the dim starlight the barren flats below the post, the willow patches along the stream, the plashing waters of the ford, the still and glassy surface of the shadowy pool, were speedily all alive with dark and darting forms intermingled in odd confusion. From the eastward side, from officers' row, Plume and his white-coated subordinates hastened to the southward face, realizing instantly what must have occurred—the long-prophesied rush of Apache prisoners for freedom. Yet how hopeless, how mad, how utterly absurd was the effort! What earthly chance had they—poor, manacled, shackled, ball-burdened wretches—to escape from two hundred fleet-footed, unhampered, stalwart young soldiery, rejoicing really in the fun and excitement of the thing? One after another the shackled fugitives were run down and overhauled, some not half across the parade, some in the shadows of the office and storehouses, some down among the shrubbery toward the lighted store, some among the shanties of Sudsville, some, lightest weighted of all, far away as the lower pool, and so one after another, the grimy, sullen, swarthy lot were slowly lugged back to the unsavory precincts wherein, for long weeks and months, they had slept or stealthily communed through the hours of the night. Three or four had been cut or slashed. Three or four soldiers had serious hurts, scratches or bruises as their fruits of the affray. But after all, the malefactors, miscreants, and incorrigibles of the Apache tribe had profited little by their wild and defiant essay—profited little, that is, if personal freedom was what they sought.

But was it? said wise heads of the garrison, as they looked the situation over. Shannon and some of his ilk were doing much independent trailing by aid of their lanterns. Taps should have been sounded at ten, but wasn't by any means, for "lights out" was the last thing to be thought of. Little by little it dawned upon Plume and his supporters that, instead of scattering, as Indian tactics demanded on all previous exploits of the kind, there had been one grand, concerted rush to the southward—planned, doubtless, for the purpose of drawing the whole garrison thither in pursuit, while three pairs of moccasined feet slipped swiftly around to the rear of the guard-house, out beyond the dim corrals, and around to a point back of "C" Troop stables, where other little hoofs had been impatiently tossing up the sands until suddenly loosed and sent bounding away to where the North Star hung low over the sheeny white mantle of San Francisco mountain. Natzie, the girl queen, was gone from the guard-house: Punch, the Lady Angela's pet pony, was gone from the corral, and who would say there had not been collusion?

"One thing is certain," said the grave-faced post commander, as, with his officers, he left the knot of troopers and troopers' wives hovering late about the guard-house, "one thing is certain; with Wren's own troopers hot on the heels of Angela's pony we'll have our Apache princess back, sure as the morning sun."

"Like hell!" said Mother Shaughnessy.

CHAPTER XXVI

"WOMAN-WALK-NO-MORE"

More morning suns than could be counted in the field of
the flag had come, and gone, but not a sign of Natzie.
Wren's own troopers, hot on Punch's flashing heels, were
cooling their own as best they could through the arid days
that followed. Wren himself was now recovered
sufficiently to be told of much that had been going on,—
not all,—and it was Angela who constantly hovered about
him, for Janet was taking a needed rest. Blakely, too, was
on the mend, sitting up hours of every day and "being
very lovely" in manner to all the Sanders household, for
thither had he demanded to be moved even sooner than it
was prudent to move him at all. Go he would, and
Graham had to order it. Pat Mullins was once again "for
duty." Even Todd, the bewildered victim of Natzie's knife,
was stretching his legs on the hospital porch. There had
come a lull in all martial proceedings at the post, and only
two sensations. One of these latter was the formal
investigation by the inspector general of the conditions
surrounding the stabbing at Camp Sandy of Privates
Mullins and Todd of the—th U. S. Cavalry. The other was
the discovery, one bright, brilliant, winter morning that
Natzie's friend and savior, Angela's Punch, was back in
his stall, looking every bit as saucy and "fit" as ever he

Charles King

did in his life. What surprised many folk in the garrison was that it surprised Angela not at all. "I thought Punch would come back," said she, in demure unconcern, and the girls at least, began to understand, and were wild to question. Only Kate Sanders, however, knew how welcome was the pet pony's coming. But what had come that was far from welcome was a coldness between Angela and Kate Sanders.

Byrne himself had arrived, and the "inquisition" had begun. No examinations under oath, no laborious recordings of question and answer, no crowd of curious listeners. The veteran inspector took each man in turn and heard his tale and jotted down his notes, and, where he thought it wise, cross-questioned over and again. One after another, Truman and Todd, Wren and Mullins, told their stories, bringing forth little that was new beyond the fact that Todd was sure it was Elise he heard that night "jabbering with Downs" on Blakely's porch. Todd felt sure that it was she who brought him whisky, and Byrne let him prattle on. It was not evidence, yet it might lead the way to light. In like manner was Mullins sure now "'Twas two ladies" stabbed him when he would have striven to stop the foremost. Byrne asked did he think they were ladies when first he set eyes on them, and Pat owned up that he thought it was some of the girls from Sudsville; it might even be Norah as one of them, coming home late from the laundresses' quarters, and trying to play him a trick. He owned to it that he grabbed the foremost, seeing at that moment no other, and thinking to win the forfeit of a kiss, and Byrne gravely assured him 'twas no shame in it, so long as Norah never found it out.

But Byrne asked Plume two questions that puzzled and worried him greatly. How much whisky had he missed? and how much opium could have been given him the night of Mrs. Plume's unconscious escapade? The major well remembered that his demijohn had grown suddenly light, and that he had found himself surprisingly heavy, dull, and drowsy. The retrospect added to his gloom and depression. Byrne had not reoccupied his old room at Plume's, now that madame and Elise were once more under the major's roof, and even in extending the customary invitation, Plume felt confident that Byrne could not and should not accept. The position he had taken with regard to Elise, her ladyship's companion and confidante, was sufficient in itself to make him, in the eyes of that lady, an unacceptable guest, but it never occurred to her, although it had to Plume, that there might be even deeper reasons. Then, too, the relations between the commander and the inspector, although each was scrupulously courteous, were now necessarily strained. Plume could not but feel that his conduct of post affairs was in a measure a matter of scrutiny. He knew that his treatment of Natzie was disapproved by nine out of ten of his command. He felt, rather than knew, that some of his people had connived at her escape, and though that escape had been a relief to everybody at Sandy, the manner of her taking off was to him a mystery and a rankling sore.

Last man to be examined was Blakely, and now indeed there was light. He had been sitting up each day for several hours; his wounds were healing well; the fever and prostration that ensued had left him weak and very thin and pale, but he had the soldier's best medicine—the consciousness of duties thoroughly and well performed. He knew that, though Wren might carry his personal antipathy to the extent of official injustice, as officers higher in rank than Wren have been known to do, the truth concerning the recent campaign must come to light, and his connection therewith be made a matter of record, as it was already a matter of fact. Wren had not yet submitted his written report. Wren and the post commander were still on terms severely official; but, to the few brother officers with whom the captain talked at all upon the stirring events through which he and his troop had so recently passed, he had made little mention of Blakely. Not so, however, the men; not so Wales Arnold, the ranchman. To hear these worthies talk, the Bugologist, next to "Princess Natzie," was the central figure of the Red Rock campaign—the one officer, "where all had done so well," whose deeds merited conspicuous mention. Byrne knew this better than Wren. Plume knew it not as well as Byrne, perhaps. Sanders, Lynn, and Duane had heard the soldier stories in a dozen ways, and it stung them that their regimental comrade should so doggedly refuse to open his lips and give Blakely his due. It is not silence that usually hurts a man, it is speech; yet here was a case to the contrary.

Now just in proportion as the Wrens would have nothing to say in praise of Blakely, the Sanders household would have nothing *but* praise to say. Kate's honest heart was hot with anger at Angela, because the girl shrank from the subject as she would from evil speaking, lying, and slandering, and here again, to paraphrase the Irishman, too much heat had produced the coldness already referred to. Sanders scoffed at the idea of Natzie's infatuation being sufficient ground for family ostracism. "If there is a man alive who owes more than Wren does to Blakely, I'm a crab," said he, "and as soon as he's well enough to listen to straight talk he'll get it from me." "If there's a girl in America as heartless as Angela Wren," said Mrs. Sanders, "I hope I never shall have to meet her." But then Mrs. Sanders, as we know, had ever been jealous of Angela on account of her own true-hearted Kate, who refused to say one word on the subject beyond what she said to Angela herself. And now they had propped their patient in his reclining-chair and arranged the little table for "the inquisitor general," as Mrs. Bridger preferred to refer to him, and left them alone together behind closed doors, and had then gone forth to find that all Camp Sandy seemed to wait with bated breath for the outcome of that interview.

Sooner than was believed possible it came. An hour, probably, before they thought the colonel could have gathered all he wished to know, that officer was on the front piazza and sending an orderly to the adjutant's office. Then came Major Plume, with quick and nervous step. There was a two-minute conference on the piazza; then both officers vanished within, were gone five minutes, and then Plume reappeared alone, went straight to his home, and slammed the door behind him, a solecism rarely known at Sandy, and presently on the hot and pulseless air there arose the sound of shrill protestation in strange vernacular. Even Wren heard the voice, and found something reminiscent in the sound of weeping and wailing that followed. The performer was unquestionably Elise—she that had won the ponderous, yet descriptive, Indian name "Woman-Walk-in-the-Night."

And while this episode was still unexpired the orderly went for Lieutenant Truman, and Truman, with two orderlies, for a box, a bulky little chest, strapped heavily with iron, and this they lugged into Sanders's hall and came out heated and mystified. Three hours later, close-veiled and in droopy desolation, "Mademoiselle Lebrun" was bundled into a waiting ambulance and started under sufficient escort, and the care of the hospital matron, *en route* for Prescott, while Dr. Graham was summoned to attend Mrs. Plume, and grimly went. "The mean part of the whole business," said Mrs. Bridger, "is that nobody knows *what* it means." There was no one along the line, except poor Mrs. Plume, to regret that sudden and enforced departure, but there was regret universal all over the post when it was learned, still later in the afternoon, that one of the best soldiers and sergeants in the entire garrison had taken the horse of one of the herd guard and galloped away on the trail of the banished one. Sergeant Shannon, at sunset parade, was reported absent without leave.

Major Plume had come forth from his quarters at the sounding of the retreat, accurately dressed as ever, white-gloved, and wearing his saber. He seemed to realize that all eyes would be upon him. He had, indeed, been tempted again to turn over the command to the senior captain, but wisely thought better of it, and determined to face the music. He looked very sad and gray, however. He returned scrupulously the salute of the four company commanders as, in turn, each came forward to report the result of the evening roll-call; Cutler and Westervelt first, their companies being the nearest, then Lieutenant Lynn, temporarily in charge of Wren's troop, its captain and first lieutenant being still "on sick report." The sight of this young officer set the major to thinking of that evening not so many moons agone when Captain Wren himself appeared and in resonant, far-carrying tone announced "Lieutenant Blakely, sir, is absent." He had been thinking much of Blakely through the solemn afternoon, as he wandered nervously about his darkened quarters, sometimes tiptoeing to the bedside of his feebly moaning, petulant wife, sometimes pacing the library and hall. He had been again for half an hour closeted with Byrne and the Bugologist, certain letters being under inspection. He hardly heard the young officer, Lynn, as he said "Troop 'C,' all present, sir." He was looking beyond him at Captain Sanders, coming striding over the barren parade, with import in his eye. Plume felt that there was trouble ahead before ever Sanders reached the prescribed six paces, halted, raised his hand in salute, and, just as did Wren on that earlier occasion, announced in tones intended to be heard over and beyond the post commander: "Sergeant Shannon, sir, with one government horse, absent without leave."

Plume went a shade white, and bit his lips before he could steady himself to question. Well he knew that this new devilment was due in some way to that spirit of evil so long harbored by his wife, and suffered by himself. All the story of the strife she had stirred in the garrison had reached him days before. Downs's drunkenness and desertion, beyond doubt, were chargeable to her, as well as another and worse crime, unless all indications were at fault. Then there was the breach between Carmody and Shannon, formerly stanch friends and comrades, and now Carmody lay buried beneath the rocks in Bear Canon, and Shannon, as gallant and useful a sergeant as ever served, had thrown to the winds his record of the past and his hopes for the future, and gone in mad pursuit of a worthless hoyden. And all because Clarice would have that woman with her wherever she might go.

"When did this happen?" he presently asked.

"Just after stable call, sir. The horses were all returned to the corral except the herd guard's. The men marched over, as usual, with their halters. Shannon fell out as they entered the gate, took young Bennett's rein as he stood ready to lead in after them, mounted and rode round back of the wall, leaving Bennett so surprised that he didn't know what to say. He never suspected anything wrong until Shannon failed to reappear. Then he followed round back of the corral, found the sergeant's stable frock lying halfway out toward the bluff, and saw a streak of dust toward Bowlder Point. Then he came and reported."

Plume, after a moment's silence, turned abruptly. He had suffered much that day, and to think of his wife lying stricken and whimpering, professing herself a sorely injured woman because compelled at last to part with her maid, angered him beyond the point of toleration. Tossing his saber to the China boy, he went straightway aloft, failing to note in the dim light that two soft-hearted sympathizers were cooing by the gentle sufferer's side.

"Well, Clarice," he broke in abruptly, "we are never to hear the end of that she-cat's doings! My best sergeant has stolen a horse and gone galloping after her." It is always our best we lose when our better half is to blame, nor is it the way of brutal man to minimize the calamity on such occasions. It did not better matters that her much-wronged ladyship should speedily reply: "It's a wonder you don't charge the Indian outbreak to poor Elise. I don't believe she had a thing to do with your sergeant's stealing."

"You wouldn't believe she stole my whisky and gave it to Downs, though you admitted she told you she had to go back that night for something she'd dropped. You wouldn't believe she married that rascally gambler at St. Louis before her first husband was out of the way! You shielded and swore by her, and brought her out here, and all the time the proofs were here in Blakely's hands. It was *she*, I suppose, who broke off—"

But here, indeed, was it high time to break off. The visitors were now visibly rising in all proper embarrassment, for Mrs. Plume had started up, with staring eyes. "Proofs!" she cried, "in Blakely's hands! Why, she told me—my own letters!—my—" And then brutal man was brought to his senses and made to see how heartless and cruel was his conduct, for Mrs. Plume went into a fit and Mrs. Lynn for the doctor.

That was a wild night at Sandy. Two young matrons had made up their minds that it was shameful to leave poor Mrs. Plume without anybody to listen to her, when she might so long for sympathetic hearers, and have so much to tell. They had entered as soon as the major came forth and, softly tapping at the stricken one's door, had been with her barely five minutes when he came tearing back, and all this tremendous scene occurred before they could put in a word to prevent, which, of course, they were dying to do. But what *hadn't* they heard in that swift moment! Between the two of them—and Mrs. Bridger was the other—their agitation was such that it all had to be told. Then, like the measles, one revelation led to another, but it was several days before the garrison settled down in possession of an array of facts sufficient to keep it in gossip for many a month. Meanwhile, many a change had come over the scene.

At Prescott, then the Territorial capital, Elise Layton, *nee* Lebrun, was held without bail because it couldn't be had, charged with obtaining money under false pretenses, bigamy as a side issue, and arson as a possible backstop. The sleep-walking theory, as advanced in favor of Mrs. Plume, had been reluctantly abandoned, it appearing that, however dazed and "doped" she may have been through the treatment of that deft-fingered, unscrupulous maid, she was sufficiently wide awake to know well whither she had gone at that woman's urging, to make a last effort to recover certain letters of vital importance. At Blakely's door Clarice had "lost her nerve" and insisted on returning, but not so Elise. She went again, and had well-nigh gotten Downs drunk enough to do as she demanded.

Frankly, sadly, Plume went to Blakely, told him of his wife's admissions, and asked him what papers of hers he retained. For a moment Blakely had blazed with indignation, but Plume's sorrow, and utter innocence of wrong intent, stilled his wrath and led to his answer: "Every letter of Mrs. Plume's I burned before she was married, and I so assured her. She herself wrote asking me to burn rather than return them, but there were letters and papers I could not burn, brought to me by a poor devil that woman Elise had married, tricked into jail, and then deserted. He disappeared afterward, and even Pinkerton's people haven't been able to find him. Those papers are his property. You and Colonel Byrne are the only men who have seen them, though they were somewhat exposed just after the fire. She made three attempts to get me to give them up to her. Then, I believe, she strove to get Downs to steal them, and gave him the money with which to desert and bring them to her. He couldn't get into the iron box; couldn't lug it out, and somehow, probably, set fire to the place, scratching matches in there. Perhaps she even persuaded him to do that as a last resort. He knew I could get out safely. At all events, he was scared out of his wits and deserted with what he had. It was in trying to make his way eastward by the Wingate road that there came the last of poor Ups and Downs."

And so the story of this baleful influence over a weak, half-drugged girl, her mistress, became known to Plume and gradually to others. It was easy for Elise to make her believe that, in spite of the word of a gentleman, her impulsive love letters were still held by Blakely because he had never forgiven her. It was Elise, indeed, who had roused her jealousy and had done her best to break that engagement with Blakely and to lead to the match with the handsome and devoted major. Intrigue and lying were as the breath of the woman's nostrils. She lived in them.

But Sandy was never to see her again. "Woman-Walk-in-the-Night" was "Woman-Walk-no-More."

And now the friendless creature stood charged with more crimes than would fill the meager space of a Territorial jail, and yet the one originally laid at her door, though never publicly announced, was now omitted entirely—that of assault with deadly weapon, possibly with intent to kill. Even Mother Shaughnessy and Norah were silenced, and Pat Mullins put to confusion. Even the latest punctured patient at the hospital, Private Todd, had to serve as evidence in behalf of Elise, for Graham, post surgeon, had calmly declared that the same weapon that so nearly killed Pat Mullins had as nearly and neatly done the deed for Todd—the keen Apache knife of Princess Natzie.

"The heathen child was making her usual night visit to her white lover," said Wren grimly, having in mind the womanly shape he had seen that starlit morning at Blakely's rear door.

"You're right in one guess, R-robert Wren," was the prompt answer of his friend and fellow Scot, who glared at Janet rather than his convalescent as he spoke. "And ye're wrang in twanty. She *was* tryin', and didn't know the way. She *was* tryin', for she had his watch and pocket-book. You're wrang if ye think she was ever there before or after. The slut you saw cryin' at his back door was that quean Elise, an' ye well know there was no love lost between them. Go say yer prayers, man, for every wicked thought ye've had of him—or of that poor child. Between them they saved your Angela!"

CHAPTER XXVII

THE PARTING BY THE WATERS

"Some day I may tell Miss Angela—but never you," had Mr. Blakely said, before setting forth on his perilous essay to find Angela's father, and with native tenacity Miss Wren the elder had remembered the words and nourished her wrath. It was strange, indeed, that Plume, an officer and a gentleman, should have bethought him of the "austere vestal" as a companion witness to Blakely's supposed iniquity; but, between these two natures,—one strong, one weak,—there had sprung up the strange sympathy that is born of a common, deep-rooted, yet ill-defined antipathy—one for which neither she nor he could yet give good reason, and of which each was secretly ashamed. Each, for reasons of her or his own, cordially disliked the Bugologist, and each could not but welcome evidence to warrant such dislike. It is human nature. Janet Wren had strong convictions that the man was immoral, if for no other reason than that he obviously sought Angela and as obviously avoided her. Janet had believed him capable of carrying on a *liaison* with the dame who had jilted him, and had had to see that theory crushed. Then she would have it that, if not the mistress, he dallied with the maid, and when it began to transpire that virulent hatred was the only passion felt for him by that baffling and detestable daughter of Belial, there came actual joy to the soul of the Scotchwoman that, after all, her intuition had not been at fault. He was immoral as she would have him, even more so, for he had taken base advantage of the young and presumably innocent. She craved some proof, and Plume knew it, and, seeing her there alone in her dejection, had bidden her come and look—with the result described.

His own feeling toward Blakely is difficult to explain. Kind friends had told him at St. Louis how inseparable had been Clarice and this very superior young officer. She had admitted to him the "flirtation," but denied all regard for Blakely, yet Plume speedily found her moody, fitful, and unhappy, and made up his mind that Blakely was at the bottom of it. Her desire to go to far-away Arizona could have no other explanation. And though in no way whatever, by look, word, or deed, had Blakely transgressed the strictest rule in his bearing toward the major's wife, both major and wife became incensed at him,—Plume because he believed the Bugologist still cherished a tender passion for his wife—or she for him; Clarice, it must be owned, because she knew well he did not. Plume sought to find a flaw in his subordinate's moral armor to warrant the aversion that he felt, and was balked at every turn. It was with joy almost fierce he discovered what he thought to be proof that the subaltern was no saint, and, never stopping to give his better nature time to rise and rebuke him, he had summoned Janet. It was to sting Blakely, more than to punish the girl, he had ordered Natzie to the guard-room. Then, as the hours wore on and he realized how contemptible had been his conduct, the sense of shame well-nigh crushed him, and though it galled him to think that some of his own kind, probably, had connived at Natzie's escape, he thanked God the girl was gone. And now having convinced herself that here at last she had positive proof of Mr. Blakely's depravity, Aunt Janet had not scrupled to bear it to Angela, with sharp and surprising result. A good girl, a dutiful girl, was Angela, as we have seen, but she, too, had her share of fighting Scotch blood and a bent for revolt that needed only a reason. For days Aunt Janet had bidden her shun the young man, first naming Mrs. Plume and then Elsie as the cause and corespondent. One after another Graham had demolished these possibilities, to the end that even Wren was ashamed of his unworthy suspicions. Then it was Natzie who was the prey of Blakely's immorality, and for that, Janet declared, quite as much as for stabbing the soldier, the girl had been sent to the cells. It was late in the day when she managed to find Angela away from her father, who, realizing what Natzie had done and suffered to save his own ewe lamb, was now in keen distress of mind because powerless to raise a hand to aid her. He wondered that Angela seemed so unresponsive—that she did not flare up in protest at such degrading punishment for the girl who had saved her life. He little knew how his daughter's heart was burning within her. He never dreamed that she, too, was suffering—torn by conflicting emotions. It was a sore thing to find that in her bene-factress lived an unsuspected rival.

Just before sunset she had left him and gone to her room to change her dress for the evening, and Janet's first swoop was upon her brother. Once before during the exciting day she had had a moment to herself and him. She had so constantly fanned the flame of his belief in Blakely's gallantries as even to throttle the sense of gratitude he felt, and, in spite of herself, that she felt for that officer's daring and successful services during the campaign. She felt, and he felt, that they must disapprove of Blakely—must stamp out any nascent regard that Angela might cherish for him, and to this end would never in her presence admit that he had been instrumental in the rescue of his captain, much less his captain's daughter. Hurriedly Janet had told him what she and Plume had seen, and left him to ponder over it. Now she came to induce him to bid her tell it all to Angela. "Now that, that other—affair—seems disproved," said she, "she'll be thinking there's no reason why she shouldn't be thinking of him," and dejectedly the Scotchman bade her do as seemed best. Women, he reasoned, could better read each other's hearts.

And so Janet had gone and had thought to shock, and had most impressively detailed what she had witnessed—I fear me Janet scrupled not to embroider a bit, so much is permissible to the "unco guid" when so very much is at stake. And Angela went on brushing out her beautiful hair without a sign of emotion. To the scandal of Scotch maidenhood she seemed unimpressed by the depravity of the pair. To the surprise of Aunt Janet she heard her without interruption to the uttermost word, and then— wished to know if Aunt Janet thought the major would let her send Natzie something for supper.

Whatever the girl may have thought of this new and possible complication, she determined that no soul should read that it cost her a pang. She declined to discuss it. She did what she had not done before that day—went forth in search of Kate Sanders. Aunt Janet was astonished that her niece should wish to send food to that—that trollop. What would she have thought could she have heard what passed a few moments later? In the dusk and the gloaming Kate Sanders was in conversation on the side veranda with a tall sergeant of her father's troop. "Ask her?" Kate was saying. "Of course I'll ask her. Why, here she comes now!" Will it be believed that Sergeant Shannon wished Miss Angela's permission to "take Punch out for a little exercise," a thing he had never ventured to ask before, and that Angela Wren eagerly said, "Yes." Poor Shannon! He did not know that night how soon he would be borrowing a horse on his own account, nor that two brave girls would nearly cry their eyes out over it, when they were barely on speaking terms.

Of him there came sad news but the day after his crack-brained, Quixotic essay. Infatuated with Elise, and believing in her promise to marry him, he had placed his savings in her hands, even as had Downs and Carmody. He had heard the story of her visiting Blakely by night, and scouted it. He heard, in a maze of astonishment, that she was being sent to Prescott under guard for delivery to the civil authorities, and taking the first horse he could lay hands on, he galloped in chase. He had overtaken the ambulance on Cherry Creek, and with moving tears she had besought him to save her. Faithful to their trust, the guard had to interpose, but, late at night, they reached Stemmer's ranch; were met there by a relief guard sent down by Captain Stout; and the big sergeant who came in charge, with special instructions from Stout's own lips, was a new king who knew not Joseph, and who sternly bade Shannon keep his distance. Hot words followed, for the trooper sergeant would stand no hectoring from an equal in rank. Shannon's heart was already lost, and now he lost his head. He struck a fellow-sergeant who stood charged with an important duty, and even his own comrades could not interpose when the infantrymen threw themselves upon the raging Irish soldier and hammered him hard before they could subdue and bind him, but bind him they did. Sadly the trooper guard went back to Sandy, bringing the "borrowed" horse and the bad news that Shannon had been arrested for assaulting Sergeant Bull, and all men knew that court-martial and disgrace must follow. It was Shannon's last run on the road he knew so well. Soldiers of rank came forward to plead for him and bear witness to his worth and services, and the general commanding remitted most of the sentence, restoring to him everything the court had decreed forfeited except the chevrons. They had to go, yet could soon be regained. But no man could restore to him the pride and self-respect that went when he realized that he was only one of several plucked and deluded victims of a female sharper. While the Frenchwoman ogled and languished behind the bars, Shannon wandered out into the world again, a deserter from the troop he was ashamed to face, an unfollowed, unsought fugitive among the mining camps in the Sierras. "Three stout soldiers stricken from the rolls—two of them gone to their last account," mused poor Plume, as at last he led his unhappy wife away to the sea, "and all the work of one woman!"

Yes, Mrs. Plume was gone now for good and all, her devoted, yet sore-hearted major with her, and Wren was sufficiently recovered to be up and taking the air on his veranda, where Sanders sometimes stopped to see him, and "pass the time of day," but cut his visits short and spoke of everything but what was uppermost in his mind, because his better half persuaded him that only ill would come from preaching. Then, late one wonderful day, the interesting invalid, Mr. Neil Blakely himself, was "paraded" upon the piazza in the Sanders's special reclining-chair, and Kate and Mrs. Sanders beamed, while nearly all society at the post came and purred and congratulated and took sidelong glances up the row to where Angela but a while before was reading to her grim old father, but where the father now read alone, for Angela had gone, as was her custom at the hour, to her own little room, and thither did Janet conceive it her duty to follow, and there to investigate.

"It won't be long now before that young man will be hobbling around the post, I suppose. How do you expect to avoid him?" said the elder maiden, looking with uncompromising austerity at her niece. Angela as before had just shaken loose her wealth of billowy tresses and was carefully brushing them. She did not turn from the contemplation of her double in the mirror before her; she did not hesitate in her reply. It was brief, calm, and to the point.

"I shall not avoid him."

"Angela! And after all I—your father and I—have told you!" And Aunt Janet began to bristle.

"Two-thirds of what you told me, Aunt Janet, proved to be without foundation. Now I doubt—the rest of it." And Aunt Janet saw the big eyes beginning to fill; saw the twitching at the corners of the soft, sensitive lips; saw the trembling of the slender, white hand, and the ominous tapping of the slender, shapely foot, but there wasn't a symptom of fear or flinching. The blood of the Wrens was up for battle. The child was a woman grown. The day of revolt had come at last.

"Angela Wr-r-ren!" rolled Aunt Janet. "D'you mean you're going to *see* him?—speak to him?"

"I'm going to see him and—thank him, Aunt Janet." And now the girl had turned and faced the astounded woman at the door. "You may spare yourself any words upon the subject."

The captain was seated in loneliness and mental perturbation just where Angela had left him, but no longer pretending to read. His back was toward the southern end of the row. He had not even seen the cause of the impromptu reception at the Sanders's. He read what was taking place when Angela began to lose her voice, to stumble over her words; and, peering at her under his bushy eyebrows, he saw that the face he loved was flushing, that her young bosom was swiftly rising and falling, the beautiful brown eyes wandering from the page. Even before the glad voices from below came ringing to his ears, he read in his daughter's face the tumult in her guileless heart, and then she suddenly caught herself and hurried back to the words that seemed swimming in space before her. But the effort was vain. Rising quickly, and with brave effort steadying her voice, she said, "I'll run and dress now, father, dear," and was gone, leaving him to face the problem thrust upon him. Had he known that Janet, too, had heard from the covert of the screened and shaded window of the little parlor, and then that she had followed, he would have shouted for his German "striker" and sent a mandate to his sister that she could not fail to understand. He did not know that she had been with Angela until he heard her footstep and saw her face at the hall doorway. She had not even to roll her r's before the story was told.

Two days now he had lived in much distress of mind. Before quitting the post Major Plume had laboriously gone the rounds, saying good-by to every officer and lady. Two officers he had asked to see alone—the captain and first lieutenant of Troop "C." Janet knew of this, and should have known it meant amende and reconciliation, perhaps revelation, but because her brother saw fit to sit and ponder, she saw fit to cling unflinchingly to her preconceived ideas and to act according to them. With Graham she was exceeding wroth for daring to defend such persons as Lieutenant Blakely and "that Indian squaw." It was akin to opposing weak-minded theories to positive knowledge of facts. She had seen with her own eyes the ignorant, but no less abandoned, creature kneeling at Blakely's bedside, her black head pillowed close to his breast. She had seen her spring up in fury at being caught—what else could have so enraged her that she should seek to knife the intruders? argued Janet. She believed, or professed to believe, that but for the vigilance of poor Todd, now quite happy in his convalescence, the young savage would have murdered both the major and herself. She did not care what Dr. Graham said. She had seen, and seeing, with Janet, was believing.

But she knew her brother well, and knew that since Graham's impetuous outbreak he had been wavering sadly, and since Plume's parting visit had been plunged in a mental slough of doubt and distress. Once before his stubborn Scotch nature had had to strike its colors and surrender to his own subaltern, and now the same struggle was on again, for what Plume said, and said in presence of grim old Graham, fairly startled him:

"You are not the only one to whom I owe amende and apology, Captain Wren. I wronged you, when you were shielding—my wife—at no little cost to yourself. I wronged Blakely in several ways, and I have had to go and tell him so and beg his pardon. The meanest thing I ever did was bringing Miss Wren in there to spy on him, unless it was in sending that girl to the guard-house. I'd beg her pardon, too, if she could be found. Yes, I see you look glum, Wren, but we've all been wrong, I reckon. There's no mystery about it now."

And then Plume told his tale and Wren meekly listened. It might well be, said he, that Natzie loved Blakely. All her people did. She had been watching him from the willows as he slept that day at the pool. He had forbidden her following him, forbidden her coming to the post, and she feared to wake him, yet when she saw the two prospectors, that had been at Hart's, ride over toward the sleeping officer she was startled. She saw them watching, whispering together. Then they rode down and tied their horses among the trees a hundred yards below, and came crouching along the bank. She was up in an instant and over the stream at the shallows, and that scared them off long enough to let her reach him. Even then she dare not wake him for fear of his anger at her disobedience, but his coat was open, his watch and wallet easy to take. She quickly seized them—the little picture-case being within the wallet at the moment—and sped back to her covert. Then Angela had come cantering down the sandy road; had gone on down stream, passing even the prowling prospectors, and after a few minutes had returned and dismounted among the willows above where Blakely lay—Angela whom poor Natzie believed to be Blakely's sister. Natzie supposed her looking for her brother, and wondered why she waited. Natzie finally signaled and pointed when she saw that Angela was going in disappointment at not finding him. Natzie witnessed Angela's theft of the net and her laughing ride away. By this time the prospectors had given up and gone about their business, and then, while she was wondering how best to restore the property, Lola and Alchisay had come with the annoying news that the agent was angered and had sent trailers after her. They were even then only a little way up stream. The three then made a run for the rocks to the east, and there remained in hiding. That night Natzie had done her best to find her way to Blakely with the property, and the rest they knew. The watch was dropped in the struggle on the *mesa* when Mullins was stabbed, the picture-case that morning at the major's quarters.

"Was it Blakely told you all this, sir?" Wren had asked, still wrong-headed and suspicious.

"No, Wren. It was I told Blakely. All this was given me by Lola's father, the interpreter, back from Chevlon's Fork only yesterday. I sent him to try to persuade Natzie and her kinsfolk to return. I have promised them immunity."

Then Plume and Graham had gone, leaving Wren to brood and ponder, and this had he been doing two mortal days and nights without definite result, and now came Janet to bring things to a head. In grim and ominous silence he listened to her recital, saying never a word until her final appeal:

"R-r-robert, is our girlie going daft, do you think? She solemnly said to me—to me—but a minute ago, 'I mean to go to him myself—and thank him!'"

And solemnly the soldier looked up from his reclining-chair and studied his sister's amazed and anxious face. Then he took her thin, white hand between his own thin, brown paws and patted it gently. She recoiled slowly as she saw contrition, not condemnation, in his blinking eyes.

"God forgive us all, Janet! It's what I ought to have done days ago."

* * * * *

Another cloudless afternoon had come, and, under the willows at the edge of the pool, a young girl sat day-dreaming, though the day was nearly done. All in the valley was wrapped in shadow, though the cliffs and turrets across the stream were resplendent in a radiance of slanting sunshine. Not a whisper of breeze stirred the drooping foliage along the sandy shores, or ruffled the liquid mirror surface. Not a sound, save drowsy hum of beetle or soft murmur of rippling waters among the pebbly shadows below, broke the vast silence of the scene. Just where Angela was seated that October day on which our story opened, she was seated now, with the greyhounds stretched sprawling in the warm sands at her feet, with Punch blinking lazily and switching his long tail in the thick of the willows.

And somebody else was there, close at hand. The shadows of the westward heights had gradually risen to the crest of the rocky cliffs across the stream. A soft, prolonged call of distant trumpet summoned homeward for the coming night the scattered herds and herd guards of the post, and, rising suddenly, her hand upon a swift-throbbing heart, her red lips parted in eagerness or excitement uncontrollable, Angela stood intently listening. Over among the thickets across the pool the voice of an Indian girl was uplifted in some weird, uncanny song. The voice was shrill, yet not unmusical. The song was savage, yet not lacking some crude harmony. She could not see the singer, but she knew. Natzie's people had returned to the agency, accepting the olive branch that Plume had tendered them—Natzie herself was here.

At the first sound of the uplifted voice an Apache boy, crouching in the shrubbery at the edge of the pool, rose quickly to his feet, and, swift and noiseless, stole away into the thicket. If he thought to conceal himself or his purpose his caution was needless. Angela neither saw nor heard him. Neither was it the song nor the singer that now arrested her attention. So still was the air, so deep was the silence of nature, that even on such sandy roads and bridlepaths as traversed the winding valley, the faintest hoof-beat was carried far. Another horse, another rider, was quickly coming. Tonto, the big hound nearest her, lifted his shapely head and listened a moment, then went bounding away through the willows, followed swiftly by his mate. They knew the hoof-beats, and joyously ran to meet and welcome the rider. Angela knew them quite as well, but could neither run to meet, nor could she fly.

Only twice, as yet, had she opportunity to see or to thank Neil Blakely, and a week had passed since her straight-forward challenge to Aunt Janet. As soon as he could walk unaided, save by his stick, Wren had gone stumping down the line to Sanders's quarters and asked for Mr. Blakely, with whom he had an uninterrupted talk of half an hour. Within two days thereafter Mr. Blakely in person returned the call, being received with awful state and solemnity by Miss Wren herself. Angela, summoned by her father's voice, came flitting down a moment later, and there in the little army parlor, where first she had sought to "entertain" him until the captain should appear, our Angela was once again brought face to face with him who had meanwhile risked his life in the effort to rescue her father, and again in the effort to find and rescue her. A fine blush mantled her winsome face as she entered, and, without a glance at Janet, went straightway to their visitor, with extended hand.

"I am so glad to see you again, Mr. Blakely," she bravely began. "I have—so much—to thank you—" but her brown eyes fell before the fire in the blue and her whole being thrilled at the fervor of his handclasp. She drew her hand away, the color mounting higher, then snuggled to her father's side with intent to take his arm; but, realizing suddenly how her own was trembling, grasped instead the back of a chair. Blakely was saying something, she knew not what, nor could she ever recall much that anyone said during the brief ten minutes of his stay, for there sat Aunt Janet, bolt upright, after the fashion of fifty years gone by, a formidable picture indeed, and Angela wondered that anyone could say anything at all.

Next time they met she was riding home and he sat on the south veranda with Mrs. Sanders and Kate. She would have ridden by with just a nod and smile; but, at sight of her, he "hobbled" down the steps and came hurriedly out to speak, whereupon Mrs. Sanders, who knew much better, followed to "help him," as she said. "Help, indeed!" quoth angry Kate, usually most dutiful of daughters. "You'd only hinder!" But even that presence had not stopped his saying: "The doctor promises I may ride Hart's single-footer in a day or two, Miss Angela, and then—"

And now it was a "single-footer" coming, the only one at Sandy. Of course it might be Hart, not Blakely, and yet Blakely had seen her as she rode away. It was Blakely's voice—how seldom she had heard, yet how well she knew it! answering the joyous welcome of the hounds. It was Blakely who came riding straight in among the willows, a radiance in his thin and lately pallid face— Blakely who quickly, yet awkwardly, dismounted, for it still caused him pain, and then, forgetful of his horse, came instantly to her as she stood there, smiling, yet tremulous. The hand that sought hers fairly shook, but that, said Angela, though she well knew better, might have been from weakness or from riding. For a moment he did not speak. It was she who began. She thought he should know at once.

"Did you—hear her singing—too?" she hazarded.

"Hear?—Who?" he replied, grudgingly letting go the hand because it pulled with such determination.

"Why—Natzie, I suppose. At least—I haven't seen her," she stammered, her cheeks all crimson now.

"Natzie, indeed!" he answered, in surprise, turning slowly and studying the opposite willows. "It is only a day or two since they came in. I thought she'd soon be down." Obviously her coming caused him neither embarrassment nor concern. "She still has a notecase of mine. I suppose you heard?" And his clear blue eyes were fastened on her lovely, downcast face.

"Something. Not much," she answered, drawing back a little, for he stood so close to her she could have heard the beating of his heart—but for her own. All was silence over there in the opposite willows, but so it was the day Natzie had so suddenly appeared from nowhere, and he saw the hurried glance she sent across the pool.

"Has she worried you?" he began, "has she been—" spying, he was going to say, and she knew it, and grew redder still with vexation. Natzie could claim at least that she was not without a shining example had she come there to spy, but Blakely had that to say to her that deserved undivided attention, and there is a time when even one's preserver and greatest benefactor may be *de trop.*

"Will you wait—one moment?" he suddenly asked. "I'll go to the rocks yonder and call her," and then, almost as suddenly, the voice was again uplifted in the same weird, barbaric song, and the singer had gone from the depths of the opposite thicket and was somewhere farther up stream, still hidden from their gaze—still, possibly, ignorant of Angela's presence. The brown eyes were at the moment following the tall, white form, moving slowly through the winding, faintly-worn pathway toward the upper shallows where, like stepping stones, the big rocks stretched from shore to shore, and she was startled to note that the moment the song began he stopped short a second or two, listened intently, then almost sprang forward in his haste to reach the crossing. Another minute and he was out of sight among the shrubbery. Another, and she heard the single shot of a revolver, and there he stood at the rocky point, a smoking pistol in his hand. Instantly the song ceased, and then his voice was uplifted, calling, "Natzie! Natzie!" With breathless interest Angela gazed and, presently, parting the shrubbery with her little brown hands, the Indian girl stepped forth into the light and stood in silence, her great black eyes fixed mournfully upon him. Could this be their mountain princess—the daring, the resolute, the commanding? Could this be the fierce, lissome, panther-like creature before whose blow two of their stoutest men had fallen? There was dejection inexpressible in her very attitude. There was no longer bravery or adornment in her dress. There was no more of queen—of chieftain's daughter—in this downcast child of the desert.

He called again, "Natzie," and held forth his hand. Her head had drooped upon her breast, but, once again, she looked upon him, and then, with one slow, hesitant, backward glance about her, stepped forward, her little, moccasined feet flitting from rock to rock across the murmuring shallows until she stood before him. Then he spoke, but she only shook her head and let it droop again, her hands passively clasping. He knew too little of her tongue to plead with her. He knew, perhaps, too little of womankind to appreciate what he was doing. Finding words useless, he gently took her hand and drew her with him, and passively she obeyed, and for a moment they disappeared from Angela's view. Then presently the tall, white form came again in sight, slowly leading the unresisting child, until, in another moment, they stepped within the little open space among the willows. At the same instant Angela arose, and the daughter of the soldier and the daughter of the savage, the one with timid yet hopeful welcome and greeting in her lovely face, the other with sudden amaze, scorn, passion, and jealous fury in her burning eyes, stood a breathless moment confronted. Then, all in a second, with one half-stifled, inarticulate cry, Natzie wrenched her hand from that of Blakely, and, with the spring of a tigress, bounded away. Just at the edge of the pool she halted, whirled about, tore from her bosom a flat, oblong packet and hurled it at his feet; then, with the dart of a frightened deer, drove through the northward willows. Angela saw her run blindly up the bank, leaping thence to the rocks below, bounding from one to another with the wild grace of the antelope. Another instant and she had reached the opposite shore, and there, tossing her arms wildly above her head, her black tresses streaming behind her, with a cry that was almost a scream, she plunged into the heart of the thicket; the stubborn branches closed behind her, and our Apache queen was gone. As they met, so had they parted, by the waters of the pool.

When Blakely turned again to Angela she, too, was gone. He found her a little later, her arms twined about her pony's neck, her face buried in his mane, and sobbing as though her heart would break.

On a soft, starlit evening within the week, no longer weeping, but leaning on Blakely's arm, Angela stood at the edge of the bluff, looking far out over the Red Rock country to the northeast. The sentry had reported a distant signal fire, and several of the younger people had strolled out to see. Whatever it was that had caused the report had vanished by the time they reached the post, so, presently, Kate Sanders started the homeward move, and now even the sentry had disappeared in the darkness. When Angela, too, would have returned, his arm restrained. She knew it would. She knew he had not spoken that evening at the willows because of her tears. She knew he had been patient, forbearing, gentle, yet well she knew he meant now to speak and wait no longer.

"Do you remember," he began, "when I said that some day I should tell you—but never your aunt—who it was that came to my quarters that night—and why she came?" and though she sought to remove her hand from his arm he would not let it go.

"You *did* tell me," she answered, her eyelids drooping.

"I *did*!—when?"

Though the face was downcast, the sensitive lips began to quiver with merriment and mischief.

"The same day you took me for—your mother—and asked me to sing for you."

"Angela!" he cried, in amaze, and turning quickly toward her, "What can you mean?"

"Just what I say. You began as though I were your sister, then your mother. I think, perhaps, if we'd had another hour together it would have been grandmother." She was shaking with suppressed laughter now, or was it violent trembling, for his heart, like hers, was bounding.

"I must indeed have been delirious," he answered now, not laughing, not even smiling. He had possessed himself of that other hand, despite its fluttering effort. His voice was deep and grave and tremulous. "I called you anything but what I most longed to call you—what I pray God I may call you, Angela—my wife!"

L'ENVOI

There was a wedding at Sandy that winter when Pat
Mullins took his discharge, and his land warrant, and a
claim up the Beaver, and Norah Shaughnessy to wife.
There was another, many a mile from Sandy, when the
May blossoms were showering in the orchard of a fair old
homestead in the distant East, and then Neil Blakely took
his bride to see "the land of the leal" after the little peep at
the lands that now she shared with him. There is one room
in the beautiful old Colonial mansion that they soon
learned to call "father's," in anticipation of the time when
he should retire and come to hang the old saber on the
older mantel and spend his declining years with them.
There is another, sacred to Aunt Janet, where she was
often welcomed, a woman long since reconciled to
Angela's once "obnoxious," but ever devoted admirer.
There were some points in which Aunt Janet suffered
sore. She had views of her own upon the rearing and
management of children, and these views she did at first
oppose to those of Angela, but not for long. In this, as in
her choice of a husband, Angela had to read her
declaration of independence to the elder woman.

There is another room filled with relics of their frontier
days,—Indian weapons, blankets, beadwork,—and among
these, in a sort of shrine of its own, there hangs a portrait

Charles King

made by a famous artist from a little tintype, taken by some wandering photographer about the old Apache reservation. Wren wrote them, ere the regiment left Arizona, that she who had been their rescuer, and then so long disappeared, finally wedded a young brave of the Chiricahua band and went with him to Mexico. That portrait is the only relic they have of a never forgotten benefactress—Natzie, their Apache Princess.

THE END

Choose from Thousands of 1stWorldLibrary Classics By

A. M. Barnard
Ada Leverson
Adolphus William Ward
Aesop
Agatha Christie
Alexander Aaronsohn
Alexander Kielland
Alexandre Dumas
Alfred Gatty
Alfred Ollivant
Alice Duer Miller
Alice Turner Curtis
Alice Dunbar
Allen Chapman
Alleyne Ireland
Ambrose Bierce
Amelia E. Barr
Amory H. Bradford
Andrew Lang
Andrew McFarland Davis
Andy Adams
Angela Brazil
Anna Alice Chapin
Anna Sewell
Annie Besant
Annie Hamilton Donnell
Annie Payson Call
Annie Roe Carr
Annonaymous
Anton Chekhov
Archibald Lee Fletcher
Arnold Bennett
Arthur C. Benson
Arthur Conan Doyle
Arthur M. Winfield
Arthur Ransome
Arthur Schnitzler
Arthur Train
Atticus
B.H. Baden-Powell
B. M. Bower
B. C. Chatterjee
Baroness Emmuska Orczy
Baroness Orczy
Basil King
Bayard Taylor
Ben Macomber
Bertha Muzzy Bower
Bjornstjerne Bjornson

Booth Tarkington
Boyd Cable
Bram Stoker
C. Collodi
C. E. Orr
C. M. Ingleby
Carolyn Wells
Catherine Parr Traill
Charles A. Eastman
Charles Amory Beach
Charles Dickens
Charles Dudley Warner
Charles Farrar Browne
Charles Ives
Charles Kingsley
Charles Klein
Charles Hanson Towne
Charles Lathrop Pack
Charles Romyn Dake
Charles Whibley
Charles Willing Beale
Charlotte M. Braeme
Charlotte M. Yonge
Charlotte Perkins Stetson
Clair W. Hayes
Clarence Day Jr.
Clarence E. Mulford
Clemence Housman
Confucius
Coningsby Dawson
Cornelis DeWitt Wilcox
Cyril Burleigh
D. H. Lawrence
Daniel Defoe
David Garnett
Dinah Craik
Don Carlos Janes
Donald Keyhoe
Dorothy Kilner
Dougan Clark
Douglas Fairbanks
E. Nesbit
E. P. Roe
E. Phillips Oppenheim
E. S. Brooks
Earl Barnes
Edgar Rice Burroughs
Edith Van Dyne
Edith Wharton

Edward Everett Hale
Edward J. O'Biren
Edward S. Ellis
Edwin L. Arnold
Eleanor Atkins
Eleanor Hallowell Abbott
Eliot Gregory
Elizabeth Gaskell
Elizabeth McCracken
Elizabeth Von Arnim
Ellem Key
Emerson Hough
Emilie F. Carlen
Emily Bronte
Emily Dickinson
Enid Bagnold
Enilor Macartney Lane
Erasmus W. Jones
Ernie Howard Pie
Ethel May Dell
Ethel Turner
Ethel Watts Mumford
Eugene Sue
Eugenie Foa
Eugene Wood
Eustace Hale Ball
Evelyn Everett-green
Everard Cotes
F. H. Cheley
F. J. Cross
F. Marion Crawford
Fannie E. Newberry
Federick Austin Ogg
Ferdinand Ossendowski
Fergus Hume
Florence A. Kilpatrick
Fremont B. Deering
Francis Bacon
Francis Darwin
Frances Hodgson Burnett
Frances Parkinson Keyes
Frank Gee Patchin
Frank Harris
Frank Jewett Mather
Frank L. Packard
Frank V. Webster
Frederic Stewart Isham
Frederick Trevor Hill
Frederick Winslow Taylor

Friedrich Kerst
Friedrich Nietzsche
Fyodor Dostoyevsky
G.A. Henty
G.K. Chesterton
Gabrielle E. Jackson
Garrett P. Serviss
Gaston Leroux
George A. Warren
George Ade
Geroge Bernard Shaw
George Cary Eggleston
George Durston
George Ebers
George Eliot
George Gissing
George MacDonald
George Meredith
George Orwell
George Sylvester Viereck
George Tucker
George W. Cable
George Wharton James
Gertrude Atherton
Gordon Casserly
Grace E. King
Grace Gallatin
Grace Greenwood
Grant Allen
Guillermo A. Sherwell
Gulielma Zollinger
Gustav Flaubert
H. A. Cody
H. B. Irving
H.C. Bailey
H. G. Wells
H. H. Munro
H. Irving Hancock
H. R. Naylor
H. Rider Haggard
H. W. C. Davis
Haldeman Julius
Hall Caine
Hamilton Wright Mabie
Hans Christian Andersen
Harold Avery
Harold McGrath
Harriet Beecher Stowe
Harry Castlemon
Harry Coghill
Harry Houidini

Hayden Carruth
Helent Hunt Jackson
Helen Nicolay
Hendrik Conscience
Hendy David Thoreau
Henri Barbusse
Henrik Ibsen
Henry Adams
Henry Ford
Henry Frost
Henry James
Henry Jones Ford
Henry Seton Merriman
Henry W Longfellow
Herbert A. Giles
Herbert Carter
Herbert N. Casson
Herman Hesse
Hildegard G. Frey
Homer
Honore De Balzac
Horace B. Day
Horace Walpole
Horatio Alger Jr.
Howard Pyle
Howard R. Garis
Hugh Lofting
Hugh Walpole
Humphry Ward
Ian Maclaren
Inez Haynes Gillmore
Irving Bacheller
Isabel Cecilia Williams
Isabel Hornibrook
Israel Abrahams
Ivan Turgenev
J.G.Austin
J. Henri Fabre
J. M. Barrie
J. M. Walsh
J. Macdonald Oxley
J. R. Miller
J. S. Fletcher
J. S. Knowles
J. Storer Clouston
J. W. Duffield
Jack London
Jacob Abbott
James Allen
James Andrews
James Baldwin

James Branch Cabell
James DeMille
James Joyce
James Lane Allen
James Lane Allen
James Oliver Curwood
James Oppenheim
James Otis
James R. Driscoll
Jane Abbott
Jane Austen
Jane L. Stewart
Janet Aldridge
Jens Peter Jacobsen
Jerome K. Jerome
Jessie Graham Flower
John Buchan
John Burroughs
John Cournos
John F. Kennedy
John Gay
John Glasworthy
John Habberton
John Joy Bell
John Kendrick Bangs
John Milton
John Philip Sousa
John Taintor Foote
Jonas Lauritz Idemil Lie
Jonathan Swift
Joseph A. Altsheler
Joseph Carey
Joseph Conrad
Joseph E. Badger Jr
Joseph Hergesheimer
Joseph Jacobs
Jules Vernes
Julian Hawthrone
Julie A Lippmann
Justin Huntly McCarthy
Kakuzo Okakura
Karle Wilson Baker
Kate Chopin
Kenneth Grahame
Kenneth McGaffey
Kate Langley Bosher
Kate Langley Bosher
Katherine Cecil Thurston
Katherine Stokes
L. A. Abbot
L. T. Meade

L. Frank Baum
Latta Griswold
Laura Dent Crane
Laura Lee Hope
Laurence Housman
Lawrence Beasley
Leo Tolstoy
Leonid Andreyev
Lewis Carroll
Lewis Sperry Chafer
Lilian Bell
Lloyd Osbourne
Louis Hughes
Louis Joseph Vance
Louis Tracy
Louisa May Alcott
Lucy Fitch Perkins
Lucy Maud Montgomery
Luther Benson
Lydia Miller Middleton
Lyndon Orr
M. Corvus
M. H. Adams
Margaret E. Sangster
Margret Howth
Margaret Vandercook
Margaret W. Hungerford
Margret Penrose
Maria Edgeworth
Maria Thompson Daviess
Mariano Azuela
Marion Polk Angellotti
Mark Overton
Mark Twain
Mary Austin
Mary Catherine Crowley
Mary Cole
Mary Hastings Bradley
Mary Roberts Rinehart
Mary Rowlandson
M. Wollstonecraft Shelley
Maud Lindsay
Max Beerbohm
Myra Kelly
Nathaniel Hawthrone
Nicolo Machiavelli
O. F. Walton
Oscar Wilde

Owen Johnson
P.G. Wodehouse
Paul and Mabel Thorne
Paul G. Tomlinson
Paul Severing
Percy Brebner
Percy Keese Fitzhugh
Peter B. Kyne
Plato
Quincy Allen
R. Derby Holmes
R. L. Stevenson
R. S. Ball
Rabindranath Tagore
Rahul Alvares
Ralph Bonehill
Ralph Henry Barbour
Ralph Victor
Ralph Waldo Emmerson
Rene Descartes
Ray Cummings
Rex Beach
Rex E. Beach
Richard Harding Davis
Richard Jefferies
Richard Le Gallienne
Robert Barr
Robert Frost
Robert Gordon Anderson
Robert L. Drake
Robert Lansing
Robert Lynd
Robert Michael Ballantyne
Robert W. Chambers
Rosa Nouchette Carey
Rudyard Kipling
Saint Augustine
Samuel B. Allison
Samuel Hopkins Adams
Sarah Bernhardt
Sarah C. Hallowell
Selma Lagerlof
Sherwood Anderson
Sigmund Freud
Standish O'Grady
Stanley Weyman
Stella Benson
Stella M. Francis

Stephen Crane
Stewart Edward White
Stijn Streuvels
Swami Abhedananda
Swami Parmananda
T. S. Ackland
T. S. Arthur
The Princess Der Ling
Thomas A. Janvier
Thomas A Kempis
Thomas Anderton
Thomas Bailey Aldrich
Thomas Bulfinch
Thomas De Quincey
Thomas Dixon
Thomas H. Huxley
Thomas Hardy
Thomas More
Thornton W. Burgess
U. S. Grant
Upton Sinclair
Valentine Williams
Various Authors
Vaughan Kester
Victor Appleton
Victor G. Durham
Victoria Cross
Virginia Woolf
Wadsworth Camp
Walter Camp
Walter Scott
Washington Irving
Wilbur Lawton
Wilkie Collins
Willa Cather
Willard F. Baker
William Dean Howells
William le Queux
W. Makepeace Thackeray
William W. Walter
William Shakespeare
Winston Churchill
Yei Theodora Ozaki
Yogi Ramacharaka
Young E. Allison
Zane Grey